Praise for the ...
and Agatha award–nominated
Gaslight Mysteries

"This long-lasting series . . . has lost none of its interest or attraction . . . Thompson has always vividly shown the life of the rich and the very poor of the city . . . This is a strong tale, emotionally and historically, and a puzzling mystery."
—*RT Book Reviews* (4 ½ stars, Top Pick)

"Tantalizing."
—Catherine Coulter, #1 *New York Times* bestselling author of *The End Game*

"Victoria Thompson shines . . . Anne Perry and Caleb Carr fans, rejoice!"
—Tamar Myers, national bestselling author of *The Girl Who Married an Eagle*

"Fast-paced . . . Another Victorian page-turner!"
—Robin Paige, national bestselling author of *Death on the Lizard*

"*Gangs of New York*, eat your heart out—this book is the real thing."
—*Mystery Scene*

"A fascinating window into a bygone era."
—*Kirkus Reviews*

"Thompson vividly re-creates the gaslit world of old New York."
—*Publishers Weekly*

"Sarah Brandt makes an intriguing sleuth, and [Thompson's] Gaslight series is a consistent winner."
—*Booklist*

MURDER ON
AMSTERDAM
AVENUE

A Gaslight Mystery

Victoria Thompson

BERKLEY PRIME CRIME, NEW YORK

An imprint of Penguin Random House LLC
375 Hudson Street, New York, New York 10014

MURDER ON AMSTERDAM AVENUE

A Berkley Prime Crime Book / published by arrangement with the author

ISBN: 978-0-425-26048-7

PUBLISHING HISTORY
Berkley Prime Crime hardcover edition / May 2015
Berkley Prime Crime mass-market edition / May 2016

PRINTED IN THE UNITED STATES OF AMERICA

10 9 8 7 6 5 4 3 2 1

Cover illustration by Karen Chandler.

Penguin
Random
House

To my new editor, Michelle Vega.
Thanks for loving Frank and Sarah!

I

"CHARLES OAKES IS DEAD."

Sarah looked up at her mother in surprise. They were sitting at her kitchen table, and Sarah had spent the last half hour bringing her mother up to date on the arrangements she and her fiancé, Frank Malloy, had decided upon for their wedding and their future life. She hadn't expected to hear about a death. "Is Charles the son? The one who was a few years older than I?"

"Sadly, yes."

"Oh dear. I thought maybe you meant his father."

"No, his father is Gerald."

"How did he die? Was it an accident?"

"No, he was taken ill and . . ." Her mother shrugged. Sometimes people just died, and no one knew why. As a nurse, Sarah understood that even better than most.

"Was he married?" Sarah had lost touch with most of her

old friends when she'd eloped with her first husband, a lowly physician, and turned her back on her family's wealth and social position.

"Yes, just over a year, I believe. No children, though, which is sad because he was an only child."

"It's always sad when a young person dies." Neither of them spoke of Sarah's sister, who had died young, but Sarah could almost feel Maggie's presence in the room.

Her mother toyed with her empty coffee cup for a moment, carefully not meeting Sarah's eye.

"Mother, what is it?"

She sighed. "I have to pay a condolence call on the family. I was hoping you'd go with me."

Sarah actually winced. She'd been afraid of this. Not of an old friend dying, but of being drawn back into her mother's world of high society with its strict and meaningless rules and obligations.

"I know you haven't seen them in years," her mother hurried on before Sarah could protest. "But you and Mr. Malloy are going to have to find your place in society now, and starting with your old friends seems like a natural way to begin."

"My *old friend* Charles is dead," Sarah reminded her.

"You know what I mean. I know you think my life is silly—"

"Oh, Mother, I don't—"

"Don't bother denying it. And you're right, a lot of the things I do aren't very important, but you and Mr. Malloy will need friends when you marry. Maybe you think your life isn't going to change very much just because you'll be wealthy, but you'll see, Sarah. People you know now won't want to associate with you anymore. They'll either be jealous or they'll assume you think yourselves too good for them."

"But we won't!"

"Of course you won't, but they'll think it anyway. You've seen it already. Mr. Malloy had to leave the police force, and his poor mother had to leave her old neighborhood."

Once the story of Malloy's sudden change of fortune had appeared in the newspapers, the Malloys had indeed been forced to leave the neighborhood where they'd lived since Mrs. Malloy had come over from Ireland as a young girl. "But that was just because the reporters wouldn't leave them alone."

"And because all her old friends wouldn't even speak to her anymore unless they were asking for money. Sarah, when you're . . ." She gestured vaguely.

"Rich?" Sarah supplied.

"I was going to say a member of the privileged classes, but yes, *wealthy*. When you're wealthy, the only people who feel comfortable with you are people just like you. Believe me, you will feel the same."

As much as she hoped otherwise, Sarah was afraid her mother was right. "So paying a condolence call on the Oakes family is to be my first step back into your world?"

"It's your world, too, or at least it was for most of your life. And yes, it could be. Charles's widow will need friends."

Sarah knew when she was beaten. "When did you want to go?"

"This afternoon if you're free. I need to go home and change, and I can send the carriage back for you."

"That's not necessary. I'll change here and go home with you. At least I have some appropriate clothes now." Sarah and her mother had started buying her trousseau. As a widowed midwife, her wardrobe had been much more practical and utilitarian than fashionable, so she'd been slowly adding new items.

Less than a half hour later, Sarah had changed into a stylish suit of myrtle green batiste in deference to the early fall weather. Since Sarah's daughter, Catherine, and her nursemaid, Maeve, were off visiting the park, they were able to get away without too much fuss.

"Do you think you'll keep a carriage when you're married?" her mother asked as her own carried them away from Sarah's Bank Street home.

"Our house has a mews, although the previous owners hadn't used the stables for a long time. Keeping horses in the city is such a lot of bother, though. Now tell me about Charles's family. I remember there's something unusual about his mother, but I can't remember what."

"She's Southern."

"Oh, that's right. Where is she from again?"

"Georgia, I think."

"Now I remember. Charles was always ashamed of that, I think, or maybe just embarrassed. He was teased, I know."

"Of course he was. After the war, people were angry and bitter. So many young men died or were maimed, and of course they blamed the South for starting it all."

"Well, they did start it all by seceding from the Union."

Her mother smiled sadly. "Gerald liked to remind them that *Jenny* didn't start it and that she was just as much a victim as they were. Even still, many people hated Jenny on principle, without ever bothering to meet her."

"But how on earth did she ever get to New York in the first place?"

"Gerald sent her. Oh, it was all very romantic, although it was also very tragic."

"Great romances are often tragic," Sarah said. "Like Romeo and Juliet."

"Fortunately, Gerald and Jenny's ended much better than that one."

"So he must have met her when he was in the army."

"I've been trying to remember the whole story, but it's been a long time since I heard it. Jenny's family owned a plantation. I'm sure of that, at least. Gerald was with General Sherman, and of course they were burning all the plantations as they marched to the sea, so it must have been Georgia. When they got to Jenny's home, she was the only one of her family left alive."

"How awful! She must have been just a child."

"Fifteen or sixteen, if I remember correctly."

"And she was there all alone?"

"It was a plantation, so they had slaves. Some of them had stayed, but when our troops burned the house, they had no place to go, so they followed the Union army. I understand that a lot of slaves did that."

"And Jenny went with them?"

"Apparently. I don't remember the details. Probably, she had no choice, and at some point, Gerald noticed her. She really was a beautiful young woman. He was smitten, and he must have understood that such a beauty wouldn't remain innocent for long when surrounded by thousands of soldiers, so he claimed her for himself."

"Oh my, this *is* a romantic story. So he sent her North?"

"After he married her."

"He married her? After just meeting her?"

"He had to, because it was the only way to ensure that his family would accept her, and even then . . . Well, as you can imagine, they were none too pleased, but what could they do? Gerald's father had to travel down into the South to fetch her home. You can't believe how dangerous that was during the war. They may have hoped Gerald would come to his senses when the war ended and he finally got home, but she was already with child. So they pretended not to notice the social snubs, and eventually, people got used to her."

"And Charles was their only child."

"Yes. I expect Jenny will be devastated."

"And you said he was married. His wife will be, too."

"I'm sorry to drag you into this, Sarah, but I just couldn't bear to face it alone."

"You could have just turned down the corner of your card and had your maid carry it in for you." Such a gesture often replaced a visit when such a visit might be awkward or unpleasant.

Her mother's lovely face hardened for a moment. "I couldn't possibly do that. I know what it's like to lose a child."

"Oh, Mother, I'm so sorry," Sarah said. "I didn't think—"

"It's all right. But it's true. I always try to give comfort in situations like this. It's the least I can do, no matter how little I might enjoy it. Besides, Gerald and your father have been friends since childhood. And they both belong to the Knickerbocker Club, of course. So no matter what I think of Jenny—"

"Wait, you don't like Jenny either?"

"No, but not because she's a Southerner. I don't like her because I don't like her."

"Oh. That makes sense."

Her mother sighed. "She's a difficult person to know."

"I'm sure she is, and is it any wonder? She lost her entire family and moved to a city she'd never seen before with people she'd never met who hated her on sight."

"Southerners are supposed to be charming. She didn't have to make it more difficult by being aloof."

"Maybe she was just shy. Or terrified. She was still a child."

"That was over thirty years ago. She's no longer a child, and she can't still be terrified."

Sarah wondered if that were true.

THE OAKES FAMILY LIVED ON AMSTERDAM AVENUE, JUST a few blocks from Sarah's parents. The neighborhood was quietly prosperous. Understated town houses crowded the sidewalks with their marble steps before rising in stately elegance. These weren't the monstrous mansions of the Vanderbilts or the Astors on Fifth Avenue. These were homes in which families lived for generations with the dignity, modesty, and money inherited from their thrifty Dutch ancestors.

A black wreath on the front door told the world that the Oakes family was in mourning. The maid admitted them, and after a perfunctory inquiry to see if Mrs. Oakes was "at home," Sarah and her mother followed the maid upstairs to the formal parlor.

Not everyone could wear black well, but Sarah decided that Jenny Oakes could probably wear anything well. She must be nearing fifty, but her skin was still flawless and her melted-chocolate eyes revealed no trace of her age. Her raven hair lay completely tamed against her well-shaped head, showing no betraying gray. Sarah would have guessed her to be at least ten years younger than she must be. If Mrs. Oakes plucked the gray hairs to maintain that fiction, who could blame her?

"Jenny," her mother was saying. "I'm so very sorry."

Mrs. Oakes rose from where she'd been perched on the sofa in this perfectly appointed room. She wore a gown of unrelieved black, a black handkerchief clutched in one hand.

She offered her cheek for Mrs. Decker's kiss and said, "Thank you for coming, Elizabeth."

Sarah heard just the slightest trace of the South in Mrs. Oakes's voice. Thirty years in the North had almost worn it away.

"I've brought Sarah with me," her mother said. "You remember her, don't you?"

"Of course, although it's been a long time, I think."

"Yes, it has," Sarah acknowledged, giving Mrs. Oakes her hand. The woman was a bit taller than she and held herself like a queen, although Sarah noticed in passing that her dress wasn't new or anywhere close to it. Every society woman had a good, black dress in her wardrobe for mourning emergencies. Death struck with alarming frequency and often without warning, so one had to be prepared. Obviously, Mrs. Oakes hadn't needed her mourning dress in quite a while. "I'm so sorry to hear about Charles. I remember him well."

Mrs. Oakes invited them to sit down and offered them tea.

When the maid had come with it and gone again, Sarah said, "I understand Charles had been ill."

"Not really. He . . . he thought he'd eaten something that didn't agree with him at first, especially when he was better the next day. By the time we realized how ill he really was and sent for the doctor . . ."

Sarah watched the woman's face for any sign of grief and saw none. If she felt the pain of her only son's loss, she hid it well. Of course, her mother would remind her of the lessons of her youth when she was taught it was unseemly to show emotions.

Her mother was murmuring something sympathetic when the parlor doors opened. A young woman wearing a very new and stylish black gown stepped into the room. The widow, Sarah guessed, although she didn't look particularly

grief stricken. She seemed pretty enough, although her pet-
ulant expression made it hard to really tell.

"Elizabeth, you remember my daughter-in-law, Hannah,
don't you? She was a Kingsley."

Sarah had almost forgotten the habit the old families had
of giving a person's pedigree.

Jenny introduced her guests. Hannah nodded stiffly at
Elizabeth, then glanced at Sarah before silently dismissing her
as someone of no importance. Then she made her way over
and dutifully sat down on the sofa beside her mother-in-law.
She was at least five years younger than Sarah, so their paths
would never have crossed growing up. If she had been weeping
for her dead husband, her eyes gave no indication of it.

Sarah's mother offered her condolences, but Hannah
hadn't quite mastered her mother-in-law's restraint.

"Someone should be sorry for me," she snapped. "It's all
so unfair."

Jenny gave her a sharp glance but Hannah never saw it.

"We were invited to go to Newport this summer," she continued, "but Charles said we couldn't go. Now we're in mourning, and I won't be able to go anyplace at all for a whole year."

"Charles didn't die just to inconvenience you, my dear," Jenny
said with the barest trace of venom.

Sarah glanced at her mother, whose wide eyes betrayed
her shock at such inappropriate behavior. She tried to smooth
things over. "I'm sure not going to Newport was a disappointment."

"It certainly was," Hannah said. "And the worst part was
that we couldn't go because Charles said he had to go to
work."

"Charles had been appointed superintendent of the Manhattan State Hospital," Jenny said, giving Hannah another
glare, although Hannah didn't appear to notice.

"Yes, I saw it mentioned in the newspapers," Sarah's mother said. "It was a very nice write-up about him and the hospital, too."

"They call it a hospital," Hannah said, "but it's really an asylum. A place for crazy people. Can you imagine? What would Charles know about crazy people?"

"It was an administrative position," Jenny said, more to Sarah and her mother than to Hannah. "His job was to manage the institution, not deal with the patients."

"It doesn't matter," Hannah said. "I still don't know why we couldn't go to Newport. The season there is only two months. That's not very long to be away."

Sarah's mother had had enough of Hannah. She turned back to Jenny. "I remember hearing about Charles's appointment. You must have been very proud."

Some emotion Sarah couldn't identify flickered over Jenny's face, causing a tightness around her mouth. "Charles has many friends in the city."

Or maybe she wasn't so proud.

Sarah's mother quickly began inquiring about funeral arrangements, which seemed cheerful by comparison to Hannah's inappropriate bitterness over her husband's inconvenient death. They managed to finish their visit without another outburst from the young widow, and gratefully followed the maid who came to show them out.

Sarah was quietly wondering if it was possible for her to withdraw from society completely after she and Malloy married, when the maid startled them both by stopping dead in her tracks. She turned to face them instead of leading them down the stairs.

"Excuse me, Mrs. Decker, but Mr. Oakes asked if you could see him in the library for a few minutes before you leave."

"Why, certainly," she replied, giving Sarah a puzzled glance. "My daughter, too?"

"Yes, ma'am. This way, please."

She led them down the hallway, away from the stairs that would have taken them to the front door at street level. She opened one of the doors and announced them.

The library was a comfortable room with large leather armchairs and rows of bookshelves. The air smelled faintly of tobacco. A middle-aged man greeted them warmly. Sarah's mother gave him both her hands and offered her cheek for a kiss.

"I'm so terribly sorry, Gerald," she said.

"It's a cruel trick of fate when a child dies," he said, blinking at the tears neither his wife nor his daughter-in-law had bothered to shed. "You expect to bury your parents, but never your children."

"I know," she said, and Sarah knew she did. "You remember my daughter, Sarah."

"Of course. Mrs. Brandt, isn't it?"

"Yes," Sarah said in surprise. He would have had no reason to have remembered her married name. She expressed her condolences, and he thanked her.

"Please, sit down. I won't keep you long, but I have a favor to ask."

They each took one of the armchairs that sat grouped together in front of the unlit fireplace. The soft leather enveloped Sarah, and she thought perhaps she should get some chairs like this for her new house. She would have to mention it to Malloy.

"You know we'll be happy to do anything for you and Jenny, Gerald," her mother was saying. "All you need to do is ask."

"Actually, Mrs. Brandt is the one I must ask," he said.

"Me?" Sarah asked in surprise.

"Well, you and your fiancé. You're engaged to Frank Malloy, aren't you?"

"Yes," she said, thinking he couldn't possibly have remembered that tidbit of information from casually reading the society pages of the newspapers.

"I know what Mr. Malloy did for the club, Mrs. Brandt. The Knickerbocker Club," he added in case she didn't know. "He handled a sensitive situation discreetly, and all the members were very grateful."

"I'll be sure and tell him you said so."

"Please do. And of course we know about his . . . his recent good fortune. As you can imagine, it has been a topic of interest to all of us."

"I can easily imagine that," Sarah said with a small smile. It had been a topic of interest to many people.

"I say all this so you know that I understand he is no longer with the police and that he no longer needs to earn his living, but I am wondering if you think he would be willing to assist me in another matter that is even more sensitive than the one he handled at the club."

Sarah's mind was racing as she tried to figure out where this conversation was taking her. "I really can't speak for Mr. Malloy," she hedged, although she could easily imagine he would be thrilled to do anything besides oversee the renovations to their house, which had been his sole occupation for the past few months. "But I will be happy to pass along your request. Can you give me some idea of what you'd like him to help you with?"

"Yes. I'd like him to investigate my son's murder."

AT FIRST FRANK THOUGHT THE KNOCKING WAS JUST more hammering from the workmen who were somewhere in the bowels of his monstrosity of a house doing something to, hopefully, make it fit for habitation, if he lived long enough to ever see the end of it. He tried to remind himself that eventually, the house would be finished, and he and Sarah would be married, and she'd live here with him. Unfortunately, he'd begun to give up hope that would ever happen, because, at this rate, the house was never going to be finished.

After a few minutes, he finally realized the knocking was coming from the front door, though, and he made his way to answer it.

The front hallway didn't look too bad, he acknowledged, glancing around as he approached the door. Except for some dust, which was unavoidable as long as the workmen were here, it was almost presentable. If only the doorbell worked. He'd asked the workmen to fix it at least a dozen times, to no avail. Who knows how many visitors had given up and gone away because he hadn't heard them knock? A lot, he hoped, since the only people who knocked on his door nowadays were reporters looking for a story or people looking for a handout.

Frank threw open the door, ready to do battle with whoever was there to ask him for something, and he caught himself just in time. "Sarah."

She smiled the way she always smiled when she saw him, and he had to resist the overwhelming urge to take her in his arms, because her mother was standing right beside her.

"Mrs. Decker, how nice to see you." He stood back and motioned them inside.

"It's lovely to see you, too," Mrs. Decker said.

Sarah gave him a peck on the cheek and a knowing smirk as she passed. Both women looked around appreciatively as he closed the door behind them.

"It's starting to look very nice," Mrs. Decker said.

Just then someone upstairs started pounding, raising a deafening racket. Frank motioned them into the room he'd just left and closed the door. They could still hear the pounding, but they could also now hear one another, too.

"This is going to be Mrs. Malloy's sitting room," Sarah told her mother. "And her bedroom is through there. We made her a suite down here so she wouldn't have to manage the stairs."

"It's lovely," Mrs. Decker said.

"She made me bring all her old furniture," Frank felt obligated to explain, because it didn't really look *that* lovely.

"Which was very sensible," Mrs. Decker said, always the lady. "You wouldn't want to put anything new in here until the workmen are finished. Where is your mother?"

"She's at school with Brian."

"She still stays with him every day?"

"She helps out there," Frank explained, "and she's learning to sign, too, so she can talk to him."

"That's such a wonderful thing," Mrs. Decker said. "We should all learn to sign now that Brian will be a member of our family."

Frank knew he was probably gaping at her in surprise at the thought that she would actually want to learn sign language to talk with his deaf son, but she was much too polite to notice.

"Uh, why don't you sit down," he managed after a moment. "Can I get you something?"

"Oh my, no. I wouldn't think of sending you to the kitchen for anything," Sarah said, still giving him that knowing smirk as she and her mother sat down on his mother's old sofa. "Besides, we're here on business."

"What kind of business?"

"Gerald Oakes wants to hire you to investigate his son's murder."

"*Possible* murder," Mrs. Decker added quickly. "Actually, he wants you to figure out if his son was murdered or if he died a natural death."

Frank sank down in one of his mother's old chairs. "Who is Gerald Oakes?"

"He's a member of the Knickerbocker Club," Sarah said.

"And an old friend of our family," Mrs. Decker said.

"And he knows all about you and what you did for the club," Sarah said.

"And he also knows your current situation," Mrs. Decker said, "so he didn't want to insult you by offering to hire you, but he thought you would appreciate a businesslike arrangement of some sort."

The women were making him a little dizzy. "You said he wants to find out if his son was murdered. How did he die?"

"It was sudden," Sarah explained. She looked especially beautiful today, he noticed, but then, he thought she looked especially beautiful every day. "He became ill, vomiting and other unpleasant things, apparently."

"He thought he'd eaten something bad," Mrs. Decker said.

"When he didn't get any better over the next few days, they called in the doctor, but he died shortly afterward."

"So Oakes thinks his son was poisoned?" Frank asked.

"Wouldn't you?" Mrs. Decker asked.

He gave her a tolerant smile. "It probably wouldn't be my first thought unless I had a reason to think someone wanted him dead. Did someone want this fellow . . . What's his name?"

"Charles Oakes," Sarah said. "He's . . . he *was* only a few years older than I, and otherwise in good health."

"Tell him about the milk," Mrs. Decker said.

"Yes, tell me about the milk," he said with a grin.

"The night he died, he'd asked for a glass of warm milk," Sarah said. "He drank most of it, and at some point later, while the doctor was working on him, the glass got knocked over. No one noticed it until the next morning."

"There wasn't much milk left, apparently," Mrs. Decker said, "but the cat—his wife has this pet cat—had apparently lapped up what was left."

"And they found the cat under Charles's bed, dead," Sarah said.

"After the undertaker had come for Charles's body the next morning," Mrs. Decker added.

"That's interesting," Frank said.

"Of course, it doesn't prove anything," Sarah said. "Sometimes cats just die."

"And sometimes people just die," Mrs. Decker said.

"But when they both die after drinking the same glass of milk, you have to wonder," Frank said.

"Exactly," Mrs. Decker said.

She looked much too excited for somebody talking about an old friend being poisoned. Frank knew he shouldn't encourage her morbid fascination, but he couldn't help himself. "What did the doctor say?"

"He said gastric fever. He didn't know about the cat, of course," Mrs. Decker said.

"I asked Mr. Oakes where they took the body, and he said it's at a funeral home now," Sarah said.

"So they didn't do an autopsy?" he asked.

Sarah shook her head. "No, and it's probably too late now, isn't it?"

"If the body is already embalmed . . ." Frank shrugged.

"And the milk glass has long since been washed and put away," Sarah said.

"Does Mr. Oakes have any reason to think somebody wanted his son dead?"

The two women exchanged a glance, then Sarah said, "He didn't want to discuss that with two gently bred ladies, but I think if you are willing to help him, he would discuss it with you."

"If there's no proof he was poisoned, I don't know what I can do," Frank said.

At some point, the pounding had apparently stopped, which Frank hadn't noticed until it suddenly started up again, making him wince.

"You won't know until you talk to him," Sarah said, "and helping him would give you a reason to get out of the house."

Frank sighed. "Do you think he's still at home?"

FRANK STEPPED OUT OF THE CAB ON AMSTERDAM AVENUE and looked up at the Oakes house. Once he would have been intimidated to enter the home of one of the wealthier families in the city. Knowing Sarah Brandt had brought him into many such homes, however, and if he'd learned nothing else, he'd learned that rich people suffered from most of the same problems as poor people. Rich people also killed each other as often as poor people. They were just a little neater about it.

Frank rang the doorbell and thought again how he needed to remind the workmen to fix his. A maid answered and looked him up and down. He couldn't do much about his Irish face, but he knew his suit told her he was somebody to be taken seriously. Sarah's father had sent him to his own tailor to make sure he looked like the millionaire he now was.

"Frank Malloy to see Mr. Oakes. He's expecting me," he said.

He'd occasionally been told to use the back door when calling on houses like this, but today the maid let him in without a protest and only kept him waiting a few minutes while she asked her employer if he was at home for Mr. Malloy.

Oakes was in a room Frank suspected he spent a lot of time in. Bookshelves lined the walls and the chairs were oversize and well-worn. The lingering scent of tobacco told him no females frequented this sanctuary.

Oakes was a handsome man in his fifties. He'd developed a slight paunch but otherwise seemed fit. His blond hair was graying at the temples, and he looked like he hadn't slept much the night before.

"Mr. Malloy, thank you for coming."

"Mrs. Brandt said you were anxious to talk to me."

"Indeed, I am. Please sit down. Can I get you something? I have bourbon and some excellent Scotch."

Frank didn't usually drink in the middle of the day, but Oakes looked like he could use one, so he said, "Bourbon."

Oakes poured their drinks into some leaded crystal tumblers, then sat down opposite him. The chairs were as comfortable as they looked, and Frank wished he were here for just a social call. "I'm sorry about your son."

A spasm of pain flickered across Oakes's face, but he squared his shoulders as if steeling himself for a fight. "Thank you. Charles was my only child. Do you have children, Mr. Malloy?"

"A son."

"Then you can imagine what it's like."

"Mrs. Brandt said you're concerned about the circumstances of your son's death."

Oakes took a fortifying sip of his whiskey. "I'm very much afraid he was poisoned."

"Mrs. Brandt also told me about the milk and the cat, but I'd like to hear from you exactly what happened."

"I wasn't there for everything, you understand. Charles felt ill one afternoon. He vomited, and he assumed he'd eaten something bad."

"Was he at home that day?"

"No, he'd been out all day. He returned home when he was taken ill. He didn't feel like eating much, and over the next day, he got better. That was Sunday. By Monday, he was well enough that he went out again."

"But he wasn't really better," Frank said.

"No. The same thing happened again. He became ill and returned home. He couldn't keep anything down, but he complained that his throat was burning and asked for some milk to soothe it."

"Who brought him the milk?"

"I have no idea. One of the maids, probably."

Frank nodded. "So he drank it?"

"Yes. Actually, I didn't know about the milk until much later, the next day in fact. All I knew was that he started vomiting again. He also had the bloody flux and was in a great deal of pain. We sent for our physician, and he tried giving Charles some medicine, but he died within the hour."

"And the cat?"

"Yes, Hannah had this cat. The thing went missing, but we thought maybe it was just frightened by all the disturbance when Charles died or maybe that it had gotten out somehow. The maid found it when she was cleaning Charles's room after . . . after they took him away."

Oakes took another sip of his whiskey, and Frank waited

for him to compose himself. "I understand the milk glass had spilled."

"Yes. Charles was in a lot of pain at the end and delirious as well. He was thrashing around, and I suppose the glass got knocked to the floor. It had rolled under the bed, you see. When the maid reached under to get it, she saw the cat."

Frank had dealt with poisonings before, and this certainly sounded like a possible case of it. He wondered if Oakes had thought beyond that, though. "I can see why you think he was poisoned."

He perked up at that. "Then you agree?"

"It's not for me to agree or disagree. Maybe he was poisoned, but knowing *how* someone died is only the beginning in a murder investigation. The important question is *why*."

"Why someone killed him, you mean?"

"Yes, and because your son was killed here, in his own home, an even more important question is *who* . . . because the killer must be someone who lives here with you."

Oakes frowned. "But no one lives here except our family and our servants."

"And if your son really was poisoned, it's very likely one of them did it, because only people in the house had access to the glass of milk."

Frank watched the emotions play across his face. The horror of thinking someone in his own house had killed his son, the reluctance to believe such a thing, and finally, a resolve Frank hadn't expected to see.

"I need to know why my son died, Mr. Malloy, and I'm willing to deal with any consequences that knowledge may bring. Will you help me?"

How could he refuse? "Of course."

"Then where will you start?"

"Do you have the glass the milk was in?"

"Yes, but it's been washed and put away."

"And I suppose you had your son's body embalmed."

"Yes. Everyone does nowadays."

Frank sighed. Only one thing left. "Then what became of the cat?"

2

THE STOREFRONT GAVE LITTLE INDICATION OF THE BUSI-ness being conducted inside, Frank noticed. Just a modest sign, slightly faded, that said: TITUS WESLEY, CORONER.

Frank wasn't sure what he expected, but it was certainly not the young man who emerged from a back room when the bell over the door announced his arrival in the shop. Wearing a stained leather apron over his clothes, he was wiping his hands on a filthy towel. Tall, scrawny, and horse-faced, he grinned at the way Frank was holding the odiferous sack out at arm's length.

"What have you brought me?" he asked pleasantly. "Something dead, by the smell of it."

"A cat," Frank said, setting the sack on the floor and stepping away, although the shop was much too small for him to escape the stench, short of leaving entirely.

The young man raised his eyebrows. "I don't handle animals. Usually people just throw them in the river or the street cleaners pick them up."

"It's evidence in a murder investigation," he said. "Doc Haynes told me you could help me determine if the cat was poisoned."

The young man laid the towel he'd been using on the counter that ran along one side wall. "Why didn't Haynes do it himself, then?"

"It's not an official police investigation, so I asked him to recommend someone as good as he is."

The young man straightened at the compliment. New York had dozens of men who called themselves coroners and who took care of the thousands of people who died each year in the city. Most of them had no medical training at all, and they would determine any cause of death their clients requested for the right price, no matter what the condition of the body indicated. Frank had always requested Doc Haynes for murder investigations because he knew Doc would give him an accurate cause of death.

"You're not a copper, then," he said, looking Frank over. Not many cops could afford the suit Frank wore.

"Not anymore."

"So you want to find out who murdered this cat?" he asked with some amusement.

"A man died after drinking a glass of milk. The cat lapped up what was left and then it died, too."

"Ah, I see! This sounds like an interesting case, Mr. . . . ?"

"Malloy. I'm a private investigator." Frank liked the way that title rolled off his tongue. He no longer inspired fear, as he had when he'd been a detective sergeant with the New York Police, but he also no longer inspired contempt for being part of the police force either.

"Titus Wesley, at your service, Mr. Malloy."

Frank was relieved he didn't offer to shake hands. "I know this is out of your usual line, but my client is willing to pay for your services, the same as if it was human."

"Why don't you just let me examine the dead man?"

"He's been embalmed."

Wesley shrugged. "I still might be able to tell something. If they didn't discard his organs, I'd like to have a look at them, too."

"I'll write down the name of the undertaker for you."

"And you'd better have someone from the family tell them it's all right for me to see him. Undertakers can be a possessive lot."

"I'll do that." Frank pulled a small notebook and a pencil from his coat pocket and scribbled down the information, then tore out the page and handed it to Wesley.

Wesley eyed the sack. "How long has the cat been dead?"

"A couple days. They'd buried it in the yard."

"Good thing or we might never be able to prove the poisoning."

Frank gave him one of the calling cards Sarah had ordered for him. At the time, he hadn't been able to imagine using them, but now . . . "How long until you'll know something?"

"Tomorrow evening."

"I'll come back then. If you need me before, that's where you'll find me."

"YOU'RE GETTING AN AUTOPSY ON A CAT?" SARAH ASKED when Malloy had finished telling her about his afternoon.

They were sitting at her kitchen table as they had been doing every weekday evening since the Malloys had moved into the house down the street where they would all live together when Sarah and Malloy married. Malloy would have dinner with his family, and Sarah with hers. After his mother put Brian to bed and Sarah's daughter, Catherine, was asleep, he'd walk down to visit with her for a few hours. It was a strange courtship, but Sarah cherished their time alone.

"You should have seen the coroner's face when I told him."

"I'm sure Dr. Haynes was thrilled."

"He would have been, but he couldn't do it. Too busy. He sent me to a fellow named Titus Wesley."

"He's a coroner?" she asked with a frown.

"Doc Haynes says he's a real doctor, and he knows what he's doing."

"Too bad he can't look at Charles's body."

"He's going to try. He said he still might find something."

"I hope he finds nothing," Sarah said. "I just hate the idea that poor Charles was poisoned. Who would do such a horrible thing?"

"A woman."

"What?"

"Poison is a woman's weapon."

Sarah glared at him. "That's unfair."

"Maybe, but it's also true. Women aren't usually strong enough to kill with their hands, like men can, or with a weapon like a knife or a club, and women hardly ever know how to shoot a gun. They also don't usually kill in the heat of passion unless it's self-defense or they're defending a child or someone weaker."

"So you're saying women take their time and plan murders."

"As a general rule. They also don't like to make a mess."

Sarah had to smile at that. "Of course not! They're the ones who'd have to clean it up."

"Poison is a great equalizer. A tiny woman can bring down a man twice her size with very little effort at all."

"I'd never thought of it that way before, but I suppose you're right. So who do you think killed Charles? Assuming he really was poisoned, of course."

"I won't know that until I know more about who lives in the house. What can you tell me about the family?"

"Oh, it's a wonderful story of how his parents met." She told him what her mother had said about the two and their wartime romance.

Malloy leaned back in his chair when she'd finished, frowning. "I guess you think it was all very romantic."

"And you don't?"

"I can see it might have seemed that way from the girl's side. She'd lost her home and her family and everything she'd ever known. Then a handsome young soldier saves her."

"I know. It's like a fairy tale from her point of view, but are you saying it's not the same from his?"

"I don't know. Maybe it was. Maybe rich young men like the idea of saving a young girl in trouble."

"A damsel in distress," Sarah said.

"And she was certainly that. I've never been a rich young man, but I wouldn't want a wife who only married me because she didn't have any other choice."

"I can't imagine they saw it that way. Surely they were in love."

"If she was pretty, he probably *thought* he was. I wonder what she thought."

Sarah smiled again. "I do know that young men can be as silly as young girls about love."

"So maybe they *were* in love, but you said his family wasn't happy about it."

"How could they be? They didn't know anything about her, and she probably came to them with little more than the clothes on her back. They may have even suspected that she tricked him somehow."

"Maybe she did. She had a baby right away, after all. You've met her. What do you think?"

"It's funny you should ask. I thought she was remarkably composed for a woman who had lost her only child. Of course, I was taught from birth not to let my emotions get the better of me in public. No one wants to see a woman cry."

"That's true enough, but do you think she was just being proper or do you think she didn't love her son?"

"I can't imagine a mother not loving her son."

Malloy gave her a crooked smile. "I'm sure you can't. You even love my son."

"He's very lovable. But you love my daughter, so we're even."

"Yes, we are, but no closer to knowing who might have poisoned Charles Oakes. What about his wife?"

"She's a piece of work. All she could talk about was how angry she was that Charles wouldn't take her to Newport this past summer and now she's in mourning and won't be able to go anywhere at all."

"Why wouldn't he take her to Newport?"

"Because he couldn't leave his job."

Malloy blinked in surprise. "He had a job?"

"Yes, he'd been appointed as superintendent of the Manhattan State Hospital."

"The Asylum? Oh, that's right. I read about him in the newspapers when it happened. So that was Charles Oakes. But why would he want a job like that?"

Sarah had to think about that for a minute. "I imagine he needed the income."

"I thought his family was rich."

"His family is *old*, and they once were wealthy, but sometimes . . . Well, we don't talk about it, but sometimes the
family money runs out or is lost in bad investments or what
have you. A lot of families were hurt in the financial panic
in ninety-three. Why do you think Theodore took a position
as police commissioner?"

"You mean he'd lost his fortune?"

"The Roosevelts—at least his branch of the family—have
to earn their keep, yes."

"Is that what happened to the Oakes family?"

"I don't know for sure, and I would never be so rude as to
ask them," she added before he could suggest it. "But now
that you mention it, I did notice that Mrs. Oakes's mourning
gown was past its prime. And maybe Charles didn't take his
wife to Newport because he couldn't afford to."

"So Charles decided to run the Asylum. That's an odd
choice."

"I doubt he *had* a choice. Young men like him often don't
have any skills when it comes to earning a living, so they ask
their friends for help finding something. If you're asking for
a favor from your friends, you have to take what's available."

"Oh, like when Tammany Hall gets jobs for the people
who do them favors."

"Exactly, except I'm sure Charles went to his Republican
friends instead of Boss Croker."

"And now the family has lost its wage earner. That's a
pity."

"And it also means his family didn't have much reason to
want him dead."

"Unless his wife was a lot madder about not going to
Newport than he expected."

"Ordinarily, I'd take you to task for saying something like
that about a poor widow, but in this case . . ."

He perked up at that. "Do you think she really might've killed him?"

"You always tell me not to decide someone is innocent just because I like them, so I'm not going to decide she's a killer just because I *don't* like her."

"Ah, but you're not saying she couldn't possibly have done it either."

"No, I'm not, but good heavens, they've only been married a year. She's hardly had time to grow to hate him that much."

"How long do you think it takes?" he asked with interest.

"I have no idea."

That made him grin. "So who else lives in the house who might've learned to hate poor Charles?"

"Besides the servants and his parents, I don't know."

"Are Gerald's parents still alive?"

Sarah tried to remember. "I haven't really kept track of my parents' friends, but I think his mother is."

"You didn't see her when you were there?"

"No, she probably isn't receiving visitors. I was surprised Jenny Oakes was, in fact. Most of the time when there's a death, the family just lets people drop off their cards and doesn't see anyone at all except at the funeral. I suppose we should attend, shouldn't we?"

"I suppose we should. It's day after tomorrow, isn't it?"

"Yes. You'll have an opportunity to see the family for yourself."

"I can hardly wait. Now come over here and sit on my lap for a while before I have to go home."

FRANK WAS STARTING TO WISH HE'D MADE ARRANGE-ments to visit Charles Oakes's body along with the coroner Wesley. The day had been a series of construction disasters

as the workmen installed a second bathroom upstairs in the
suite of rooms Sarah and Frank had claimed for their own.
He was just about to lose his temper completely and order
all of them out of the house when someone knocked on the
front door, reminding him again about the broken doorbell.

Ready to shout at some nosy reporter or some bum looking for a handout, he found a soldier on his doorstep instead.
He needed a moment to recognize him.

"Gino! I didn't know you were back from Cuba," he said,
absurdly happy to see the young man.

Gino grinned. "We've been back for a few weeks. They
kept us out on Long Island for a while before we got discharged." He'd resigned from the police department several
months ago to fight with Theodore Roosevelt's Rough Riders in the war with Spain. Mercifully, the combat had only
lasted a few weeks before the Spanish had been soundly
beaten, at least according to the newspapers.

"Come in. Don't mind the mess. We've got workmen
fixing the place up. How'd you find me?"

"They told me at Police Headquarters. Everybody knows
where you live now."

Frank led him into his mother's parlor. "Are you back on
the force again, then?"

"No, I . . . Not yet."

Frank motioned for him to sit down on the sofa. "I hardly
knew you in your uniform, and you're awfully brown."

"I got sunburned. All the Rough Riders did. Cuba is . . .
Well, it's not like anything I've ever seen before. If hell is
any hotter, I'll be surprised."

"You look good," Frank said, exaggerating a little. Gino
looked thinner and tired. "Your mother told me you came
through without a scratch."

"I was lucky." The boy's dark eyes clouded. Many of the Rough Riders had not come back from Cuba.

"We all read about your charge up San Juan Hill," Frank said, hoping to lighten the mood a bit.

"It was really Kettle Hill. Colonel Roosevelt said San Juan Hill sounded better, so that's what the newspapers called it. It was the next hill over, so we figured it didn't matter."

"Whatever it was, it made Roosevelt a hero. They're talking to him about running for governor."

"He'll be good at it. I thought he did some stupid things when he was police commissioner, but he was a good soldier. He took care of his men and kept us out of trouble whenever he could."

"Are you glad you left the police and joined up?"

Gino met Frank's gaze directly for the first time. "I am. When the colonel said he wanted policemen and athletes in his regiment, well, I figured I could qualify. I didn't know who else would be there, though. Mr. Malloy, I served with the sons of millionaires from Fifth Avenue and cowboys from Texas. We even had some Indians. But Colonel Roosevelt, he treated us all the same, and we treated each other all the same, too. All that mattered was if you could fight."

"I'm sure you did well, Gino. And you beat the Spanish."

He shook his head. "I don't know that the Cubans even noticed. They didn't even seem grateful that we came. I never saw people so poor. I thought things were bad in Mulberry Bend and places like that, but you've never seen anything like the way those people live. They didn't have anything at all. They'd follow the army around and steal whatever we set down. They took our food and our equipment and our clothes, whatever they could carry away. I'm not sure they even cared who was ruling them."

Frank didn't know what to say to that. The newspapers hadn't mentioned anything about the Cubans or how they lived. All the stories had been about the bravery of the American forces and how quickly they'd beaten the Spanish army. "But you said you're glad you went."

Gino nodded. "I learned a lot, but . . . I'd never seen a man die before. That may sound funny, because we've seen lots of dead people, but I never saw someone actually die."

"You lost a lot of good men."

Gino looked away, and Frank thought he must be remembering those men. After a moment, though, he forced a grin. "So, what have you been doing while I was gone?"

"Trying to stay out of sight. You wouldn't believe how many people have asked me for money."

"Are you serious? People ask you for money?"

"All the time. I had to move my mother and Brian here even though the house isn't ready yet, just so they wouldn't be bothered anymore."

"Where are they?" he asked, glancing around.

"At the deaf school. Ma takes him every day and stays there, helping out."

"And you just sit here all by yourself?"

"I'm supervising the workmen." As if to illustrate his point, someone started pounding upstairs somewhere.

"Do you miss the police work at all?"

Frank had been asked to leave the police department when they found out he'd come into a fortune. "I miss the work. I don't miss the rest of it."

Gino grinned. "Me, too. Especially after the army. If you think the department was bad, the army was ten times worse. They couldn't even get supplies to us, and they only issued us one suit of clothes and one blanket each, so if anything happened . . ." His eyes clouded again. "I'll never forget when we carried the wounded to the hospital tents or where the hospital was supposed to be, at least. The wounded men had lost their packs, and the doctors cut off their bloody clothes to bandage them up, and then they didn't have so much as a shirt to put on them. The wounded were just laying in a field, right on the ground, buck naked most of them. If it hadn't been for that lady, Clara Barton . . ."

"I read about her in the newspapers."

"She sent her people out to buy bolts of fabric, and they cut it up to make sheets so the men didn't have to lay on the bare ground. And the nurses she brought with her, well, I don't know how many more men would've died if they hadn't been there." He stared off again, lost in the dark place Frank couldn't see.

"Have you talked to the chief?" Frank asked, trying to draw him back. "I'm sure he'll give you your old job back if you want it."

"That's just it. I'm not sure I do want it."

Frank didn't want to point out that job opportunities for the son of Italian immigrants weren't too plentiful in the city. "You don't have to decide today, you know. You can take some time to get used to being home again. I'm sure things will look different to you in a few weeks."

"Things look different to me now, Mr. Malloy. I saw men die, men even younger than I am. They never got a chance to do anything with their lives. I feel like I owe them something because I lived and they didn't."

"What do you think you owe them?"

"I . . . I don't know exactly, but I remember when I first joined the police, I thought I'd help make the city a better place."

"You thought you'd get rid of the criminals," Frank guessed. "Lock them up and throw away the key."

"Yeah. It sounds stupid now, doesn't it?"

"No, it doesn't," Frank said gently. "We both know it isn't going to happen, but that doesn't mean we should quit trying."

"Are you still trying?"

Frank sighed, suddenly realizing that he was. "As a matter of fact, I just took a new case yesterday."

For the first time since he'd walked in the door, Gino's eyes lit with interest. "A case? You're not back on the force, are you?"

"No, of course not. One of Mr. Decker's friends asked me to investigate his son's death, though. We think he was poisoned."

"You're a private detective, then," Gino said. "Just like when we found those missing girls."

"I guess I am, at least right now."

"And you think he was poisoned?" Gino leaned forward, his eyes alive now in a way they hadn't been just a minute ago. "Who do you think did it?"

Frank leaned back in his own chair and studied the young man for a few seconds. "I'm not sure I should discuss the case with you."

Gino stiffened, obviously offended. "Why not?"

"Because if you're with the police—"

"I'm not with the police!"

Frank rubbed his chin, pretending to consider the matter. "On the other hand, if you worked for me, I could tell you."

"What do you mean, if I worked for you?"

"Well, I'm probably going to need some help with this case, and you're not doing anything right now . . ."

Now he was really offended. "Wait, I didn't come here looking for a handout or anything."

"I haven't offered you a handout. I'll pay you if you want to help me work on the case. This friend of Mr. Decker's is going to pay me, after all. What do you think?"

Plainly, Gino didn't know what to think. "I . . . Are you sure?"

"Am I sure of what? That you're a good investigator? I know that you used to be, and unless something happened to you down in Cuba that made you forget everything you used to know, then I'm sure you'll be able to help with this."

"I haven't forgotten anything," he insisted. "I wasn't gone *that* long."

Frank grinned. "Well, then, you need to go home and change into some regular clothes and meet me at the coroner's office to find out if this fellow was poisoned or not."

"And if he wasn't?"

Frank shrugged. "Then we'll find another case to keep us busy."

Gino was waiting for him outside Titus Wesley's storefront office. He wore a brown suit, neatly pressed but a little tight in the shoulders, Frank noticed. Gino's time in the army had put some muscle on him. His shirt collar was new and his tie neat. He even wore his bowler hat down low on his forehead instead of perched on the back of his head, as so many young men did. He was taking the private detective business seriously.

"Why didn't you use Doc Haynes for the autopsy?" Gino asked by way of greeting.

"He's too busy. Besides, when I started, I only had a dead cat. Doc wasn't too happy about wasting his time on a cat."

"Why didn't the family just go to the police in the first place?"

Gino had clearly been thinking about the case while he'd been off changing his clothes. "The father, Mr. Oakes, didn't want to alarm the women. There's a wife and a mother and maybe a grandmother, too. No sense getting them all upset for no reason, at least until he's sure."

Frank pushed open the door to Wesley's shop, setting the bell to jangling. The sickening smell of death enveloped them. Frank hadn't noticed it before, since he'd just carried a dead cat halfway across town the first time he'd been here. He'd blamed the smell on that.

"Wesley, you here?"

Gino, he noticed, was looking a little green.

Wesley came out from the back room, once again wiping his hands on a filthy rag, and greeted them. Frank introduced Gino, and the young man didn't offer to shake hands. Frank couldn't blame him.

"Donatelli here is going to be assisting me," Frank explained. "Did you find out anything?"

"Oh yes. The undertaker wasn't too happy with me, I can tell you that, but I got the dead man's organs. They hadn't even removed them, thank God. They were able to sew him back up, as good as new, so no one will ever suspect that not all of him went into the ground. They complained bitterly about the extra work, though."

"And was he poisoned?"

Wesley frowned. "You have to understand that coroners don't automatically look for traces of poison. Unless it's something obvious, like the mouth and throat are burned from something caustic, we never assume someone's been poisoned."

"How do you find out, then?" Frank asked.

"Most of the time we don't. I suspect that there are hundreds of people poisoned every year, and the killer is never even suspected because no one looked for it at autopsy or no autopsy was even performed."

"Or the coroner was paid not to notice it," Frank guessed.

Wesley gave him a small nod of acknowledgment. "In this case, however, someone did suspect, so I looked for it especially."

"And what did you find?"

"I didn't have much to work with, you understand. I could see the stomach and throat were irritated, but from what you described of his last hours, that's what I would've expected. I didn't see any ulcers or other damage, so if I was looking for a poison, I suspected arsenic. It's very easy to obtain and doesn't leave much trace unless the person has been poisoned over a long period of time. From what you told me, it sounds like this Oakes fellow was only sick for a few days, so I didn't expect to see any traces of long-term exposure."

"How long would it have to be going on before you'd find that?" Gino asked.

Frank looked at him in surprise, but Wesley was already responding. "A few weeks at least. Then I'd find it in the liver and kidneys. If it was longer, say a month or more, then I could find it in the fingernails and hair."

"In the fingernails?"

"Yeah, there would be lines. The hair is the same, except there's no lines."

Gino frowned. "How could somebody be taking arsenic for weeks or months and not die?"

"Small amounts of arsenic will just make you sick. It builds up in the body over time, though, and eventually the organs begin to fail."

"Why would somebody give a person a dose too small to kill them, though?"

Wesley grinned, obviously enjoying the conversation. "You'd have to ask that 'somebody,' but maybe they aren't sure how much would be a fatal dose, so they don't give the victim enough at first. Or maybe the person has a tolerance for it. Some people do, and the amount that would kill me in an hour might only make you a little sick."

"Or," Frank said, glad to see his new assistant was curious but wanting to move the interview along, "the killer might want it to look like the victim had some mysterious illness the doctors couldn't cure and eventually died of it."

"Oh, so no one would suspect poison," Gino said.

"That's right. So was it arsenic?" Frank asked.

"Oh yes. I did the Marsh test where you put the material on a zinc plate covered with sulfuric acid—"

"This Marsh test," Frank interrupted him, not interested in the details. "Is it something that's scientifically official?"

"You mean, would it be accepted in court?"

"I guess that's what I mean."

"Yes. It's been around since the thirties, and the test is good on even the smallest amount of arsenic. I was also able to test the contents of the cat's stomach, and I found arsenic there, too."

Frank knew he shouldn't be pleased to hear that Charles Oakes had been poisoned. This meant a lot more heartache for the Oakes family. On the other hand, it also meant he didn't have to spend all his days sitting in his new house, listening to the workmen pounding away.

"If someone was getting poisoned, though, wouldn't they notice the taste?" Gino asked.

"With some poisons, yes, but arsenic doesn't have a taste."

"So it might've been put into anything he drank," Frank said.

"Yes or anything he ate. It can take some time to work, too. Some poisons cause an immediate reaction, but with arsenic, depending on how big the dose is, the victim can go anywhere from half an hour to a whole day before they start showing a reaction."

"So even though our victim first got sick when he was away from home, he might've gotten poisoned there," Frank said.

"Yes, but from what we know about the milk and the dead cat, it looks like he got the final, fatal dose at home the night he died," Wesley said.

Frank told Wesley where to send his bill, and he and Gino stepped out onto the sidewalk and the noticeably fresher air.

"How does he stand the stench?" Gino asked.

"He probably doesn't even smell it anymore."

"What do we do now?"

"Well, I've got to go tell Mr. Oakes that his son was murdered."

"Can I go with you?"

Frank hated to dampen his enthusiasm, but he couldn't bring a stranger to the Oakes house, at least not yet. "I want to see Oakes alone. There's no telling how he'll take the news, even if he's expecting it, and he obviously is or he wouldn't have hired me to investigate. Suspecting your son was murdered and finding out for sure that he was are two different things, though. Add to that the fact that he was killed in their house, so the killer must be someone close, well, Oakes might change his mind about finding out who did it. I don't think he'd want a stranger there while we're discussing the possibilities."

Gino nodded, obviously trying to hide his disappointment. "That makes sense."

"I'm thinking I need to tell Mrs. Brandt what we found out, though. She'll be wondering, and I don't want her doing anything silly, like going to call on Mrs. Oakes to find out."

As Frank had expected, Gino visibly brightened at the prospect of seeing Sarah. "You won't mind if I go with you to Mrs. Brandt's, will you?"

"I won't have time to see her before I go to visit Oakes. I want to get to him before the family sits down to supper. I was thinking you could go see Mrs. Brandt without me, though. You know as much as I do about the case now."

"I'd be happy to do that," he said, looking *more* than happy to do that.

"And maybe Maeve will give you a kiss to welcome you home."

"Wha . . . Why would she do that?" Gino stammered, blushing furiously.

"No reason I can think of," Frank confessed, "but a man can hope."

Frank and Sarah had more than once discussed the apparent attraction between Sarah's nursemaid and the young policeman. Judging from Gino's reaction just now, they'd been right about his feelings for the young lady. Her feelings were still not nearly as certain, at least not so far as Frank could tell. Knowing Maeve, though, she'd lead Gino on a merry chase, no matter what.

"Oh well, I see," Gino said, although he plainly didn't see anything at all. "I'll go right over and tell Mrs. Brandt what we know so far."

"You do that and tell her I'll come by later to tell her what happened with Oakes."

"Should I wait there until you come?"

"No, it'll be late, but come to my house in the morning. We'll all go to Charles Oakes's funeral tomorrow."

3

Sarah and Maeve were in the kitchen, discussing what to have for supper, when someone rang the doorbell.

"Is it a baby?" Sarah's daughter, Catherine, asked from where she'd been sitting at the kitchen table listening to their discussion.

"I thought you were sending all your patients to other midwives now," Maeve said.

"I am, but you'll remember that sometimes people just come knocking on my door with no warning because a woman went into labor and they know I'm a midwife. If it's truly an emergency, I can't refuse to help."

"I hope it's not a baby," Catherine said. "Because then we'll just have sandwiches for supper."

Sarah was still smiling when she reached the front door. A young man's silhouette showed through the glass, so she was very much afraid she really was being summoned to a delivery. Young men were most often the ones sent to fetch a midwife.

When she opened the door, however, she saw that this young man was smiling much too widely to be involved in the anxiety of an imminent birth. She needed a moment to recognize him.

"Gino! You're back!" Without a thought for propriety, she grabbed his hand, pulled him inside, and threw her arms around him. "I'm so glad to see you," she said as she released him to find him blushing furiously but looking very pleased. She held him at arm's length and looked him up and down. "I hardly recognized you without your police uniform. You're thinner."

"That's what my mother noticed first, too," he said. "The army food was pretty bad."

"But you're home and not wounded. That's all that matters. Maeve! Catherine!" she called, "Gino is here."

But Catherine was already running through the front room, having heard Sarah greeting him. Maeve, she noticed, was close behind, coming as fast as her youthful dignity allowed.

Catherine skidded to a stop when she reached him and frowned up at him, probably as confused as Sarah at seeing him in something other than his patrolman's uniform.

"Don't I get a hug?" he asked, bending down to pick her up.

"Are you really Officer Donatelli?" she asked.

"Of course I am," he said, making her smile again. She giggled and threw her slender arms around his neck.

By then Maeve had reached him, too, and although her smile wasn't nearly as wide as Catherine's, her eyes were shining. "Welcome home," she said as he set Catherine down.

"It's good to be home," he replied.

Now they were both blushing, and Sarah let them stare

at each other for a minute or two before rescuing them. "Please come in, Gino, and I hope you can stay for supper. It's nothing fancy since we weren't expecting you, but you have to stay and tell us all about your adventures in Cuba."

"I'd be happy to, but Mr. Malloy actually sent me to tell you what the coroner discovered."

"How did you happen to be assigned that duty?" Sarah asked in surprise.

"I called on him this morning at your new house—which looks like it will be very nice when it's finished—and he hired me to help him on the case."

"Aren't you going back to the police department?"

"No, not . . . not right away, at least."

"That sounds like something else we'll need to discuss when we've finished supper." Sarah glanced meaningfully at Catherine. "Meanwhile, give me your hat and come into the kitchen while we fix us all something to eat."

When Gino had taken a seat at the kitchen table, Catherine snuggled up in his lap. Sarah and Maeve started pulling things out of the pantry and the icebox to see what they could put together. Sarah peeled potatoes while Maeve sliced some cold ham.

"We read all about the Rough Riders in the newspapers," Maeve said.

"Not everything they said in the newspapers was true," he replied. He proceeded to tell them all about the charge up the hill that wasn't really San Juan Hill and how Theodore Roosevelt had carried several spare pairs of spectacles with him in case one got broken because he couldn't see a blessed thing without them. By the time he was finished, the girls were laughing, although Sarah suspected no one had thought the battle was humorous at the time. At some point in the story, Maeve had abandoned her cooking and taken a seat across the table from him so she could hang on his every word.

Sarah chopped up some onions and fried them with the potatoes as Gino continued with his tales of the wonders he'd seen in Cuba, such as crabs as big as dinner plates that ate anything left unattended, and the incompetence of the army, which had supplied the soldiers with shoes that fell apart the instant they got wet.

By the time they'd finished eating, Gino had convinced the girls that the brief war with Spain had been little more than a lark.

When they'd cleared the dishes away, Maeve said, "I'll take Catherine upstairs now so you can talk. It's very nice to have you home again, Officer Donatelli."

Sarah didn't miss the disappointment on Gino's face, so she said, "I'll call you back down when we're finished, Maeve, so you can say good night."

Maeve hurried Catherine away before Sarah could judge Maeve's opinion of this plan, but at least she hadn't objected. Sarah noted that Gino watched them go until they were out of sight, then turned back to Sarah.

"Thank you for supper."

"Thank you for coming. Now tell me why you haven't rejoined the police department."

"I . . . I, uh, just got back to the city yesterday. I wanted to spend some time with my family first."

"And yet here you are, not with your family, and you've already agreed to work with Malloy on a case. So obviously, you aren't reluctant to go back to work. You're just reluctant to go back to police work."

Gino gave her a little grin. "I kept thinking about the last case I worked on with Mr. Malloy. Those women . . .

The police didn't seem to care, and what would've happened to them if Mr. Malloy hadn't gone looking for them?"

Sarah didn't want to know the answer to that question. "So you've decided to help him again."

"When he told me what happened to your friend, well, I could see why the family didn't want to get the police involved. But I could also see why Mr. Oakes wants to find out for sure what happened to his son."

"Malloy is only doing this because Mr. Oakes is a friend of my father's, you know. What will you do after this is over?"

Gino gave her an odd look, but before she could figure it out, it vanished. "I don't know, but maybe by then, I'll have figured it out. Mr. Malloy wanted you to know that the coroner—his name is Titus Wesley—was able to get Charles Oakes's organs . . ." He stopped, mortified. "I'm sorry, Mrs. Brandt. I just realized that's not a fit topic for you to hear about."

Sarah smiled at his chagrin. "Don't be silly. I'm a nurse and a midwife. I know more about organs than you ever will. Just forget I'm a lady for the time being."

"All right," he said, although he didn't look happy about it. "Wesley got Oakes's organs from the undertaker. He was able to test what he . . . what he found in Oakes's stomach and what was in the cat's stomach, too. It was arsenic."

"He's absolutely sure?"

"He said he did the Marsh test, whatever that is, and he's sure. He said it would be accepted in court, too."

"Then I guess he's sure. This is terrible news, of course. It means someone poisoned poor Charles, probably on purpose."

"Was he a good friend of yours, Mrs. Brandt?"

"Not really a friend. An acquaintance, I guess. We knew

each other because our parents were friends. He's a few years older than I, so our paths didn't cross much growing up, and of course, I haven't been in society for years."

"I guess you and Mr. Malloy will be now that he's a millionaire."

Sarah sighed. "My mother would like nothing better, but I can't imagine Mr. Malloy being interested in that, can you?"

"No," he said with a grin, "but don't you want to?"

"Not really. I haven't missed it at all, if you want the truth."

"Then what will you do if you're not a midwife and you're not doing whatever it is rich ladies do all day?"

"That, my dear Gino, is an excellent question, and like you, I hope to figure it out very soon. So what is Malloy doing right now that he had to send you here in his place?"

"Oh, he went over to see Mr. Oakes and give him the news about the arsenic. He said to tell you he'll come see you later."

"He'd better."

"So what do you know about the Oakes family that might help us figure out who killed this Charles?"

Sarah told him what she knew about his mother and his wife and her impressions of them.

"Did the family ever accept Mrs. Oakes? The mother, I mean," Gino asked.

"They didn't really have a choice, did they?"

"I guess they didn't, and maybe they put on a good show for outsiders, but did they really accept her as one of their own after they got over the shock of having a Johnny Reb for a daughter-in-law?"

"*Johnny Reb?*" Sarah teased. "Where did you hear that expression?"

"We learned about the War between the States in school,"

he defended himself. "The question is, do they still think of her like that?"

"I'm sure her husband doesn't."

"What about her in-laws? Isn't the old mother still alive at least?"

"I think so. We'll find out tomorrow at the funeral. I guess she could have made life difficult for Jenny, couldn't she? But she would have had to at least tolerate her."

"Being tolerated is almost worse than being hated outright," Gino said. "At least when someone hates you, you know where you stand."

"You sound like you know this from personal experience."

Gino smiled mirthlessly. "When Colonel Roosevelt insisted on hiring men for the police force who weren't Irish, he thought he was doing a good thing. Nobody else did, though. The old-timers on the force never wanted us, but they had to accept us and work with us, at least as long as the colonel was there. That didn't stop them from assigning us the worst duties or treating us like we didn't belong, though, and sometimes they pretended not to hear when one of us sent out a call for help. They complain that you don't do a good job, and they get jealous if you do the job better than they do."

"I think I understand why you're not happy about returning to the police."

Gino shrugged. "It's the same most places for the Italians."

"Just as it's that way for the Irish in other occupations."

"That's kind of funny, isn't it?"

"I'm not sure it's funny at all, but I know what you mean. You'd think the Irish would be kind to others since they've suffered so much discrimination themselves."

"Not many people are kind at all," Gino said. "Which is why we need men like Mr. Malloy to set things right again."

"Why, Gino, I think that's the nicest compliment anyone could receive."

"It's not a compliment. It's why I want to work with him."

"I can see that." And Sarah was starting to see more than that, too. She understood that Gino saw this case as the beginning of something for him. Had Malloy said something to make Gino think he'd be continuing this habit he had recently developed of stepping in when people didn't trust the police to handle something? And would that be such a bad thing if he decided to fill his days helping other people find justice?

No, it would not be a bad thing at all. She wouldn't let on that she'd figured this out however. Malloy might not have figured it out himself yet, but when he did, he would have to tell her himself. She could hardly wait.

"You still haven't answered my question, Mrs. Brandt. Can you think of anybody who would've wanted to kill Charles Oakes?"

"Not yet, Gino, but I have every confidence that we will figure it out."

MR. OAKES RECEIVED FRANK IN HIS LIBRARY AGAIN. HE had poured a whiskey for Frank, and he handed it to him the moment he sat down. Oakes had already started on his, Frank noticed.

"Thank you for giving the coroner permission to examine your son's body," Frank said.

"I didn't tell his wife or his mother. I saw no need to distress them, so I'd appreciate it if you didn't mention it either."

Frank couldn't make a promise like that. If they eventually had to prove Charles had been murdered, the truth would come out. "I can understand your concern."

Oakes took a sip of his whiskey. Frank wondered if he always used liquor to soothe the rough edges of his life. After a moment Oakes said, "What did your man find?"

"Just as you suspected, Charles was poisoned. The coroner found traces of arsenic in him and in the cat, too."

A spasm of pain twisted Oakes's face, but he recovered quickly. "All my life, I have taken great pleasure in being right, until now."

"I'm sorry, Mr. Oakes. I was hoping I would have better news for you."

"Arsenic, did you say? Not some exotic poison?"

"I'm afraid not. It's so readily available, just about anyone could have access to it. Practically every home in the city has a box of it somewhere. The question is, who also had access to Charles?"

"Anyone in this house, of course. He was also away from home all day when he first fell ill, and I'm not sure we even know where he spent that time."

Frank didn't remind him that the cat, who had died from the same poison, had never left the house. "I guess the real question is, what do you want to do now? You can always pretend you didn't know and bury your son with no scandal."

"And let a killer go free?" he asked, outraged. "And what if Charles is just the first victim? Suppose the killer is some madman who intends to keep on killing indiscriminately? How could I live with myself if someone else died because I wanted to shield my family from gossip?"

"We don't know that Charles was killed 'indiscriminately.' He may have been killed deliberately, by someone who knew him well."

"But why? Oh, Malloy, I know you warned me that the killer would most likely be someone in this house, but I've been racking my brain ever since, trying to think of any

reason someone here would want him dead, and nothing
could be more ridiculous. You can't think his mother or his
wife poisoned him, or his grandmother either for that matter. And the servants have all been with us for years. If one
of them had run mad enough to do something like this,
someone would surely have noticed."

Frank decided not to inform Oakes that most people were
murdered by someone very close to them, like a wife or a
mother or an angry servant. And madmen usually killed
viciously, not with the secret cunning of a poisoner. From
what Sarah had told him about the wife, Frank was willing
to put his money on her, sight unseen. "You're right, it's hard
to believe someone close to him could have done it, which is
why an investigation like this is so painful. A lot of innocent
people will be upset that they were considered suspects, no
matter how unlikely. And if it turns out to be someone you
trusted, you'll have to live with the guilt of not having seen
their treachery in time."

"And if I do nothing, I will have to live with the knowledge that my son's killer is enjoying life and freedom while
he lies in an early grave. Which is worse?"

"That's a question only you can answer, Mr. Oakes."

"Then I will answer it, Mr. Malloy. Charles was my only
child. There will never be another, and he left no heirs, so
my line ends with me. Whatever Charles might have accomplished in his life will never happen now. Whatever his children might have accomplished will never happen. I have to
live the rest of my life knowing there is no future, no one to
remember me when I am gone and no one to carry on my
name or bear the weight of my hopes and dreams. I want the
person who stole all this from me to be punished. I want
them to suffer as my family has suffered."

"Even if the killer is part of your family?"

"He is not, I promise you that, Mr. Malloy. And even if I am wrong, even if the killer proves to be someone dear to me, I will rejoice to see him punished for taking Charles. Under those conditions, are you willing to continue the investigation?"

"Are you sure you don't want to call in the police now that we know it was murder?"

"And have my family's name plastered all over the newspapers? I've seen what Hearst and Pulitzer will do to sell newspapers, the lies they'll tell and the innocent people they will vilify. No, I want this investigation to remain private until you have identified the killer and have enough proof to take it to the district attorney."

"They'll still write about it in the newspapers," Frank said.

"But only about the trial, because they won't know about it until then, which means that they won't have the opportunity to publish rumors and conjecture for months leading up to it."

He was right, as far as he went. There would still be rumors and scandal, of course, but if Frank could prove who the killer was, perhaps even get a confession, the damage would be limited. "All right. Then I'll do everything I can to find the person who killed your son," Frank said.

"Do you think you might fail?" Oakes asked in alarm.

As a matter of fact, Frank didn't think he'd have much trouble at all, considering the killer was probably in the house with them at that very moment, but he said, "The killer will do everything he can to keep from getting caught, so we have to be more clever than he is. I can't promise I'll find him, but if I fail, you'll understand why."

"I suppose that is all I can ask, Mr. Malloy. Thank you."

"You will have to tell your family that Charles was poisoned."

Oakes winced. "Is that really necessary?"

"They'll want to know who I am and why I'm asking questions. And you'll have to instruct your servants to talk to me. They won't want to say anything about the family to an outsider, but they're the ones who will know where Charles was the day he first got sick and who brought him the poisoned milk and who had access to it before he drank it."

"Good God." Oakes raised a hand to his forehead, and Frank saw it was trembling. "I didn't realize . . . and we have the funeral tomorrow . . ."

"We can wait until after the funeral to start. It might even help to let the killer think we have no idea what really happened. He could get careless."

"I would appreciate it if you could delay. Tomorrow will be difficult enough without upsetting everyone beforehand."

"Mrs. Brandt and I are planning to attend the funeral, if that's all right."

"Of course."

"Mrs. Brandt would probably have attended anyway, as an old friend of the family, but I'll be watching the other mourners to see if anyone is acting suspiciously."

"At the funeral? What could they possibly be doing?"

"Maybe it's what they're not doing. Someone who should be mourning who seems remarkably composed, or someone putting on a show of grief that seems out of character. I won't know until it happens. You can be watching, too, and let me know if you see something odd."

"You won't disrupt the service, will you?"

"We won't do anything at all that day except watch, I promise."

Oakes finished off his whiskey and got up to pour himself another. Frank wondered if he always drank so heavily. That's something the servants would know. The trick, of course, was getting them to answer truthfully.

SARAH HAD BEEN SITTING BY THE FRONT WINDOW, watching for Malloy so he didn't have to knock. She opened the door and let him in. He looked tired, but he kissed her with his usual level of enthusiasm.

"Thank you for sending Gino over today," she said when they'd finally made it back to the kitchen.

"I knew you'd be happy to see him, and I guessed he'd want to see Maeve. How did that go?"

"They were shy with each other at first, but when he'd finished telling me everything you'd learned from the coroner, he asked Maeve if she'd like to go for a walk. Of course I offered to put Catherine to bed so she could. He brought her back just as it was getting dark, but she didn't tell me anything about their visit."

"Do you think that's a good sign?"

"Oh yes," she said. "So tell me about your visit with Gerald Oakes."

"He wasn't surprised his son was poisoned, but he was pretty upset about it. He also isn't ready to accept that it might be someone in the house who did it."

"Is there any possibility it wasn't?"

"Not much. He got sick two days before he died, which means someone gave him a dose sometime during the day but not enough to kill him. The same thing happened again on the day he died, and he came home sick again. Those doses could have been given by anyone, but the dose that killed him the last day was in the milk, so that could only have been someone in the house."

"But Gerald still wants you to investigate?"

"Yes. He's pretty angry someone killed his only child and left him with no hope for the future."

"Family heritage is pretty important to these old families. I guess it would be particularly painful if your only son was murdered."

"He claims he wants to see the killer punished no matter who it is."

"But we know he might change his mind when he finds out who it is."

Malloy frowned. "I don't know. I got the feeling he's angry enough that he doesn't really care. Of course, he doesn't really believe it could be a family member, but he's willing to throw any of the servants to the wolves, I think."

"And you told him you'd have to question all of them?"

"Oh yes, but he asked me to wait until after the funeral."

"Of course. They'll be too busy until then anyway. Did you tell him we'll be at the funeral?"

"Yes, and he seemed glad of it. I've been thinking since then, though, that maybe Gino should go, too."

"Gino? You mean he should go with us?"

"No, separately, so we can have an extra pair of eyes watching the mourners."

"Won't that look odd? He'll stick out in that crowd, and people will know he doesn't belong."

"I was thinking Maeve could go with him. A couple wouldn't attract as much attention."

"Unless no one has ever seen them before, which they wouldn't have, and wondered who they were."

"They could make up a story. Maeve can think of one, I'm sure."

"What can I think of?" Maeve asked, wandering into the kitchen as if it were an accident, although Sarah figured she'd probably been waiting in the front room for the proper moment to intrude.

Malloy grinned at her. "A story as to why you and Gino Donatelli would be attending Charles Oakes's funeral tomorrow."

She wrinkled her nose as she considered. "Didn't he have a job at the Asylum?"

"Yes, he was the superintendent. How did you know that?"

"Gino told me. We could say we worked there and we're paying our respects, if anyone asks. But I'll bet no one will ask. Sometimes if you've got a good enough story, you're so confident that no one even challenges you."

"And society people are so polite, they might consider it rude to question someone's presence at a funeral," Sarah added.

"Unless we look like we just came for the free meal," Maeve said with a grin.

"So you're willing to go?" Malloy asked her.

"Of course. Who will watch Catherine, though?"

"I'll ask Mrs. Ellsworth," Sarah said. Her next-door neighbor was always willing to have Catherine over for a visit.

"It's settled then," Frank said. "Gino is meeting me at my house in the morning. We'll come over here and talk about what we're going to be watching for."

THE CROWD AT THE OAKES HOME WAS SMALLER THAN Frank had expected. He remembered Gino's question about whether the Oakes family had ever really accepted Jenny and wondered if the cream of New York society had ever accepted her either. Certainly, the number of well-dressed, middle-aged society people was much smaller than Frank had seen at similar funerals. A few younger men, probably Charles's friends, and their wives clustered here and there. What surprised Frank most, however, were the three men who came together. They brought no wives, and they didn't offer condolences to the family, and they gave the body of the deceased, on display in the parlor, barely a glance. Bullet-headed thugs, they wore expensive suits, but not well. Frank understood that because he didn't wear his well either. A man had to be born to wealth and grow up with its comforts to feel truly at ease in situations like this.

Frank recognized these men. Even though he'd never seen them before, he knew the type: political hacks. They hung around the fringes of power, helping out as needed, and made money from the corruption that power bred. The city was full of them. Frank's only question was why were these particular fellows at Charles Oakes's funeral?

Sarah was chatting with her parents, so Frank wandered over to where the men stood watching the crowd.

"I don't think I know you," he said to the one who appeared to be the leader.

He stared back with a cunning grin. "I don't think I know you either," he replied, earning a chuckle from one of his companions.

"Frank Malloy." He offered his hand.

"Then I do know who you are," the fellow said, shaking Frank's hand. "You're the cop what got all that money."

Frank managed not to wince. "And who are you?"

"Virgil Adderly."

The name meant nothing to Frank. "Are you a friend of Charles's?"

"Not anymore," he said, earning another chuckle which he silenced with a sharp glance at the offender. "You don't look like you'd be a friend of his either, Malloy."

"I know his father from the Knickerbocker Club." Which was absolutely true as far as it went. This fellow didn't need to know Frank wasn't a member there.

"I heard they let in Jews, but I didn't know they let in Micks. What's this world coming to?"

"I guess you met Charles at the Asylum," Frank replied in kind.

He nodded his head in acknowledgment. "I was able to help Oakes get his position there, yes."

"And now you're here to make sure he's really dead?"

"I don't think it's any business of yours why I'm here."

"It's my business if you're going to cause trouble."

"Why would I do that?"

"I don't know." Frank glanced meaningfully at his two companions. "Why did you think you'd need bodyguards at a funeral?"

His gaze hardened. "These are my business associates."

"Just make sure they don't do any *business* here."

"As I said, we're merely paying our respects."

Frank took his leave, conscious of their gaze as he made his way across the crowded parlor. Should he upset Oakes by warning him? Or could he take the man at his word that they had no intention of causing trouble? He found Sarah and her parents.

"Who are those men?" Sarah asked.

Frank looked at her father. "Do you know them?"

Felix Decker shook his head. "What are they doing here?"

"They said they know Charles because they got him the job at the Asylum."

"That's how things work, of course, but how would Charles know people like that in the first place?"

"And why have they come here?" Mrs. Decker asked with a worried frown.

"They said just to pay their respects," Frank said.

"Do you believe them?" Sarah asked.

"Of course not, but I don't think they're here to cause trouble either. It wouldn't do them any good to make trouble for a socially prominent family."

"Then why else would they be here?" Sarah asked.

Frank frowned. "I think they might be waiting for somebody. Watch the way they look up every time somebody comes in."

"Who could they be waiting for?" Mr. Decker asked.

"I guess we'll find out if that person shows up."

"And in the meantime, we should find seats because the service is going to start soon," Mrs. Decker said.

"Have you seen Gino and Maeve?" Frank asked Sarah as they moved toward the back row of the chairs that had been set up in the center of the room.

"Not yet, but you told them to wait outside until the last minute so they could watch everyone who arrived. They should come in soon, though."

Sure enough, they had just taken their seats when Gino and Maeve arrived. They looked exactly right in their cheap finery, gawking like rubes. That part had been Maeve's idea. They'd come to honor Mr. Oakes, who had been such a kind superintendent, but they weren't quite sure how to act in a big house like this. Maeve clung to Gino's arm for dear life. If Frank hadn't known better, he would have been sure she was terrified to find herself in such a fancy place. Not for the first time, Frank thought how fortunate Sarah had been to hire a nanny who had been raised by a confident man.

The two young people took seats on the opposite end of the last row of chairs and never so much as glanced at Frank and Sarah. Mrs. Decker looked over at them in surprise. "Isn't that—?"

"Shhh, Mother," Sarah whispered.

The rest of the group had found their seats, and the family now filed in to sit in the front row. Frank studied the wife, who came first. She looked suitably bereaved, although her eyes showed no sign of prolonged weeping. She'd understand that even if she secretly rejoiced that her husband was dead, she shouldn't show anything except grief on this occasion. He was looking forward to talking to her, and hoped he would have the opportunity. Men like Gerald Oakes sometimes tried to protect females from the ugliness of murder, but since Sarah already suspected her of being the killer, Frank couldn't let her off easy.

Next came Gerald and his wife. She also seemed to be bearing up pretty well, her still-beautiful face a frozen mask hiding whatever her true feelings were. For his part, Gerald looked terrible, his face splotchy and haggard. He, at least, had been weeping for his lost child.

Behind them came an elderly woman Frank hadn't seen before. She hadn't been greeting guests as they arrived. This must be Gerald's mother. She walked with a cane and leaned on the arm of a male servant until she reached her seat, although she didn't seem particularly unsteady on her feet.

As soon as the family was seated, the minister stood up and took his place behind a podium that had been set near the casket.

He welcomed them and said a few platitudes about the tragedy of Charles's death, and then he said, "Let us pray." Almost everyone bowed their heads. Frank and Sarah did not, and when he glanced over, he saw Gino and Maeve were also looking around. Interestingly, Virgil Adderly and his companions had also kept their heads raised and their eyes open.

Frank only had a second to register this when a disturbance

in the doorway distracted him. A woman had come in late but not quietly. Dressed all in black, she looked the part of a mourner, but her face betrayed not grief but fear and desperation. She glanced wildly around the room until she saw the still-open casket. An anguished cry escaped her, causing the minister to stutter in his prayer and all the mourners to lift their heads in surprise.

She didn't seem to notice everyone had turned to look at her as she took a step toward the casket and promptly fainted in a heap.

4

GINO WAS ALREADY ON HIS FEET BEFORE FRANK COULD move, but neither of them were quick enough to beat Virgil Adderly and his companions. If they really had been waiting for someone, this woman was probably the object of their anticipation. The smaller of Adderly's friends reached her first and made short work of picking her up and carrying her out of the room. Adderly and his other friend followed. It was the work of a moment, and the minister picked up his prayer right where he'd left off.

Gino glanced at Frank for direction. Someone needed to go after them. Frank shook his head and followed the men himself, taking a moment to close the parlor doors behind him. No sense disturbing the funeral any more than necessary.

The male servant who had been helping old Mrs. Oakes was trying to get them to stop so someone could minister to the stricken woman, but Adderly was intent on getting her out of there.

"Adderly, you aren't planning to kidnap that poor woman, are you?" Frank said.

Adderly looked around in surprise to see Frank following them. He signaled his friend who was carrying the unconscious woman to stop. "I'm just going to take her home. She's obviously indisposed."

"Nothing a little smelling salts won't cure," Frank said. "Oh, look, she's coming around without them."

The woman's eyes fluttered, and she moaned softly, "Charles."

"Get her out of here," Adderly snapped to the man still holding her, then turned to Frank. "You should mind your own business, Malloy."

"Charles Oakes's death is my business."

"Charles," the woman said again as she regained consciousness. She looked around in alarm. "Put me down, Amos!"

Amos looked to Adderly, who nodded curtly. Amos set her down. Now that he had a chance to really look at her, Frank could see she was a rather plain woman a bit past her prime, although her figure was good. He'd thought for a minute, right before she fainted, that she might have been Oakes's mistress, but now he realized that was unlikely.

She was looking around frantically. "Where is he? I must see him!"

"You can't see him, Ella. He didn't want anything to do with you when he was alive, and you're not going to make a fool of yourself in front of all those people."

She looked like she was going to argue with Adderly, and Frank figured an argument like that, with a female who was already on her way to being hysterical, could be very loud and unpleasant for the Oakes family.

"This isn't really a good time to see him, miss," Frank said, stepping forward.

"Who are you?" she demanded.

"A friend of Charles's." Frank ignored the glare Adderly was giving him. "You'll want to spend some time with him alone, to say good-bye." Frank was gratified to see the glimmer of hope in her muddy brown eyes. "If you let Mr. Adderly take you away now, you can come back later, after everyone's gone, and have him all to yourself."

"Oh, thank you!" she said. "Thank you so much." She turned to Adderly. "You see, Virgil, Charles's friends understand."

Adderly shot Frank a look of reluctant gratitude, then turned back to Ella. "Let me take you home now."

"And you'll bring me back later?"

"Of course," he lied.

She turned back to Frank. "Thank you, sir. You are truly a gentleman."

Frank nodded his acknowledgment and watched Adderly guide her down the stairs and out of the house with his two thugs at his heels.

Now wasn't that interesting. Adderly claimed to have helped Oakes get his patronage appointment at the Manhattan State Hospital, and maybe he had, but who was this woman Ella and how did she know Charles Oakes? She was obviously not quite right in the head either, so he also had to wonder if she might have poisoned poor Charles when she realized he didn't want anything to do with her. In his police work, he'd dealt with women who had developed an unhealthy—and unrequited—attachment to some man, and this looked like another version of that malady.

Of course, she would have had to have access to Charles in his home, which didn't seem likely, but Frank had learned not to jump to conclusions where murder was concerned.

"Mr. Malloy?" the butler said. "Thank you very much for your assistance, sir."

"Oh, you're welcome. I was glad to help."

"Would you like to go back into the service now?"

He really wanted to go after Adderly and find out more about this mysterious female, but he'd have time for that later. "I suppose so."

"Please follow me, then, sir."

AFTER THE FUNERAL AND THE MEAL, GINO AND MAEVE were waiting for them back at Sarah's parents' house, which was only a few blocks from the Oakeses' house. The Deckers greeted the young people and made everyone comfortable in the rear parlor, the room the family used most often.

"Who on earth was that woman who fainted?" Mrs. Decker asked when they were settled.

Frank noticed that Gino had taken a seat beside Maeve on the sofa. She was no longer clinging to his arm, and they seemed more comfortable together than they had been.

"Her name is Ella," Frank said. "Adderly and his friends were waiting for her to arrive."

"Is Adderly the rough-looking fellow with the two, uh, companions?" Sarah asked.

"Yes. I got the feeling they had been expecting her to arrive and make a scene, and they all seemed to know each other very well. She was upset about Charles Oakes's death and wanted to pay her respects, whatever she thought that meant, but Adderly was determined she wasn't going to make a fool of herself in front of everyone."

"She managed to make a spectacle of herself in spite of him, though," Mrs. Decker said.

"It wasn't as bad as it would've been if Adderly hadn't gotten her out of there," Frank said.

"But what relationship does she have with Charles Oakes?" Sarah asked.

"She's apparently in love with him or thinks she is, and according to what Adderly said, Oakes didn't want anything to do with her. I'd like to get her side of the story, though."

"And find out where she was when Oakes was poisoned," Gino added grimly.

"So, enough about Miss Ella. Gino, did you notice anything suspicious?"

Gino glanced at Maeve. "Maeve did."

"What was it?"

Maeve frowned. "Charles's wife. She never shed a tear."

"I think we already decided she didn't care much for her husband," Sarah said.

"But did you notice all the men—the young ones, I mean—were giving her a lot of sympathy, but not the women?"

"I saw women going up to her to express their condolences," Mrs. Decker said.

"Yes, but they didn't really talk to her. They just said how sorry they were and then walked away. The men, they took her hand and looked into her eyes and told her how she could always count on them and a lot of silly stuff that didn't mean anything except they'd be more than happy to come over and cheer her up after the funeral was over."

Mrs. Decker looked shocked. "Do you think she could have been having an affair?"

"Elizabeth," her husband scolded her. "Is that any way to talk about the poor girl?"

"It is if she was having an affair," Mrs. Decker replied.

"If she was, I couldn't tell it," Maeve said. "She didn't give

any of them secret looks or whisper to them or do anything
to show she preferred one over the others. Which made me
think none of them was special to her. But she sure enjoyed
all the attention they were paying her, and she did everything
she could to encourage it."

"So maybe she poisoned her husband so she could be free
to find someone else," Sarah said.

"That's a bit of a leap, isn't it?" her father said. "She may
have been enjoying the attention of those men, but how can
you imagine she would murder her husband just so she could
flirt a bit?"

"And she could flirt all she wanted while Charles was alive,"
Mrs. Decker said, "just as long as she didn't do any more than
flirt."

Realizing they had reached an impasse on Charles's
widow, Frank said, "What about the rest of the family? Did
anyone notice anything unusual?"

"I noticed Jenny had been crying, at least," Mrs. Decker
said. "She didn't shed more than a few tears at the service,
but I could see her eyes were swollen even though she'd tried
very hard to cover the traces."

"She wouldn't want to lose her composure in public,"
Sarah explained. "But I'm relieved to know she was mourning her son. She seemed so cold and unfeeling when we called
on her."

"But did you notice hardly anybody spoke to her after the
service?" Maeve said. "A few ladies came over and spoke to
her, but you'd think her friends would've gathered around
her or something."

"Jenny has always been . . . reserved," Mrs. Decker said.
"She's never been close friends with other society women."

"Is she shy?" Sarah asked. "She didn't seem shy when I
met her."

"I think she's just sensitive about her background," Mrs. Decker said. "Many people were rude to her when she came to the city, even after Gerald came home and the war was over."

"For some people, the war was never over," Mr. Decker said. "If you lost a son or a brother, it was hard to forgive."

"But Mrs. Oakes was just a young girl during the war," Maeve said. "Why would people blame her?"

"I'm not sure they did, not exactly," Mrs. Decker said. "If Jenny had been different . . . If she'd had some of that famous Southern charm and had tried to win people over, I think they would have eventually accepted her, but she always held herself a little apart."

"Gerald was angry about it," Mr. Decker said, surprising them all.

"He was?" his wife asked.

"Yes, he told me more than once how grateful he was that we'd befriended her. He never thought for a minute that it was any of her doing that people didn't like her, though. He thought they were just mean to her because she was from the South."

"Mr. Oakes drinks a lot."

Everyone looked at Gino in surprise.

"I thought you didn't notice anything," Frank said with some amusement.

He glanced at Maeve again. "I wanted to let Maeve go first." She shot him a glare which he ignored. "He'd been drinking before the funeral started."

"How do you know that?" Frank asked.

"I could smell it on him when we got there. I shook his hand and told him and his wife we knew his son from the hospital and what a good job he did there and all of that. He thanked me and I could smell his breath."

"It wouldn't be surprising if a man took a drink to fortify himself on the day he buried his only son," Mr. Decker said.

If Decker had meant to chasten Gino, it didn't work. "It wasn't just today. That he was drinking, I mean. I could tell from his face. Did you notice how red it was?"

"I did," Frank said. "I thought he'd been crying."

"I've seen that a lot at Police Headquarters. Well, not there exactly, but the men who work there. The ones who drink a lot, their faces get red like that, and they stay red."

Frank frowned, a little annoyed. "The Irishmen, you mean."

Gino managed not to grin. "The ones with fair skin. Gerald Oakes isn't Irish, but he has fair skin."

"He does drink," Mr. Decker said with obvious reluctance. "More than most, I suppose, but he's not a . . . a belligerent drunk. In fact, I don't think I've ever actually seen him drunk."

That was interesting, a man who drank heavily but didn't show the effects, which meant he was very used to it. Why did Gerald Oakes drink so much? Of course, a man didn't need a reason to drink, but in Frank's experience, he usually at least pretended to have one.

"What about the old woman, the grandmother?" he asked.

"What about her?" Mrs. Decker asked.

"What do we know about her? How was she acting today?"

"I only exchanged a few words with her today, so I can't say much about that, but she never liked Jenny," Mrs. Decker said. "I already told you that."

"And they've both lived together in that house all these years?" Maeve asked in wonder.

Mrs. Decker smiled kindly at the girl. "Women often don't get along with their mother-in-law, and yet they can live together for years."

Maeve glanced at Sarah, who grinned knowingly. Frank's mother would be living with them when they got married.

"When you're a family, you make the best of it and at least learn to tolerate each other," Sarah said. "Besides, it doesn't matter to us if Gerald's mother hated Jenny or not. We're looking for someone who hated Charles, or at least had a reason to want him dead."

"Maybe she hated Charles because he was Jenny's son," Gino said.

"But he was Gerald's son, too, and her grandson," Sarah said.

"What if he wasn't, though." Everyone looked at Maeve in surprise. "I know it's not a nice thing to say, but it could be true. Even if it wasn't, the grandmother might've believed it was. Maybe she didn't want Charles to inherit everything."

"There wasn't much to inherit," Mr. Decker said. This time everyone looked at him. "Charles had taken the job at the hospital because the family fortunes were in serious decline. Gerald had been asking around, trying to find something for Charles even before he married. I understand his wife had some money her father settled on her, but not enough to restore the family to their former situation."

"What happened to their money?" Sarah asked.

"The same thing that happens every time a family tries to rely on inherited money generation after generation without ever bothering to make any themselves. It only takes one wastrel in the bloodline to ruin everyone else's prospects."

"So somebody spent it all?" Gino asked.

"Gerald's father was rather . . . irresponsible."

"He gambled, didn't he?" Mrs. Decker asked.

"And drank," her husband said. "A dangerous combination."

"Did Charles drink a lot, too?" Frank asked.

Mr. Decker frowned, plainly uncomfortable with the conversation. "I didn't know him well. He wasn't a member of the club, and we didn't move in the same social circles."

"And we don't like to speak ill of the dead," Mrs. Decker added meaningfully.

Frank took the hint and changed the subject. He could find out about Charles's drinking habits from someone else. "Did anyone notice any of the mourners acting strangely?"

"You mean besides flirting with the widow?" Maeve asked, earning a scowl from Gino.

"Yes, besides that."

"It wasn't a mourner," Sarah said, "but I did see one strange thing. When I happened to go by the parlor while everyone was in the dining room eating. One of the maids was leaning over the casket."

"Paying her respects maybe," Frank said. "Mr. Oakes said all the servants have been with them for years."

"My goodness, did he really say that?" Mrs. Decker said in amazement.

"Yes, why?"

"Because if Jenny Oakes has been able to keep all her servants for years, she's a miracle worker. It seems like I'm hiring a new maid at least once a month."

"Well, that's what he said, so maybe this was someone who'd known Charles a long time."

"It seemed that way," Sarah said. "She leaned over and touched him. I couldn't see where, exactly, but it looked like she might have been stroking his face. Sort of the way a mother would her child."

"Was it one of the colored girls?" Frank asked.

"All Jenny's maids are colored," Mrs. Decker said. "Most of mine are, too. It's getting almost impossible to find a white girl who'll go into service."

"She wasn't a girl, though," Sarah said. "If she had been,

I might have suspected something romantic, but this woman was much older."

"Maybe she'd taken care of him when he was a child," Mrs. Decker said.

"That's possible, I suppose," Sarah said. "As I said, the way she touched him did look maternal. It made me very sad to see her grief."

"Would you know her if you saw her again?" Frank asked.

"I didn't get a very good look at her, but I think so."

"There can't be too many servants that age in the house at any rate," Mrs. Decker said. "You'll probably find her easily when you question the servants."

They spent the next half hour discussing the other mourners. The Deckers knew almost all of them, and none had seemed to behave oddly except the men who had paid too much attention to Hannah Oakes.

"What do we do now?" Gino asked Frank when they'd exhausted the subject of the mourners.

"Tomorrow you and I go back to the Oakes house and start questioning the family and the servants."

"What about the rest of us?" Maeve asked.

Frank smiled at her. "I thought you were supposed to be taking care of Catherine."

"And I thought you were supposed to be overseeing the workmen at your house," she countered pertly.

"Mrs. Brandt will be taking my place for a few days, so she'll really need for you to watch Catherine," he countered right back.

"But you might need us to help you talk to the women," she tried. He'd let her help on several other cases, and now he realized she had enjoyed it way too much.

"If I do, I'll let you know. In the meantime, I think we should be heading home. It's been a long day."

Mr. Decker summoned his carriage for them, and Frank had to admit it was nice to sit back and relax in comfort while the driver negotiated the crowded streets. Finding a cab was always challenging, and it was never this comfortable. Maybe he'd get a carriage, too. Of course, that meant a driver and a groom and heaven only knew who else to take care of the horses. Was it really as hard to keep servants as Mrs. Decker had said?

"What are you frowning about?" Sarah asked.

"Just thinking about servants."

"I wonder why it's so hard to keep them," Maeve said.

"It's hard work, for one thing," Sarah said. "If you're a maid, you have to be available at all hours, up early to clean and make the fires and then work all day scrubbing and dusting, and then you can't go to bed until the family does, and they might have slept until noon that day. You hardly get any time to yourself and only one afternoon a month off. You also have to live in, which means if you marry, you have to be separated from your husband or leave your job. And if you have children, you'll hardly ever get to see them. That's why the maids don't stay long. When they want to get married, they have to leave and find other work."

"If they can," Gino said.

Maeve frowned. "I thought girls didn't have to work anymore when they got married."

"If they're lucky," Sarah said.

"And white," Gino added.

"What do you mean, if they're white?" Maeve asked.

"If a man can earn enough to keep a wife and family, then his wife doesn't have to work, but it's not always easy to find work in the city, especially if you're colored," Gino said.

"Or Italian," Sarah said.

Maeve's gaze darted to Gino, who looked away.

"Or even Irish," Frank said. "Think about it. What jobs do you see colored men doing?"

Maeve opened her mouth but nothing came out for a few seconds. "I just realized I hardly ever see a colored man working at all. Elevator operator. Shining shoes."

"Waiters sometimes, and bellmen," Sarah said, "but not in the better hotels where they could make good money, because white men take those jobs. So women have to work, too, but it's almost as difficult for a colored woman to find work as for her husband, except in service."

"And then we're back to them not being able to live with their husbands and families," Maeve said. She turned to Gino. "Do Italian women have to work?"

Frank could see his face tighten. Was he worried about scaring Maeve off by making her think he couldn't provide for a wife? "Some of them, but they do outwork."

"What's that?"

"They do piecework," Sarah explained quickly, "but they do it in their homes instead of in a factory, so they can be with their children."

"I knew women did that, but I never thought about it. So why don't the colored women do that, too?"

"Because no one will give them the work."

"Why not?"

"Because," Sarah said, "they think the colored women aren't trustworthy."

"Then why do they let them live and work in their houses?"

"Don't try to make sense of it," Frank warned her. "That's just the way things are."

Maeve glanced at Gino, who'd been watching her closely. "Why are you looking at me?"

"Because I like to," he said to Frank's surprise.

Well, now, Frank would never have thought to give a reply

like that. Gino, however, obviously understood that charm would get him out of just about any jam with a pretty girl. Now Maeve was too flustered to ask any more questions that might lead her back to the difficulties Italian men faced in supporting a family.

He could see that Sarah had also understood the ploy, so she took pity on Maeve and said, "Do you have Mr. Oakes's permission to speak with Jenny and Hannah and old Mrs. Oakes?"

"Yes, but that's not the same as having *their* permission, is it?" he asked.

"I'm sure if you explain that you're investigating Charles's death, they'll help you in any way they can."

"Unless one of them killed him," Gino said with a bland little grin.

"His wife, maybe," Maeve said, having recovered her composure. "I've seen too many women who'd happily put arsenic in their husband's drink." She gave Gino a long look that made him squirm. "But I can't believe his mother would do it."

"She would have to have a very frightening reason," Sarah agreed. "And if she does, she isn't likely to confess it readily."

"Even still, not many mothers kill their sons for any reason at all," Frank said. "Now the grandmother, as Maeve reminded us, may not think Charles was Gerald's son."

"And if that's true, is she likely to confess it to you?" Sarah asked.

He tried glaring at her, but that never worked, and it didn't work now, so he just said, "Somebody needs to be at our house while they're working on it."

"But you know I'm available if you need me to speak with the women."

"And I suppose your mother is, too," he said.

That made her grin. "She'd like nothing better, I'm sure,

but I know Father would appreciate it if we could keep her out of it."

"I always want your father's appreciation," he said.

"But he won't care if I help," Maeve said.

Frank shook his head in wonder at her persistence. "I'll keep that in mind."

THE NEXT MORNING WAS SATURDAY, AND FRANK'S MOTHER answered the door when Gino arrived. Frank was still eating his breakfast in the newly finished kitchen.

"It's that Italian boy," she informed him, pronouncing it Eye-talian. "I didn't know he was home."

"He was discharged from the army a few days ago. Why didn't you bring him back here?"

She sniffed. "I didn't think millionaires entertained visitors in their kitchens."

Frank knew better than to get into a discussion with her about proper behavior for millionaires. "He's not a visitor. I've hired him to help me investigate a murder."

She pulled herself up to her full five-foot-nothing and said, "So you're just going to go around the city butting into other people's business now that you're rich and don't have anything else to do?"

"I've been hired as a private investigator," he said as patiently as he could manage. "Gino is working for me. I'm doing it as a favor for a friend of Mr. Decker."

"First you say you've been hired, and then you say you're doing somebody a favor. Which is it?"

"Both. If people don't pay you, they don't value your work, so I'm charging him, even though I don't need the money."

"But this Gino needs the money if he's just got out of the army and doesn't have a job."

"That's right, and I see I'll have to go get him myself because you're the mother of a millionaire and you don't have to work either, I guess."

"Don't be silly, Francis. Finish your breakfast." She marched out of the kitchen, looking like a stylish andiron in the dress Sarah had helped her pick out at Macy's so she'd have some fashionable clothes and wouldn't shame him. So far she'd refused to see a dressmaker or wear anything except the unrelieved black she'd worn every day since his father had died, but at least she wasn't resisting Sarah's efforts. In fact, the two of them seemed to get along famously, which worried Frank a lot. In his experience, his mother didn't get along with anyone.

A joyous shriek brought Frank to his feet as his mother returned with Gino in tow. The shriek had come from Frank's son, Brian, who was riding on Gino's shoulders. Gino hunched down so they could get through the doorway without bashing Brian's head against the lintel. The boy let out another ear-piercing cry that he couldn't hear himself because he was profoundly deaf. When they were safely in the kitchen, Gino swung the smiling boy down and set him on his feet.

Brian's small hands flew as he signed something to Gino.

"He says he felt like he was flying," Frank's mother said.

Gino reached down and ruffled the boy's hair affectionately.

She signed something to Brian, and his little face fell. "I told him he has to go play because you've got business. Now you sit down, Mr. Donatelli. Can I get you some coffee? Have you had your breakfast? There's plenty here."

"I just finished eating, but I wouldn't turn down another cup of coffee, ma'am."

While she poured the coffee, Brian sidled up to Frank and insinuated himself onto his lap, an expression of angelic innocence on his face. Probably he hoped his grandmother wouldn't notice he was still there if he stayed very quiet.

She set out the coffee and a plate of leftover biscuits. "Help yourself, Mr. Donatelli. I raised a boy, and I know they're always hungry. There's strawberry jam there, too." Without missing a beat, she signed to the boy, who shot Frank a pleading look, but Frank signed the same thing, and he shuffled off, the picture of rejection in order to make Frank feel supremely guilty, behind her.

"You're signing," Gino said.

"I've picked up a few things. Ma's made a study of it, so I'm nowhere near as good as she is, but it's easier now that I'm around the boy more."

Gino looked around. "This looks real nice."

The room had turned out well, Frank had to admit. They'd bought a new stove and icebox and the sink had a tap with hot and cold running water. The floor had shiny, new linoleum in a granite pattern, and the walls were paneled in walnut below and painted a pale green above. He wouldn't be eating in the kitchen much longer, once the dining room was finished, but he was rather proud of the way it had turned out.

"It's a lot bigger than Mrs. Brandt's kitchen," Gino said.

"We'll have a lot more people living here."

"Do you think . . . ?" Gino began, then caught himself and reached for a biscuit and started spreading it with jam.

"Do I think what?"

"I was just wondering if . . . Well, is Miss Smith going to stay on when you and Mrs. Brandt get married?"

"As far as I know. Didn't you ask her when you took her for a walk the other night?" Frank pretended not to notice how the color was rising in his neck.

"How did you know about that?"

"Mrs. Brandt told me, of course. And to answer your question, she's too young to be thinking about getting married."

Gino instantly started choking on a bite of biscuit, and
Frank waited patiently until he'd managed to swallow and
gulp down some coffee.

"I guess that means you're too young to think about getting
married, too," Frank said. "Now let's talk about how we're
going to handle questioning the people at the Oakes house."

THE MAID WAS OBVIOUSLY EXPECTING THEM, AND SHE
took them right up to the library where Mr. Oakes was
waiting.

His face, as Gino had mentioned, was red, and Frank
wondered if he'd been drinking already this morning. Frank
introduced Gino.

"I've seen you before," Oakes said as they shook hands.

"I was at the funeral."

"Yes, that's it. You were with a young lady." He frowned,
remembering. "You said you knew Charles."

"I'm sorry for that, sir."

"I wanted to have Gino there to observe," Frank said. "If
he was attending the funeral as a mourner, no one would pay
any particular attention to him."

"I see." Plainly, he didn't like it, though.

"I promise we won't deceive you again, but it was important to see if anyone at the funeral behaved strangely."

"And did they?"

"Just the woman who fainted. Do you know who she was?"

"No, but I've already chastened the servants for letting
her in. She made quite a spectacle of herself and upset my
wife and daughter-in-law terribly."

"What about the man who took her out? He said his name
is Virgil Adderly."

Oakes frowned. "I've never met the man, but I've heard

of him. He's a political hack, somebody who makes his living doing things respectable people don't want to do."

"Did he do something for Charles?"

"Not that I'm aware," Oakes said, effectively ending the discussion. "Please sit down. Can I offer you a . . . anything?"

"We're fine," Frank said, wondering if Oakes would have really poured them drinks at ten o'clock in the morning.

"So now we're going to have to speak to your staff and your family."

He winced and ran a hand over his face.

"Did you tell them I was coming today?"

Oakes sighed wearily. "I told them Charles was poisoned and that you would be investigating."

"How did they react to that?"

"How do you think they reacted?" he snapped. "My mother was nearly hysterical."

"What about your wife and daughter-in-law?"

That stopped him. He glanced away uneasily, his hands picking absently at the arms of his chair.

In the lengthening silence, Gino cast Frank a questioning look, but he just waited. In his experience, people couldn't stand silence, and they would eventually fill it, even if they had to say something incriminating.

"Hannah . . . She said . . . She said she knows who killed Charles."

5

FRANK BLINKED IN SURPRISE. "SHE SAID SHE KNOWS WHO poisoned Charles?"

"Yes."

"Who does she think did it?"

"She didn't say. Or more accurately, she wouldn't say, even though my wife demanded that she do so. We think she's just vying for attention."

"That's an odd way to get it," Frank said.

"Hannah is an odd girl. I'm not sure why Charles chose her. Or why she chose him, for that matter."

"Maybe she wanted your old family name."

"And she probably expected old family money to go along with it," Oakes said, not bothering to hide his bitterness. "I think she was unhappy with her life here."

"What will happen to her now?"

"She's welcome to stay on here, as Charles's widow, but I

can't imagine she will. To tell the truth, I expect she'll remarry as soon as propriety allows."

Frank wondered if she had decided to take matters into her own hands and free herself of an unwanted husband without the scandal or inconvenience of divorce. That would certainly explain her eagerness to point the finger at someone else as the killer. He wasn't going to suggest that to Oakes, though, at least not without some proof.

"I suppose we should see her first then," he said.

"I've put the front parlor at your disposal. I'll have the maid take you there, and send for Hannah."

"Donatelli will be questioning the servants," Frank said. "Can you give him a room as well?"

"Yes. I'll instruct my man, Zeller, to find a place for you to use. He'll bring whoever you need to talk to."

"I'd like to talk to him first, then," Gino said.

"I'll ring for the girl."

FRANK ROSE WHEN THE PARLOR DOOR OPENED. THE MAID admitted Mrs. Charles Oakes and then withdrew, closing the door behind her.

Hannah looked much as she had yesterday. Her dress was black and her light brown hair was tucked severely into a bun, although she had a fringe of curls around her face to soften the look.

"I remember you," she said without bothering to greet him. "You were at the funeral with Mrs. Brandt."

"Yes." He felt no need to explain his relationship with Sarah.

She frowned, crinkling up her nose in a way that she must have practiced in front of a mirror to be sure she still looked appealing. He'd dealt with women like her before. Everything they did was for effect. But in a world where a woman's very survival could depend on attracting a man to support her, he supposed she was justified.

"Won't you sit down?" he asked, indicating the second of a pair of armchairs that sat in front of the fireplace.

She took the offered chair without comment, perching on the edge as if she didn't want to get too comfortable or wanted to be able to escape quickly. Her back ramrod straight, she stared at him with a smug expression that almost looked defiant.

"I suppose Father Oakes told you that I know who killed Charles," she said as Frank sat down in the other chair.

"He told me you thought you did, yes."

"Oh, I know. I'm sure of it."

"And who do you think it is?"

"That new girl, Daisy. I knew she was trouble the minute I saw her. She's insolent. She looks me right in the eye, bold as you please, whenever I speak to her."

"This Daisy, she's one of the maids?"

"Yes, I suppose. I don't know what she does exactly. I've never seen her doing any work, but I suppose she must. That's what servants do, isn't it?"

Frank didn't bother to answer her. "She's new, you say?" So much for Gerald Oakes's claim that all the servants had been with them for years.

"Yes. I don't know how long she's been here. No one consults me about anything, least of all the hiring of staff, but it hasn't been long."

"And what makes you think she killed Charles?"

"Well, it has to be her, doesn't it? She's new."

This was interesting reasoning, probably the same kind Oakes himself would have used if he'd realized they had a new servant. "Do you mind answering a few questions for me, so I can get an idea of exactly what happened to your husband?"

She stiffened even more, although he would've thought that impossible. "I'm sure I don't know anything that will help."

"You might know something you don't realize you know. You do want to help us find out who poisoned Charles, don't you?"

She wrinkled her nose again. "I'm not sure that I do."

"Why not?" Frank asked, trying not to sound as shocked as he felt. Even if she herself was the killer, surely she would at least pretend an interest in getting justice for her husband.

"Because I don't want my name in every newspaper in town. I've seen what happens when there's a sensational crime and the newspapers start reporting on it. It's the females who always get the worst of it, too. The female is always portrayed as some immoral Jezebel who lured some poor man to his doom or seduced some poor man to murder his rival."

Unfortunately, she was absolutely correct. "That's exactly why Mr. Oakes asked me to investigate, though. He wants to keep this out of the newspapers."

"You'll forgive me if I don't trust you, Mr. . . ."

"Malloy," he supplied.

"Mr. Malloy. If someone is tried for Charles's murder, it will be reported in the newspapers, and as Charles's wife, I will most likely be portrayed unfairly and my reputation ruined."

"Would you rather see your husband's killer go free?"

"Certainly not, but finding the killer won't bring him back and it might do irreparable harm to those he left behind."

"So you're not willing to help me?"

"How can you say that? I already told you who the killer is."

"Did you see her poison Charles?"

She took a minute, and Frank thought perhaps she was

trying to decide whether to lie or not. Finally, she said, "No, not exactly."

"Then I'm going to need some proof, so will you start by answering my questions?"

She wasn't happy. Probably, she was used to getting her way because most men would succumb to her charms. "I suppose," she said without much enthusiasm. "If I can, that is."

"Thank you." He tried a smile, but she didn't return it. She was completely put out with him because he had failed to be charmed. "Do you remember exactly when Charles first became sick?"

She had to think about that for a moment. "On Saturday, I think. Two days before he died."

"When exactly? Do you know?"

"I . . . I didn't see him that day until dinner. He must have been at the . . . the hospital all day," she said. The word *hospital* seemed to leave a bad taste in her mouth.

Frank couldn't imagine Charles worked all day on Saturday, but he didn't bother to correct her. "Was he sick when he got home?"

"He didn't eat much at dinner, as I recall. His mother made a fuss about it, and he said he wasn't hungry, that he didn't feel well."

That was interesting. So Charles was already sick when he came home.

"How did he feel overnight?"

"I'm sure I have no idea. He very considerately slept in his dressing room so he wouldn't disturb me."

"And did you see him in the morning?"

"Of course I did."

"How was he then?"

"Better, I think, although he didn't attend church with us."

"And how was he feeling by evening?"

"Better still, I'm sure."

"And did you see him on Monday morning?"

"No, I did not. He had already left the house when I got up."

"But he obviously felt well enough to go out."

"Yes, but he came home early. He was ill again, and this time his mother put him in one of the guest rooms. We didn't know if he had something the rest of us could catch, you see."

"And who looked after him?"

"The servants, I suppose. I was afraid of catching whatever he had, so I didn't go near him."

"So you don't know which servants were looking after him?"

He expected her to say Daisy had been the one, but she said, "I have no idea. I'm sure Zeller can tell you. He manages the staff."

"When did you realize that Charles was dead?"

She had the grace to flinch at the baldness of the question. "I . . . Well, there was a crisis of some kind, and they called for the doctor. I was in my room, and I heard the commotion. Everything got very quiet after a while, though, and then Mother Oakes came to tell me he was gone."

"Do you know a woman named Ella?"

She did the wrinkled nose again. "Ella who?"

"I don't know her last name, but she was in love with your husband."

"That's preposterous."

"What is? The idea that someone was in love with him?"

"Oh, I suppose that's possible, but it's preposterous what you're suggesting."

"What am I suggesting?"

"That Charles had a mistress. Oh my, is that the woman who fainted at the service yesterday?"

"Yes, did you recognize her?"

"Not at all. I thought she must be someone from the hospital."

"A patient, you mean?"

Her eyes widened. "Oh my, I didn't think of that! But I don't think they allow the patients out, do they? No, I thought perhaps she worked there as a matron or something. She certainly wasn't a friend of the family."

"How do you know?"

"By the way she was dressed, of course. I wouldn't expect a man to notice, but it was obvious to me and every other female in the room."

"I see. So you think it is preposterous to imagine that your husband had a mistress."

"Yes, I do."

"Even when I tell you that the wife is usually the last one to know about it?"

"I assure you, I have no experience with mistresses at all, but I know my husband. I can't imagine him being unfaithful to me, but even if he was, he would never have wasted his time with that woman."

Frank shared her opinion, but he wasn't going to let her know it.

"Really, Mr. Malloy, I'm finding this whole thing very upsetting. First you refuse to take my word when I tell you who killed my husband, and now you're accusing the poor man of having a mistress. I'm afraid I must put an end to

this interview. My nerves simply cannot stand it another
minute."

"I'm sorry if I upset you, Mrs. Oakes," he lied, rising as
she stood. "And thank you for your help."

"You should do more than thank me. You should find
that Daisy woman and get her out of this house before she
kills someone else."

As Gino followed the butler into the servants'
area of the house, he tried to guess how old the man was. He
stood erect and walked with a firm step, even though his hair
was gray. He had wrinkles around his eyes, but his jaw was
still firm, so he wasn't as old as Gino had first thought.

"This way," Zeller said, holding a door open for him.

The room was small and lined floor to ceiling with
built-in cabinets. A table and four chairs were the only fur-
nishings, although it didn't look like a dining room.

"This is my domain," he said. "Please, sit down."

Gino pulled out a chair and sat. Zeller took the chair opposite. Gino immediately sensed that something was different
from all the other times he'd questioned people about a case.
Of course, he'd seldom questioned people in houses like this,
but that wasn't it, he realized. The difference was that in the
past, every single time, he'd been a policeman, and people had
been afraid of him. Their fear had automatically given him an
advantage. This man, however, was not afraid of him at all.
In fact, Gino thought this butler might actually feel superior
to him. At best, he was only willing to cooperate because his
employer had instructed him to.

Now Gino would find out just how good he was at this
detecting business.

"How long have you worked for Mr. Oakes, Mr. Zeller?" Gino asked.

"Just Zeller, please. I've been here almost twenty-one years."

"Then you know the family pretty well."

"I suppose I do."

"I think Mr. Oakes told you that his son was poisoned. We believe it was arsenic." Zeller flinched at this, but didn't lower his gaze. He felt no obvious guilt then. Gino decided to get right to the point. "First of all, I need to know where you keep the arsenic."

Zeller blinked in surprise. "We don't keep it at all."

"What does that mean?"

"It means we don't . . . Actually, as long as I've worked here, we've never kept poison of any kind in the house."

"Not even for rats?"

"Mrs. Oakes, Mrs. Prudence Oakes, that is, would never allow it in the house. Ever since she became mistress of the house years ago, she has forbidden it. Since I've been here, we've used traps for rats when the need arose."

That was very interesting. It meant that whoever had killed Charles had made a special effort to acquire the poison. If they could find out who had done that . . . But that would have to wait until later. "I need to know everything that happened from the time he got sick until he died."

"I wasn't with him the entire time, of course, but I can tell you what I do know."

"That'll be good enough. So let's start with when Mr. Oakes first got sick. When was the first you knew about that?"

"The first I knew that he didn't feel well was when he came home Saturday evening, two days before the day he died."

"So he was fine when he left that morning?"

"As far as I know, yes. He usually dresses himself unless it's a formal occasion, so I don't see him until he comes downstairs. That morning he seemed well."

"Where did he go that day?"

"I am not in the habit of asking Mr. Charles his plans."

"Can you give me an idea of some of the places he might have gone?"

"He might have gone to his office or his club. You will have to confirm that with the people there, though."

"And was he already not feeling well when he got home or did that happen after supper?"

"He told me he'd become ill that afternoon. He thought perhaps he'd eaten something at noon that didn't agree with him."

"And did he eat supper with the rest of the family?"

"He sat down with them, but I don't believe he ate very much."

"And did he get better or worse that evening?"

"He seemed to recover somewhat, although he didn't attend church with the family the next morning."

"Was he all right the rest of that day?"

"He seemed to be recovering, and on Monday morning, he went out again as usual."

"To his office?"

"So I assume, although he might have gone to his club or someplace else."

"And when did he come back?"

"In the middle of the afternoon. This time he was quite ill and went straight to bed."

"When you say he was quite ill, what do you mean?"

"Really, it's very unpleasant to discuss this."

"I'm sure it is, but it's important that I know exactly what happened."

"He was . . . vomiting and his bowels were . . . Well, he had no control over them. Mrs. Oakes, his mother, had us put him in one of the guest rooms."

"Instead of his own room? Why was that?"

For the first time, Zeller's gaze flickered away. "So as not to disturb his wife."

Gino made a mental note to follow up on this piece of information. "Who was taking care of him?"

"Uh . . . some of the maids. Several, in fact."

"Not his wife? Or his mother?"

"His mother was there, but his wife . . . she was afraid of contagion." Once again his gaze had flickered away.

"Which maids?"

"Well, probably all of them, at one time or another. There was laundry and we changed the bed linen several times and—"

"Which ones?" Gino said in the voice he used to use to intimidate people.

It didn't seem to work on Zeller, but he said, "Daisy was there the most. He . . . Mr. Charles asked for her in particular."

Ah, Gino thought. This might be the older woman Mrs. Brandt had seen by the casket.

"This Daisy, she's been with the family for a long time?"

"No. As a matter of fact, she's only been with us a few months."

So Mrs. Decker had been right about the Oakeses not keeping their staff—at least the maids—for years. Daisy was new, and yet Charles Oakes had asked for her to care for him in his dying agonies and this man had tried to avoid mentioning her by name in what appeared to be an effort to protect her from Gino's suspicion.

"Tell me about the glass of milk that Charles requested."

"I don't know what to tell you. He said his throat was burning and asked for some warm milk to soothe it."

"Who brought it up?"

"One of the girls. I couldn't tell you which one."

"Could it have been Daisy?"

"It's possible, but I don't think she would have left him."

"Would she have been in the room with him when he drank it?"

"I couldn't say for sure. I wasn't there myself, you see."

And he didn't want to implicate Daisy any more than necessary either. "Who decided to call the doctor?"

"Mrs. Oakes did. Mr. Charles became violent and the girls couldn't control him anymore, so I went to help them, and she sent for the doctor."

"And this happened after he drank the milk?"

"I believe so, yes. I saw the glass on the bedside table."

"Was it empty then?"

"Nearly so. I believe there was still a bit in the bottom."

"Do you remember it getting knocked over?"

"No, but as I said, Mr. Charles became very violent, thrashing around. He couldn't seem to understand what I was saying to him, and the things he said didn't make any sense. In all the confusion, the glass was probably knocked to the floor and no one noticed."

And if it hadn't been, someone might have gotten away with murder. "I'll need to speak with all the maids who were in the sick room that night, and I'd like to start with Daisy."

CHARLES OAKES'S MOTHER DID NOT LOOK LIKE A WOMAN who had recently lost her only child. She betrayed no emotion whatever as she accepted Frank's apology for bothering her

and took the chair her daughter-in-law had occupied earlier.
She also sat erect, although she didn't give the impression
she wanted to flee so much as being annoyed at having to
endure this.

"I'm very sorry about your son, Mrs. Oakes. It must have
been a shock to find out he was poisoned."

"No worse than the shock of having him die in the first
place, Mr. Malloy." She was, he noticed, still a very handsome
woman except for the coldness in her eyes.

"Your daughter-in-law thinks one of your maids is responsible."

Her lips tightened at this, her only discernible reaction.
"Hannah is a foolish girl. You shouldn't take her seriously."

Frank had already come to that conclusion. "Why do you
think she blames Daisy?"

"You will have to ask her that."

"Daisy is new, isn't she?"

"She hasn't been with us very long, if that's what you mean."

Now Frank was curious. "How is that different from
being new?"

She was silent so long, Frank thought she wasn't going to
reply at all, no matter how much time he gave her, but his
patience finally paid off. "You will probably hear this from
someone else, so I suppose I should be the one to tell you
first. I knew Daisy when . . . We grew up together in
Georgia."

Frank remembered her story well. "She was a slave on
your plantation."

"On my family's plantation, yes."

"How did she end up here, after all this time?"

Once again, she hesitated. Frank could see she wasn't
accustomed to sharing her private business with strangers,
and she certainly wasn't enjoying the opportunity. When she

did begin to speak, she did so haltingly, as if choosing her words with care lest she betray something she would rather keep hidden. Frank wondered what that might be.

"I met my husband when he arrived with the Yankee troops to burn our home," she said with an amazing lack of bitterness. "I escaped with a few of the house servants. The field hands had long since run off, and we were the only ones left."

"What about the rest of your family?"

"The family was all dead, and I couldn't stay there alone."

"What about your neighbors?"

"They were in the same situation, Mr. Malloy. Houses burned, servants scattered, nothing to eat. So we followed the Yankee army. At least they fed us."

"And Mr. Oakes fell in love with you."

"Yes. We were married, and he sent me North, to his family."

"And what about your . . . servants?" he asked, using the word she had chosen.

"I had to leave them behind. No one was giving Negroes safe passage to go North, and Gerald's family certainly didn't want them. They didn't even want me."

This time Frank caught the faintest trace of bitterness in her tone. "How did Daisy find you after all this time?"

"She remembered the name of the man I'd married, and she knew we lived in New York City. After the war, she tried to get here, but she had no money. Things were very bad in the South then, as you may know. She went as far as she could and finally settled in North Carolina. She married a man she met there. He died a few years ago, though, so she decided to try to find me again. She finally got to the city, like so many others before her, but she had no idea how enormous it was or how many people live here. It took her years to locate me, and then it was only because of the article in the newspaper about Charles's appointment to the Manhattan State Hospital."

"Were you happy to see her?"

"No, I was not, Mr. Malloy. She was a reminder of a terrible time in my life that I have tried very hard to forget."

"But you hired her."

"Of course I did. She'd had a very difficult life, and it had only become more difficult since she arrived in the city. Jobs are very scarce for Negroes here, and she is no longer young."

"Your daughter-in-law claims she hasn't seen Daisy do any work."

"I can't believe Hannah pays any attention to such things, but Daisy attends to my needs."

Frank was remembering what Sarah had seen at the funeral, the older woman leaning over Charles's casket. "I guess a lot of your servants are older since they've been with you for a long time."

"Who told you that?"

"Your husband."

She sighed with what sounded like disgust. "Zeller has been with us for years, and some of the maids may have been here as long as five years, but none longer, I'd guess."

"Why would your husband tell me they'd all been with you for years?"

This time the coldness in her eyes could have frozen his blood. "Probably because he can't tell one colored girl from another. He thinks they all look alike."

Frank blinked at the venom behind her words. He'd often heard this sentiment from other cops and countless other white people, but he'd never seen anyone angry about it. He'd also never imagined anyone would fail to recognize the faces of the people he saw every day in his own home, no matter what color they were, but here was proof it was possible.

And if Mrs. Oakes was bitter about it, how did the servants themselves feel? Did they even know? But of course they did. If he couldn't tell them apart, how could he call them by name? And if they were bitter, too . . .

"Your daughter-in-law thinks Daisy is the one who poisoned your son. Can you think of any reason why she would have?"

"You mean as revenge against me for some ancient wrong I'd done her?" she scoffed. "More likely, she would help me try to save him, since she was grateful for the kindness I had recently shown her. And that, Mr. Malloy, is exactly what she did do."

"She helped you try to save him?"

"Of course she did. She was with him all evening the night he died, holding his head while he vomited and changing his sheets when he lost control of his bodily functions."

"Giving him the milk he asked for?"

"That I don't know, but how could she? She never left his side, so someone else prepared it and carried it up from the kitchen. If she helped him drink it, she had no idea it was poisoned. I would swear to that."

"And how can you be so sure? You might've grown up with this woman, but you haven't seen her in what, thirty years? She could have changed."

"Perhaps she has, but she loved Charles like he was—"

Frank waited but she didn't finish her sentence. "Her own son?" he asked.

"Yes, like a son," she said, but Frank wondered why she'd caught herself if she was so willing to say the words.

"You said you grew up with Daisy. I guess it's hard for

Northerners to understand what it was like in the South in those days."

"Yes, it is, and I gave up trying to explain it years ago. But please understand that Daisy bore me no grudges because I had to leave her behind, and I was happy to give her a place here when she found me again. So don't imagine some bad melodrama took place in this house. If someone really did poison Charles, it wasn't Daisy."

"I'll keep that in mind. Would you help me understand when Charles first became sick? We need to figure out how he got the poison in the first place."

"I thought you'd decided it was the milk. My husband told me it killed Hannah's cat as well."

"That was the final dose, but I understand he'd been sick several days before, too."

"Yes, he said he had started feeling ill on Saturday, in the afternoon."

"Where was he that day?"

"At his club, I assume."

"But you don't know for sure?"

"No, I don't."

"And you don't know where he ate lunch that day?"

"No, I don't."

"But when he came home, not feeling well, did he suspect it was something he'd eaten?"

"I don't know what he thought. I believe his father suggested that might have been it. We weren't really aware that he was feeling ill until we sat down to eat supper, and he had no appetite."

"And he didn't get any sicker after he got home that night?"

"No. In fact, he said he was feeling better."

"And yet he spent the night in his dressing room instead of with his wife."

"She told you that?" Her lips were tight again.

"She said she didn't know how he felt during the night because he slept in the dressing room so he wouldn't disturb her."

"I see."

"What do you see, Mrs. Oakes?"

She sighed again. "My son had been sleeping in his dressing room for weeks because his wife didn't want to be disturbed."

Now it was Frank's turn to say, "I see." And he did. Charles Oakes's marriage wasn't particularly happy, and his mother wanted him to know it. The question was, why? The obvious reason was to cast suspicion on Hannah for the murder. But was that because she really suspected Hannah, or because she wanted to divert suspicion from someone else?

"I understand that your son felt so much better on Monday morning that he went to his office."

"I don't know how much better he felt, but he had some business to attend to, I believe. He made the effort to go out, but he became ill again that afternoon and had to come home. By the time he got here, he was so bad, we put him right to bed."

"In a guest room."

"Hannah insisted," she said. "She didn't want him near her. She said she was afraid of catching whatever he had, but I believe she just didn't want him being sick in her room."

Frank could understand that, although it wasn't very wifely, he supposed. He'd have to ask Sarah what she'd do in a situation like that. It might be a good idea to be prepared. "You said Daisy never left his side."

"I told you, she's very fond of him. Was. Was very fond of him," she corrected herself, and Frank saw the first flicker of real grief cross her face. "He asked for her," she added softly.

"And you were there, too?"

"Not the entire time. Several of the other girls were helping Daisy, and I was in their way. Besides, he seemed to be getting better."

"I understand he asked for the milk?"

"That's what I was told. I wasn't there."

"And you have no idea who prepared it and brought it up?"

"No, although they could tell you in the kitchen, I'm sure."

"And after he drank the milk, he got much worse."

"Yes, he started thrashing uncontrollably, and Daisy called for help."

"Daisy did? Not one of the other girls?"

"What do you mean?"

"I'm trying to figure out who was in the room when your son drank the milk."

"I told you, I wasn't there, so I don't know."

"When Daisy called for help, who came?"

"I did. Zeller, too."

"And who was there with Daisy when you got there?"

She still betrayed no emotion, but her cheeks were red. "I . . . I don't remember."

"Was she alone with him?"

"I told you, I don't remember!"

"Someone put arsenic in the milk, Mrs. Oakes."

"You don't know that for certain! He was sick for two days before that."

"Which only means he'd gotten a dose or two before, but he definitely got one that evening and it killed him."

"How can you be sure? He got sick again that afternoon, when he wasn't even here. He could have gotten it anywhere!" Her voice broke but she blinked furiously, refusing to weep.

"We know because of the cat, Mrs. Oakes. The cat that drank what was left of the milk and died under his bed."

"You're wrong, Mr. Malloy. If someone poisoned my son, they did it outside of this house and for reasons we don't know. I have no idea how it was done, but I know no one in this house would have harmed him."

"Not even his wife?"

To Frank's surprise, she laughed. It was a grating sound, full of anger and bitterness and grief. "If I thought for a moment she could have done it, I would tear her heart from her chest with my bare hands and leave you nothing for your courts of law. Unfortunately, no matter how much Hannah might have regretted her marriage and might have wanted to be free, she was never close enough to Charles during those last days to have done it. And no one else in this house would have dreamed of it. No, Mr. Malloy, if you want to find my son's killer, you'll have to look elsewhere."

6

DAISY LOOKED TERRIFIED WHEN ZELLER ESCORTED HER into the room Gino now understood was the butler's pantry. Her hair was streaked with gray, and the hands she kept wringing in distress were knobby from hard work and age. He could see she had once been an attractive woman, although the same trials that had ruined her hands had stolen all but a trace of her former beauty. Her skin was lighter than he'd expected. So light, in fact, that he might have passed her on the street and not realized she was colored.

"Don't be frightened, Daisy," Zeller was saying. "This young man just wants to ask you some questions about the night Mr. Charles died."

"Sit down, Daisy," Gino said as gently as he could. He didn't need to intimidate Daisy to get her information. In fact, if he couldn't put her at ease, he probably wouldn't get anything out of her at all.

She glanced up at Zeller, as if asking for permission to obey Gino's command. Zeller nodded and pulled out a chair for her. She sank down onto it quickly, as if she was afraid her legs would give out.

"You aren't in any trouble, Daisy," Gino said. He'd dealt with lots of people who were terrified of the police and had good reason to be. She had probably seen the police beating her neighbors and arresting them for no good reason, which they frequently did in colored neighborhoods.

She glanced up at Zeller, who still hovered over her. "You ain't going to leave me, are you, Mr. Zeller?"

Zeller glanced at Gino, who said, "He can stay if it makes you feel better, Daisy."

She nodded vigorously and clasped her hands tightly on the tabletop in a visible effort to get control of herself.

Gino tried a smile. "I just need to know what happened in Mr. Oakes's room the night he died. You were there, weren't you?"

She nodded again, then glanced at Zeller as if for approval.

"Mr. Zeller said Mr. Oakes asked for you to take care of him. Do you know why he wanted you especially, over the other maids?"

She frowned at that. "I . . ." Another glance at Zeller. "I guess 'cause I'm older than them."

Which made Gino wonder why Mrs. Oakes would have hired such an old woman as a maid. Nobody could expect her to do much work, not as much as you could get from a young woman and not for as long either. "So he thought you'd take better care of him."

"I . . . I guess so."

"Did the other girls help you?"

"They did, sir."

"Do you remember who helped?"

"Mary and Patsy. They came and . . . They helped me change the bedclothes a time or two. Mr. Charles was powerful sick." She blinked as her eyes glistened with tears, but she didn't weep.

"When Mr. Charles asked for some milk, who brought it upstairs?"

She frowned, obviously sensing this was an important question and not wanting to give the wrong answer. "I . . ."

"It's all right, Daisy. You can tell him," Zeller said.

"It was Patsy, I think. She brought it up."

"Did she heat it, too?" Gino asked.

"Oh no, sir. Cook wouldn't never allow that. She would've fixed Mr. Charles's milk her ownself."

"And did Patsy help him drink it?"

"No, sir. Mr. Charles didn't want nobody but me to help him that night." She blinked back her tears again.

"How was Mr. Charles feeling when you gave him the milk? Before he drank it, I mean."

"Some better. He'd stopped . . . being sick and all. He said he'd feel even better if he had himself some . . . some milk."

She'd caught herself. She'd started to say something else and caught herself. Gino hoped he hadn't betrayed the fact that he'd noticed. "Was the milk all Mr. Charles had to eat or drink that evening?"

"Oh yes, sir," she said too quickly. "He . . . he couldn't hold nothing down at all from the time he came home until he asked for the milk." She'd started wringing her hands again, twisting them on the tabletop. She wasn't glancing at Zeller anymore, though. He couldn't help her with this. She'd lied about something important, but Zeller didn't know about it, so he couldn't help.

Gino tried to think what Malloy would do now. What would he ask her to keep her talking so he could put her at ease again before trying to figure out the lie?

"Mr. Zeller said you haven't worked here long."

She blinked in surprise at the change of subject. "No, sir. Only a few months."

"You seem very fond of Mr. Charles for not knowing him very long."

Her eyes welled again, and this time a tear slipped out. She dashed it away with a fingertip. "I . . . He was a very nice young gentleman."

"You sound like you're from the South, Daisy. Did you just come to New York?"

Another blink at this new change of subject. "No, sir. I been here a few years now."

"Did you come here to work because Mrs. Oakes is from the South herself?"

To Gino's surprise, this made her sit up straight and turn to Zeller in alarm.

"It's all right to tell him, Daisy," he said.

"It ain't his business," she protested.

"Mr. Gerald told us to tell the truth to these men."

When she turned back to Gino, her fear had melted into wariness. "I come here to work because I used to know Mrs. Oakes when she . . . when she lived in the South."

"Daisy used to be a . . . She worked at the plantation where Mrs. Oakes grew up," Zeller said.

So Daisy had been a slave, and Mrs. Oakes had owned her. Now her reaction made some sense. "Did she remember you after all that time?"

"Of course she remembered me."

Gino didn't know much about slavery, but he wondered

how many society women in New York would remember a maid who had worked for them over thirty years ago. Not many, he'd guess, but Mrs. Oakes had recognized Daisy. Then he recalled something else. "You said you'd been in New York a few years, but you just came to work here a few months ago. Why did you wait so long to find Mrs. Oakes?"

"I didn't wait. I just couldn't find her before is all. In the South, when you come to a town, looking for somebody, you ask around and somebody will know them and point you in the right direction. Here, well, I never saw so many people, and none of them ever heard of Mrs. Oakes. I didn't have no idea where to find her until Mr. Charles got hisself the job at the hospital. It was in the newspapers, and my pastor, Mr. Nicely, saw his name."

"Did the newspaper say where Mr. Charles lived?"

"Oh no, sir. I'd told my pastor the name of the gentleman Miss Jenny had married. I remembered it from all those years ago, and Mr. Nicely thought maybe Mr. Charles was related to her, so he helped me find the house."

Gino nodded. "So what was it that made Mr. Charles so sick that last time? You said he'd tried to eat something."

He'd thought to catch her off guard, but Daisy stared at him for a long moment, her face still and as expressionless as she could make it. "I didn't say that, sir. I said all he had was the milk that Cook had heated up and Patsy carried upstairs to him."

"Oh, I must've misunderstood you. And what happened after he drank it?"

"He . . . Well, at first he seemed fine, like maybe it did him some good. He was glad to get it, too, he said. He . . ." Her voice broke, and she needed a moment to gather herself. "He thanked me for it. But it wasn't long before he started getting sick again, and he was talking, out of his head. I tried to calm him down, but he just got worse, so I called for help."

"And who came to help you?"

"Miss Jenny and Mr. Zeller came right away. Then the other girls come, too, but there was nothing they could do, so Mr. Zeller sent them away."

"Mr. Oakes didn't come?"

This time she did glance at Zeller, not sure what she should say.

"I'm not sure Mr. Oakes knew Mr. Charles had been taken so bad," Zeller said quickly. "He was downstairs, you see, and probably didn't hear Daisy calling."

Gino thought that sounded reasonable, so he couldn't figure out why Daisy wouldn't have realized that, too. He wanted to press her about the milk and what else she knew about it, but he figured Zeller wasn't going to let him frighten her. He'd made a mistake in letting the man stay, but he still needed Zeller's help questioning the rest of the staff, so he couldn't send him off now and risk offending him. There would be time later to question Daisy again when he didn't have to be quite so nice. Or when Mr. Malloy could be there to terrify her with one of his glares.

"Thank you for answering my questions, Daisy," he said. "I'm sure Mrs. Oakes is grateful to you for trying to take care of Mr. Charles."

Daisy frowned, not at all reassured by this. She looked up at Zeller. "Can I go now?"

"Yes, you may," Zeller said.

She stood up and gave a little bob of a curtsy to Gino, then fled.

"She didn't poison Mr. Charles," Zeller said.

Gino stared at the man, seeing him in a whole new light now. Why would the family's longtime butler vouch for a maid who'd only been with them a few months? "How can you be sure?"

"She was devoted to Mr. Charles and his mother. You asked if Mrs. Oakes recognized Daisy when she came to the house a few months ago. I'm not sure you understand, Mr. Donatelli. In the South, when the white people owned slaves, those slaves were often born and lived their entire lives on the very same plantation. Mrs. Oakes and Daisy grew up together as children and knew each other their whole lives until Mrs. Oakes married and came North."

Even still, Gino thought, they hadn't seen each other in over thirty years. People could change a lot in thirty years. Even if they recognized each other, how could Mrs. Oakes just take this woman into her house? For all she knew, Daisy was a thief or something even worse. She'd certainly lived a hard life since the War of the Great Rebellion. Then she'd come to New York, where Negroes didn't exactly have an easy time of it either. How could she know Daisy would be grateful and not harbor a grudge?

"Are you ready to see someone else now, sir?" Zeller asked, all polite now that he'd successfully protected Daisy from whatever he'd thought Gino might do to her.

"Yes, send in Patsy next."

FRANK HAD BEEN SITTING ALONE FOR THE PAST FEW MINutes, reviewing his interview with Jenny Oakes and wondering what he had really learned from her, when the parlor door opened and an older woman came in.

Tall and thin, her sharp features put Frank in mind of a bird. Not a harmless sparrow, though. A bird of prey.

Although he hadn't sent for her, he knew this must be Gerald's mother. Like the two previous Mrs. Oakeses, she wore black, but she wore it well, as if she were most comfortable in its protective embrace. Her hair was a silvery swirl on her head, still thick and lustrous. Her eyes were icy blue, and her lips pursed in a perpetual frown of disapproval.

He'd risen to his feet instinctively as she entered the room, and now he nodded. "Mrs. Oakes, thank you for coming to see me."

"You're the detective, I take it," she said, closing the parlor door behind her with a decisive click. "Weren't you going to send for me?"

"I was hoping you'd be able to meet with me, but I thought you might not feel up to it."

"Why? Because Charles died?" she scoffed. "I've buried my parents, my husband, three children, and a brother. If I allowed death to overwhelm me, I'd have been in my own grave long ago, Mr. . . . Whatever is your name? No one bothered to tell me."

"Malloy."

She sniffed, as if she'd expected nothing better. "Well, Mr. Malloy, you'd better ask me some questions before I decide to have a case of the vapors or whatever it is delicate females do when they don't want to be bothered."

"Then please, sit down." He indicated the easy chair where his first two visitors had sat.

"Thank you for inviting me to sit down in my own house," she snapped. "And I'll invite you to sit down, too. Then we'll be even."

When they had both taken their seats, she studied Frank for a long moment, and he let her because he wanted to study her in return. Like many older women, she'd grown thinner than was good for her. Maybe she'd been sick, although he had no intention of asking her that. He'd find out from Sarah or her mother. The crepey skin of her face sagged now, without the underlying flesh to support it. Her hands clutching the arms of the chair were spotted and clawlike, the bones showing through the papery skin. He realized she hadn't brought a cane with her, although she'd used one yesterday at the funeral.

"I've heard about you, Mr. Malloy," she said. "It's a very interesting story."

"Yes, I'm a bouncer," he said, using a derogatory term used to describe the "new money" people in the city.

"I prefer the term *arriviste*. It sounds less energetic, don't you think?"

Frank shrugged.

"Besides," she said, still pinning him with her daggerlike gaze, "Felix Decker would never allow his daughter to marry a bouncer."

"And yet she's engaged to me."

"Oh, Mr. Malloy, don't play the bumpkin with me. There's much more to you than meets the eye, or Gerald would never have brought you here."

And there was much more to Mrs. Oakes than met the eye, Frank realized. "Did you come to see me because you know who killed your grandson?"

"But I don't know who killed him, and if I did, I most certainly would not tell you. I think you should earn your fee on your own, Mr. Malloy."

Frank bit back a smile. He didn't want her to think he was laughing at her, although he found her amusing. "Charles's wife was a lot more obliging. She told me before I even asked."

"Hannah? She's a fool, and I doubt very much she knows anything about it. Whom did she name as the dastardly villain?"

"The maid Daisy."

Her expression hardened for the briefest instant as she registered the name, then smoothed out again to conceal whatever thoughts had caused the reaction. "The girl who used to belong to Jenny."

"She said they'd grown up together."

"As they did in the South. A quaint custom, don't you think, raising your slaves and your children together, as if they were cats from the same litter?"

"I don't know much about it. My family never even had servants."

"Of course they didn't," she said, although not unkindly. "Mine did, and I assure you, we would never have allowed their children to mingle with ours. Nothing good comes of that."

Frank thought she might be right. "If you aren't going to help me figure out who killed Charles, then why did you come?"

"I didn't say I wouldn't help. I'm happy to tell you what I know, although it isn't much."

"Do you know who prepared the milk that killed him?"

"One of the servants, I suppose. Someone in the kitchen. Do you really think one of our servants poisoned him?"

"I don't know, but they would have had the best opportunity to put arsenic into the milk."

"That might be true, if they had access to arsenic."

This was something they hadn't explored yet. "Why wouldn't they?"

"Because I've always had a special horror of poisons, and we don't keep them in this house."

"May I ask what caused your special horror of poisons?"

"You may not."

"And you're sure there isn't any here at all?"

"Yes, I am. You may ask anyone. They will confirm this."

Frank would certainly do just that. "But it's easy enough to get. Anybody could have gotten some."

"Yes, but why poison Charles? If a disgruntled servant is responsible, she would be more likely to poison me or my daughter-in-law or Hannah, since we're the ones most likely to make their lives miserable."

"You said 'she.' Do you think one of the maids is responsible?"

"I said 'she' because the vast majority of the servants are female. The only male who works inside the house is Zeller, and he was very fond of Charles."

"Why did Charles sleep in his dressing room?"

The wrinkles around her eyes nearly disappeared when she widened them in surprise. "Really, Mr. Malloy, you do get right to the point, don't you?"

"Actually, I thought I'd been beating around the bush a lot. I was trying to put you at ease first."

She laughed at that, a rusty sound that told him she seldom found anything amusing. "I'm beginning to see why Sarah Brandt has agreed to marry you."

"I can be even more charming than this, but I thought you'd see right through it."

"Indeed I would have. And to answer your question, I did not know that he *was* sleeping in his dressing room. Didn't you use your charm to ask Hannah herself?"

"No, because I didn't find out until after I questioned her. Mrs. Jenny Oakes told me."

"The servants would have reported it to her, of course, but no one tells me anything."

"Can you guess why?" Frank asked. "Were they quarreling about something?"

"I have no idea. Hannah may be a fool, but she was raised

properly. She would never do something so common as argue with her husband in front of other people."

Frank hesitated for a few seconds, not sure what her reaction would be to his next question, but if she stormed off, it would tell him almost as much as if she answered him. "Could she have been upset because Charles had interfered with one of the maids?"

"Good heavens, I don't believe anyone else in this world would have dared ask me such a question," she said, although she seemed pleased that he had.

"And do you know the answer?"

"I dearly wish I did, Mr. Malloy, if only to see your face when I gave it. But sadly, I do not, although my opinion is that he would not have dared. All of our maids are Negroes, you know."

Frank could have pointed out that some men would have been even more likely to take advantage of a Negro maid, since many whites considered them less than virtuous by nature. He decided he'd already shocked her enough, though, so he just waited for her to think of this herself.

After a few moments of awkward silence, she said, "The men in this house have never, to my knowledge, taken their pleasure with the servants."

"They wouldn't be likely to tell you if they did."

"No, but I would have heard. I would have pretended not to, but I would have. I can't swear to it, but as I said, I do not have any reason to think Charles betrayed Hannah with anyone at all."

"Do you think Hannah loved him?"

"Loved him? Good heavens, why would she bother with that? He had what she wanted, and she had what he needed."

"She had money, I understand."

"Not enough, unfortunately. Her father gave her a

settlement, but she couldn't buy a house in Newport and travel to Europe or hold masquerade balls and such. She wanted to be an Astor or a Vanderbilt. She thought our family connections would gain her entry into their society, but they did not. She did not accept this disappointment with pleasure, I assure you."

"I gathered she also wasn't happy with Charles's new position at the hospital."

"Heavens, no. She'd never known anyone who had to work for a living, or so she claims. She found it humiliating, for some reason. I suspect she's read too many English novels, and imagines she's part of the aristocracy."

Frank had never read any English novels at all, so he wasn't particularly familiar with the habits of the English aristocracy. "Do you think she regretted her marriage?"

"I'm sure she did, but many young women do. Very few of them murder their husbands, however."

She was right, of course. "Can you think of anyone at all who might have wanted your grandson dead?"

"Heavens no. Charles was . . . Well, one shouldn't speak ill of the dead, but he simply wasn't interesting enough to inspire someone to murder."

Now this was something Frank hadn't considered. "What do you mean by that?"

"Exactly what I said. Oh, he wasn't particularly boring, or at least no more so than the average young man of his social standing. He liked horse racing and cards and smoking cigars at his club with his friends. He didn't care about politics, and he didn't hold any strong beliefs about anything, so he rarely argued. I believe his friends would say he was 'well liked,' which sounds boring all by itself."

"But wasn't his job at the hospital a political appointment?"

She frowned at this. "I suppose it was, but if so, it wasn't based on Charles's politics. Gerald was the one who used his influence to get him the position. He's not particularly political either, but he has many friends who are."

"Would the people who helped him have expected Charles to grant favors in return?"

"I couldn't say, but what possible favors could Charles grant? I'm sure not many people are clamoring for the release of lunatics from the hospital."

"You might be surprised," Frank said, "but I'm thinking they might want someone locked up instead."

Her eyes narrowed into a shrewd glare. "Someone who isn't insane, you mean."

"I'm just guessing."

"That's a very disturbing thought, isn't it?"

"Yes, it is, but like I said, I'm just guessing. Do you think Charles had a mistress?"

"Good heavens! I wouldn't have any idea, and I'm certainly not the person Charles would have confided in about such a thing."

"But if he was spending his nights in his dressing room—"

"Please, Mr. Malloy. You're shocking me again."

Frank didn't bother to apologize, since they both knew perfectly well she wasn't shocked. "If he wasn't bothering the maids, he might have found comfort someplace else."

She considered the possibility for a moment. "Oh, wait a minute, do you mean that pathetic creature who fainted at the funeral? Surely, you can't mean her!"

"I don't mean anyone in particular," he lied. "But now that you mention it, did you know her?"

"Certainly not, but she looked as if she might be a candidate for the Asylum herself."

Frank had to agree with that. "And what about the men who took her away?"

"I don't know them either, but I saw you follow them out. Didn't you find out who they are?"

"I know their names, if that's what you mean. I haven't found out why they were at the funeral, though."

She sniffed. "Unfortunately, none of them were here the night Charles died, so we can't blame it on any of them."

Frank also found that unfortunate. It would be very tidy to be able to blame someone like Adderly or his cohorts. "So you agree, the killer must be someone in this house?"

"Certainly not, although I can't imagine how someone outside could have managed it. Still, as I said, no one here had any reason to want him dead."

"That we know of."

Her eyes widened again. "What is that supposed to mean?"

"Just what I said. The reason I haven't figured out who killed Charles is because I don't know *why* they did it . . . yet."

"And how do you propose to find out?" she asked with genuine interest.

"I'll keep asking questions until I get the answer that will tell me."

"And then you'll tell us?"

"I'll tell Mr. Oakes. He'll decide what to do next."

Once again, she pinned him with her gaze. "And if he does not, Mr. Malloy, please come to me."

FRANK FOUND GERALD OAKES IN HIS LIBRARY, A GLASS IN his hand. His eyes were bloodshot and his face as red as any drunken Irishman Frank had ever seen. Gerald set his glass down on the table beside his chair and struggled to his feet.

"What did you find out?" he asked.

"Not much yet. Mostly, I'm finding out who didn't do it."

"What did Hannah tell you?"

"She thinks Daisy did it."

Gerald frowned. "Who's Daisy?"

"The new maid," Frank said, watching Gerald's face closely. Was he too drunk to remember or did he really not pay any attention to the servants at all, as his wife had claimed. "The one who came from your wife's old plantation."

"What are you talking about?"

Frank wondered just how much Gerald Oakes had drunk. "Maybe we should sit down."

Gerald sank gratefully back into his chair while Frank took the one next to his.

"Now what's this about Jenny's plantation?"

"There's a maid who was a slave on your wife's plantation."

"That's impossible. Who told you such a thing?"

"Your wife did."

He sat back and then lifted his glass, draining what was left in one gulp. Then he set it back on the table with a thunk. "She was on the plantation? This Daisy? You're sure?"

Frank was starting to wonder how a man could live in the same house as other people and not know anything about them. Of course, he'd never had servants, so maybe that was different, but even still, wouldn't Jenny have mentioned something to her husband if someone from her past had suddenly appeared on her doorstep? "I'm sure."

"But how did she get here? And you say she just arrived?"

"A few months ago, I take it, and she probably came by ship. That's how most of the Negroes get here from the South now."

"Oh yes, of course. I didn't mean . . . I mean, I know that, but why would she suddenly appear after all these years?"

"You'll have to ask her that, I'm afraid. But her name is Daisy, and she's the one Hannah accused of killing Charles."

"Why would she do such a thing?"

"Why would Daisy kill Charles or why would Hannah accuse her?"

But Gerald wasn't listening. He was thinking or trying to. "I wonder if . . . Jenny only had a few slaves left when we found her. Years ago, in Georgia, I mean. The others had run away after the rest of her family died."

"How did her family die?" Frank asked.

Gerald looked up in surprise, and suddenly he didn't look quite so drunk. "That wasn't what happened."

"What wasn't what happened?"

"I know what you're thinking, but they weren't poisoned."

"I wasn't thinking that," Frank lied.

"The father and the older brother were killed in the war. Well, the father died in battle, and the son died of a fever in the camp. I think more soldiers died of disease than on the battlefield."

"And the rest of the family?"

"The other brother was younger. He . . . he was never strong, Jenny said. They didn't have enough to eat, and he just got weaker and weaker. When he died, the mother just gave up. Wouldn't eat or even talk, Jenny said. She was alone in that house when I found her with just the two slaves."

"Was Daisy one of them?"

"I . . . I suppose she was. It was a mother and daughter, I think. The daughter was about Jenny's age, maybe a little younger."

"Why didn't she take them North with her after you got married?"

"What use would we have had for slaves in New York? Besides, Jenny said they didn't want to go. Truth to tell, I don't think she did either, but I told her she'd never be hungry. I said she'd have fine clothes and live in a big house again. It wasn't a lie. She's had everything she could ever want, and I would've given her even more than that, if I could. You don't know what she was like then, Malloy. She was so beautiful and so fragile and so frightened. I just wanted to take her someplace safe and protect her for the rest of her life."

Frank tried to match the Jenny Oakes he knew now with the girl Gerald described. She wasn't fragile or frightened anymore, at least that he could tell, and even her beauty had faded. Had Gerald ever regretted his choice?

But this wasn't getting him any closer to Charles's killer. "I wonder if Daisy came here to get revenge on Jenny for leaving her behind."

Gerald frowned and lifted the glass to his lips again, only to discover to his annoyance that it was empty. "Would you like a drink?" he asked as he got up to refill it.

"No, thanks." Frank waited until he'd sat down again. "Are you sure the two slave women really didn't want to go North with Jenny?"

"That's what she said, but we couldn't have taken them in any case. My father had to get a pass for himself and for Jenny and travel down to fetch her. You don't know what it was like then. Even if you had a pass, you couldn't count on having safe passage. A reb might shoot you just for sport, and what good would a piece of paper do you then? I don't think my mother has ever forgiven me for forcing Father to make that trip."

Frank could easily believe that. He also noticed that Gerald hadn't answered his question about revenge. Maybe he simply didn't know, but he could be protecting someone, too. Who, though? Not Daisy, whose name he hadn't even recognized. And no one else even seemed like a likely candidate to have killed Charles. Unless Charles wasn't quite as much of a gentleman as his grandmother had insisted.

"You have a lot of young women working in the house. Did Charles ever . . ." He gestured vaguely.

"What are you asking me? If Charles ever seduced the maids? Good God, man, that's a terrible thing to say."

"A lot of men do, and a lot of men think colored women are no better than they have to be."

"Not in this house."

"Did you know Charles was sleeping in his dressing room?"

Plainly, he did not. He gaped at Frank for a long moment. "Who told you that?"

"Your wife."

He shook his head and took a long swallow from his glass. "That girl . . ." he muttered.

Frank figured he meant Hannah. "Were they fighting?"

"Hannah and Charles, you mean? Of course they were fighting, or at least she was. Nothing ever suited her. We weren't rich enough and we didn't have the right friends and they didn't get invited to the places she wanted to go and Charles wouldn't take her to Newport."

"And she didn't like him having a job."

"No, she didn't. She hated that, although she didn't object to spending his money."

"Your mother said you'd gotten him the job."

"My mother? You *have* been busy if you've spoken with her."

"She came to see me before I even asked."

"Of course she did. She must be curious. She's never met a detective before."

"And you used your influence to find him the job."

"I'd hardly call it influence. I asked some of my friends, men at the Knickerbocker Club. They were very helpful."

"And which one of them suggested you talk to Virgil Adderly?"

Once again, Gerald Oakes gaped at him. He'd denied knowing Adderly this morning, but he didn't deny it now. Instead he began to weep.

7

Frank waited. He'd learned not to comment when a man began to cry. Offering sympathy just humiliated him, and telling him to be a man made him angry.

After a few short minutes, Oakes pulled a handkerchief from his pocket, mopped his face, and blew his nose. When he'd composed himself, Frank said, "Do you think Adderly had something to do with Charles's death?"

Oakes's eyes were terrible, full of pain and guilt and horror. "If I find out that he did, I'll kill him with my bare hands."

"But you're upset because you suspect him."

Oakes stuffed the handkerchief back in his pocket. "I *want* to suspect him. There's a difference."

"Do you know of any reason he'd want to kill Charles?"

"No, of course not. Charles wasn't . . . Well, he wasn't the kind of man someone would murder. But I can't think of anyone else I know who would even think of committing a crime of this nature."

"And you think Adderly would?"

Oakes sighed. "I honestly don't know, but he strikes me as the kind of man who would do whatever is necessary."

"What do you know about him?"

"Not much. He . . . Charles needed a job, and people told me he was helpful."

"What people?"

"I told you, some men at the club. They told me he has lots of friends in the city, and he likes to do favors for people."

"And he did a favor for Charles by getting him the job at the hospital."

Oakes winced. "He said he suggested to the right people that Charles would be a good candidate for the position."

"Did you pay him?"

"No, that's the funny part. I expected I would have to pay him something, but he wouldn't hear of it. He said he was just happy to help."

No one in New York was "just happy to help." Men like Adderly worked hard to cultivate contacts so they could do favors for men who would then be in a position to do them favors in return. The question was, what favor had he asked of Charles and had Charles angered him by refusing to cooperate? Oakes wouldn't know the answer to that, though. Frank would have to find out some other way. "I see."

"What do you see? Do you think Adderly did it?"

"Personally? No, but he might be responsible. I'll need to know more about what Charles was doing these past few weeks. What can you tell me?"

"Nothing, I'm afraid. He never discussed his work with me. I think he . . . Well, Hannah was ashamed of him and didn't want to hear what he was doing, so he just didn't talk about it at all."

Frank would have to go to Charles's office and see what he could find out. Not for the first time, he felt his lack of authority. If he were still a detective sergeant with the New York City Police, he could make people talk to him. Now, he had no such power, so he'd have to rely on people's natural instincts to help others. He tried to remember the last time he'd encountered someone with that instinct, but he couldn't come up with anything.

"Are you going to see Adderly?" Oakes asked.

"Probably, unless I find out someone else did it first. But tell me one more thing. That woman with Adderly, the one who fainted at Charles's funeral, did you lie about not knowing her, too?"

"No. I never saw her before in my life. I swear it. I didn't mean to lie to you before about Adderly. I just . . . I couldn't think of any way he could be responsible."

"Until we find out exactly how Charles died, we won't know who could be responsible."

"I see that now. I won't keep anything else from you, I promise. Please, Malloy, just find out who killed my son."

FRANK FOUND GINO ALONE IN THE BUTLER'S PANTRY, scowling. "What's wrong with you?"

Gino blinked. "Me? Nothing, why?"

"You look like you lost your best friend."

"I'm just trying to figure out why anybody would want to kill Charles Oakes."

"So am I." Frank pulled out a chair and sat down across the table from him.

Gino's scowl disappeared. "Really?"

"Yeah. Everybody in his family loved him except his wife, and nobody thinks he had enough gumption to make anybody mad enough to kill him."

"That's pretty much what the servants said. Did you know one of them used to be a slave on Mrs. Oakes's plantation in Georgia?"

"Yeah, Daisy. Mrs. Oakes told me. That's who Hannah thinks killed Charles."

"Really? Did she have a reason?"

"I think she picked Daisy because she's new."

"She's new, but she loves Charles just like everybody else."

"Everybody except his wife," Frank corrected him.

"All the other maids liked him, too. I thought maybe he was having his way with them, but they said not. They got mad when I even suggested it."

"They actually got mad?"

"Yeah, but I think they were just insulted that I thought of it. All the cops in New York think every colored woman is a whore, and they wanted me to know they were respectable women."

"Oakes told me nothing like that goes on in his house, so I guess it's true. I was kind of hoping Charles threw one of them over, and she got even by putting arsenic in his bedtime milk."

"Patsy, the one who carried the milk upstairs, she was terrified I'd blame her for it. She was near hysterical before I could calm her down."

"So you don't think she did it?"

"No, and even if I did, they all told me that old Mrs. Oakes doesn't allow them to keep arsenic in the house."

"That's what she told me, too. Do they know why?"

"No, they don't, and they wish she did because there's no other good way to get rid of rats, and they're pretty put out with her over it."

"Then I guess it's true, but one of them could've bought some without telling anybody."

"I guess they could have, but not to kill Charles Oakes. They're all really sad he died."

"Except his wife."

"Really? Do you think she could've done it?"

Frank shook his head. "She's a piece of work, but Mrs. Oakes doesn't think she could have done it. She wasn't anywhere near him when he first got sick or any time after. They didn't even sleep together."

"That's strange."

"Not for rich people. Sometimes they even have separate bedrooms."

Gino frowned. "Are you and Mrs. Brandt going to have separate bedrooms?"

"That's none of your business, Gino, but absolutely not."

That made him grin. "So Charles and his wife had separate bedrooms?"

Frank told him what he had learned about the sleeping arrangements of Charles and his wife and also about the timing of Charles's illness and the delivery of the poisoned milk.

"That's what I heard, too. Patsy said she carried up the milk," Gino confirmed, "and the cook heated it up. She took it from a crock that had been delivered just that morning, and other people in the house drank out of it before and after without getting sick."

"So the milk wasn't poisoned until after it got poured. What about the cook?"

"She's in a state thinking something she did might've

poisoned Charles, so I don't think she did it either. She was practically sobbing when I got finished with her, and not because of anything I did."

"So the milk wasn't poisoned when she poured it. Then Patsy carried it up, but she didn't poison it either. Did anybody touch it or distract her or anything on the way?"

"She says not. She says she carried it straight up to the room where he was. Daisy took the glass from her and sent her away."

"Who was in the sick room?"

"She didn't see anyone but Daisy and Charles."

"I thought the butler was in there."

"He didn't come in until Charles got real bad, after he drank the milk."

Frank didn't like this at all. "Then Daisy was the last one to touch the milk before he drank it, and she was all alone with Charles so no one saw what she did."

"And she's hiding something."

Frank straightened in his chair. "How do you know?"

"She lied to me. She said she didn't give Charles anything except the milk, but I could tell she wasn't being honest."

"And you let her get away with it?"

"I let Zeller stay while I questioned her. I know!" Gino held up his hands to stop Frank's outraged protest. "I shouldn't have, but she was so scared, I was afraid she wouldn't talk at all if he didn't stay. He's . . . I think he's sweet on her or something."

"Sweet on her? What makes you say that?"

"Because of the way he treated her. He was protective of all the maids, but Daisy was the only one he wouldn't leave. He . . . I don't know, but he acted like he was worried about her, the way you'd be worried that somebody was going to hurt your sister's feelings or something."

"So he treated her like a sister?"

Gino shook his head. "A sister or a wife. A woman you care about."

"There's a difference between a sister and a wife."

"If you're asking me if he is in love with her, I don't know, but I didn't want to risk pushing her and making him mad. He could've told the other maids not to talk to me."

"You did the right thing. We'll get another chance at this Daisy."

"Maybe we should get Mrs. Brandt to talk to her. She'd probably be too scared of you, too."

"You might be right. Is there anybody else here you think we need to talk to?"

"I think I saw all the servants who know anything. What do you think we should do now?"

"What do *you* think we should do now?"

Gino sat back in surprise. "I don't know."

"Yes, you do."

"I . . . Well, I guess we should find out where Charles was and what he was doing the day he first got sick."

"And if he was doing anything that could've made somebody mad enough to kill him."

"THIS IS EXACTLY WHAT I'VE BEEN AFRAID OF," SARAH SAID.

"You've been afraid of riding in a carriage?" her mother asked as her carriage carried them through the city streets.

"Of course not. I've been afraid that you're going to draw me back into society, where I'll spend my days visiting other society ladies and drinking tea and gossiping."

"I hope you think more of me than that, Sarah. Really, I wouldn't have suggested this if I didn't think it would help Mr. Malloy find out who killed poor Charles Oakes."

Sarah didn't believe that for a minute, but she did, at least, believe her mother thought she was helping. "Tell me again why we're going to see this Mrs. Peabody?"

"Because she's known the Oakes family all her life, and she's the biggest gossip I know."

In the world of New York society, where gossip was the grease that smoothed the gears of conversation, this was quite an achievement, Sarah knew. "But what do you think she can tell us that Malloy can't find out for himself?"

"We won't know that until we hear what she has to say, will we? But I do know she's been friends with Prudence Oakes since they were in the nursery. If Charles was involved in anything unsavory, she'll have caught wind of it."

Esther Peabody lived in a comfortable home on a once-fashionable street in Murray Hill. Many of her former neighbors had moved to newer parts of the city, and all around her, their old houses were being razed for more modest brownstone town houses. Sarah understood as soon as they were ushered into Mrs. Peabody's slightly shabby parlor that she lacked the means to follow her old friends and would spend the remainder of her days living here in reduced circumstances, as many of the older families did.

Mrs. Peabody was a plump woman with the face of a cherub. She wore an old-fashioned lace cap over her graying hair, and her lavender dress spoke of a half-mourning period for her late husband that would probably never end. She perfectly matched the overstuffed and lace-doilyed decoration of the room, which had been the style of the previous generation.

She greeted Mrs. Decker warmly and seemed delighted to see Sarah, who had become an object of curiosity ever since the notice of her engagement to Frank Malloy had appeared in the newspapers.

"Have you set a date for your wedding?" Mrs. Peabody asked Sarah when they were settled on the faded horsehair sofa and had been served tea.

"Not yet. We're waiting for our house to be ready."

"And will you have a big wedding? I should love to see it," she said hopefully.

"I'm afraid it's going to be a small affair, just family and a few close friends."

"It's the second marriage for both of them," her mother said. "And Mr. Malloy isn't accustomed to being in society."

"You must tell me how you came to meet such an interesting man, Sarah," Mrs. Peabody said, and Sarah understood that this was her repayment for whatever information Mrs. Peabody would give them in return. She told a very brief version of her first encounter with Frank Malloy and how they had, together, solved the murder of a young woman Sarah had known.

"How thrilling," Mrs. Peabody said. "I can truthfully say I have never known anyone who was murdered."

"At least to your knowledge," Sarah's mother said.

Mrs. Peabody smiled over her teacup. "Quite true. One does wonder sometimes, when inconvenient spouses conveniently die, doesn't one?"

"Or a young person is suddenly taken ill," her mother said.

"And especially when the two things happen together."

Sarah's mother feigned surprise. "Are you speaking of someone in particular?"

"You know I am. You were at Charles Oakes's funeral, too."

"Do you think Hannah found him inconvenient?"

"I have no idea, although I do know she wasn't happy when he took a position at that Asylum."

"One can't fault him for wanting to provide for his family," her mother said.

"Of course not, and I understand it pays five thousand a year."

Sarah almost gasped. The amount was quite generous, of course, but what really surprised her was she didn't think she'd ever heard a woman of Mrs. Peabody's station in life mention anything so crass as how much salary someone earned.

"That seems . . . very generous," her mother said.

"Particularly when Charles hardly ever bothered to appear at his office."

Sarah had to bite her tongue to keep from demanding how she could know such a thing, reminding herself she wasn't interrogating Mrs. Peabody. She had to allow her mother to obtain the information in the customary way that gossiping women did.

"I wonder what he did with himself all day then," her mother said.

"Oh, that's easy enough to determine. He went to his club. My nephew Percy would see him there almost every day."

"Percy?" her mother said. "Is that your sister's boy?"

"Yes, Percy Littlefield."

Her mother was going to ask another question, probably about Percy's heritage, so Sarah decided to get the conversation back where she wanted it. "I wonder if Charles was at his club when he was first taken ill," she said.

"I'll have to ask Percy," Mrs. Peabody said. "Although I wouldn't be surprised if he hadn't been taken ill any number of times when he was at his club," she added with a smirk.

Her mother somehow managed to betray only mild interest. "Why is that?"

"Well, I hate to speak ill of the dead, you understand, but it was common knowledge that Charles often drank far more than was sensible and certainly more than was good for him.

Percy said that he had to be escorted home more than once after he had overindulged."

"Many young men overindulge."

"But how many of them become so ill from it that they die?"

"Oh my."

"I hope we aren't shocking you, Sarah," Mrs. Peabody said, obviously hoping that she was.

Sarah refused to react. "I was just thinking how tragic that is, for a young man's lack of control to cost him his life."

"Indeed. Although there are other ways a young man's lack of control can ruin him. His own father proved that."

"Whatever do you mean, Esther?" her mother asked.

"You know the story as well as I, how Gerald took up with that girl down South during the war. Prudence hasn't forgiven him to this day."

"Surely you exaggerate. No one can stay angry for thirty years."

"Perhaps not angry, but certainly bitter."

"Because her son fell in love?" her mother scoffed.

"Because he was tricked. Oh, you must have heard the rumors. Prudence started them herself with her carrying on when Jenny first arrived here."

"I'm afraid I didn't. What rumors do you mean?"

"The rumor that Jenny wasn't at all what she claimed to be."

"But she really was from the South. That part had to be true, because that's where Gerald found her."

"Yes, but she claimed to be the daughter of a wealthy family who had owned a plantation and slaves, but Prudence said her manners were atrocious. She had to teach her everything—how to have a conversation and entertain company, even how to shop for clothing and deal with a dress-maker."

"I'm sure her life in the South was very different, and she was so young . . ." Sarah's mother tried.

"She was old enough to have a child, which was another thing that bothered Prudence. She could never get the truth of it, whether Charles had married her and gotten her with child or if it was the other way around."

"That's a terrible thing to say," her mother said.

"Of course it is, but who could have blamed the girl? There was a war, and she'd lost everything and everyone. She wouldn't be the first to trade her virtue for some security."

Sarah couldn't keep silent any longer. "But how could she be sure her virtue would really buy her security? As you said, there was a war, and the soldiers might be gone the next day."

"Ah yes, Sarah, you are absolutely right, which is why Prudence also never quite believed that Charles was Gerald's son."

This time both Sarah and her mother did gasp.

"You can't be serious," her mother said.

"I'm perfectly serious. Of course I have no idea if Prudence's suspicions were justified, but I do know she had them. A girl who had lied about her background would lie about anything, I suppose."

"But you've known Jenny all these years," Sarah couldn't help pointing out. "Wouldn't you have suspected something yourself?"

"No one really got to know her until after Charles was born and Gerald returned home. By then, she'd learned how to conduct herself, I suppose . . . And truth to tell, no one really knows her to this day. She keeps her own counsel, as they say."

Sarah couldn't help wondering if Jenny had truly kept to herself or if the good citizens of New York had left her to herself because she was different and not really one of them.

Enough money could overcome even that, but Gerald's family
didn't have that kind of money, at least not anymore. If Mrs.
Peabody was still spreading these stories about her, others
probably were, too. Sarah felt a pang of sympathy for the young
woman Jenny had been and the lonely, middle-aged woman
she had become.

"I wonder if Hannah knew any of this when she married
Charles," her mother said.

"Oh my, I doubt it. The Kingsleys were never in our social
circle. Mr. Kingsley made his money in railroads, I believe,
and he brought his family to the city where his children
would have more opportunities to marry well. Hannah chose
Charles because she was interested in being invited to the
right houses, and she was sorely disappointed that Charles's
name didn't open those doors for her."

Sarah couldn't help wondering what Mrs. Peabody would
say if she knew Charles really had been murdered, but they
had decided not to tell her this, since his family didn't want
anyone to know. Telling Mrs. Peabody would work better
than putting it on the front page of a newspaper to make it
public knowledge.

"It's odd you should have mentioned murder, though,"
Mrs. Peabody said, "because I can't help wondering if Hannah might not have started thinking she could do better for
herself if only Charles were out of the way."

F RANK AND GINO TOOK THE NINTH AVENUE ELEVATED
train north to 104th Street. Then they got a cab to take them
across to the East Side and over the rickety bridge at 110th
Street to Wards Island and the newly minted Manhattan
State Hospital.

Most everybody still called it the Wards Island Asylum, though.

From a distance, the buildings looked impressive. Four stories of ornate brickwork with towers and arched windows, the sprawling structure could have been a university or some other revered institution. Only when the cab lurched to a stop in front of the main entrance did that impression fade.

Frank sensed rather than saw the despair that permeated the whole island. Decades ago, hundreds of thousands of bodies had been moved from cemeteries in Madison Square and Bryant Park to this desolate place for reburial. Later someone decided this small island off the East Side of Manhattan would be an excellent location for the city's insane men, so they'd built the Asylum. Recently, they'd also begun moving the female population of Blackwell's Island here, as well. When Frank went inside to inquire about speaking to someone who knew Charles Oakes, he was directed to Dr. Dent, who was the supervisor of the Women's Department.

Frank left Gino to wander around and see what he could learn from the staff or even the inmates while he spoke with Dr. Dent.

"Who did you say you are again?" Dr. Dent asked when he'd invited Frank to take one of the straight-backed chairs sitting in front of his battered desk. The room had the cluttered look of a man with too much real work to do and not enough time for managing the paperwork.

"I'm assisting Mr. Gerald Oakes in making some inquiries about the death of his son, Charles."

Dr. Dent wasn't impressed by this piece of gobbledygook. "Which means that Mr. Oakes thinks his son met with some sort of foul play, I take it."

"That's something he's concerned about, yes. Do you know

anything about Charles Oakes that might help us determine what happened to him?"

"I hardly know anything at all about Charles Oakes, as a matter of fact."

"I thought he worked here."

"That is a matter of opinion, Mr. Malloy. Oakes was appointed to a position here with much fanfare, but like many government appointments, his position was not clearly defined as to duties and responsibilities."

Frank could see this didn't sit well with the good doctor. "So you're saying he had a job here but no real work to do."

"I'm sure he could have found something, but he rarely bothered to appear, so he never had the opportunity." Was that bitterness in the doctor's voice? "What is it exactly you want to know about Mr. Oakes?"

"I was wondering if you saw him on the day when he first became ill."

"I see, because you think his illness was suspicious. Does that mean you think he was murdered somehow?"

"As a matter of fact, that's a possibility. He may have been poisoned. That's why I'd like to know if you saw him and had a medical opinion about his condition."

"I had not seen him for at least a week before he died, and he seemed perfectly fine then."

"Can you think of any reason why someone would want to poison Mr. Oakes?"

"Good God, man, that's . . . How would I know something like that?"

"We both know why a man like Charles Oakes gets appointed to a position here, and it's not because he has any interest in the patients or the treatment of the insane."

"You are absolutely right, Mr. Malloy, although Charles Oakes did have some interest in at least one of the patients."

"Really? Which one?"

"A woman named Ella Adderly."

Frank managed not to react. "What sort of interest did he take in her?"

"Not the kind you're probably thinking. We're very progressive here, Mr. Malloy, and I assure you that the female patients are not interfered with in any way by the staff. We treat insanity with the most modern methods, and many of our patients actually recover and return home to live perfectly normal lives."

"Was this Ella Adderly one of them?"

Dr. Dent sighed. "Sadly, no. That is, she may yet recover, but when she left here, she was still somewhat delusional."

"And Charles Oakes was responsible for her leaving?"

"Yes, he handled the paperwork himself and made sure the doctor who examined her provided the diagnosis necessary to get her released."

"Had he ever done this for any other patients?"

"Never. He never even expressed any interest in the other patients. As I said, he spent little time here."

"Do you have any idea why he chose this Ella Adderly for special attention?"

"Not really, although it isn't difficult to guess. Her family must have, uh, asked him to get her released."

"Is that common?"

"Mr. Malloy, when someone is judged insane and sent here for treatment, their family is usually ashamed. People don't like their friends to know. It reflects badly on the entire family, you see. They are suspected of a certain weakness or lack of moral fiber, and all the family members are tainted with the idea of 'bad blood.'"

Frank knew this perfectly well. "What does this have to do with getting the Adderly woman released?"

"Because of the taint, families often don't want their loved one returned to them. In some cases, where the individual is completely recovered, they can make up a story about where the person has been and no one is ever the wiser. But if the person isn't recovered, she will eventually call attention to herself and her condition and embarrass her family."

"So it's not likely the family will want the person back if they aren't recovered."

"No. In fact, they are usually more than happy to leave the person here with us indefinitely, even after they are completely recovered, just in case she might have a relapse someday."

"Why do you think the Adderly woman's family wanted her released?"

"I don't know, but I do know it was the worst thing they could have done. She is very fragile, and the slightest difficulty could shatter her mentally beyond repair."

"She came to Charles Oakes's funeral."

"Oh dear," Dent said, frowning. "I hope she wasn't disruptive."

"She fainted and a man named Adderly took her home. Her husband, do you think?"

"She wasn't married, which was unfortunate. We see many old maids here. When a female doesn't have the opportunity to fulfill her natural destiny as a wife and mother, especially if she is of a nervous temperament, her mind often turns inward."

Frank couldn't believe what he was hearing. "Are you saying that getting married prevents women from going insane?"

"Not precisely, no, but any individual who finds himself with no outlets for his abilities and nothing to occupy his— or her—mind and energies, may succumb to despair and lose touch with reality."

"And this is what happened to Miss Adderly?"

"I don't know the specifics of her case, and of course it can't possibly have any bearing on Charles Oakes's death, but it seems likely."

"Then why do you think her family wanted her released?"

"As I said, I have no idea. Perhaps you should ask them."

Perhaps he should. "What else was Oakes involved with? Was he in a position to give business to a particular company, for example? Or was he in charge of ordering food or supplies?"

"He might have been, had he taken any interest in the running of the hospital. I'm afraid the only time I saw him exert himself was when he was being of service to Miss Adderly and her family."

"And of course he had to bribe the doctor to get him to certify her sane enough to be released," Frank guessed.

Dent stiffened, obviously insulted. "I told you, we are very progressive here. In the old days, the physicians might have taken a bribe to get someone admitted to the hospital who wasn't insane, someone their friends or family wanted taken out of the way for some reason, but that would never happen now."

"Did that happen a lot?"

"More often than anyone would like to think. Immigrants were often judged insane simply because they didn't speak English and couldn't understand what people were saying to them. Other people might be ill with a disease that caused them to have seizures or behave oddly. They would be locked away for years and receive no treatment for what was really wrong with them. Some of them did eventually go insane, as you can imagine."

"But that doesn't happen anymore?"

"Not here, Mr. Malloy. We also are usually very careful about who we discharge. We don't want any of our patients to harm themselves or others after they leave here."

"Was this Miss Adderly someone who might do that?"

"She was quite despondent when she arrived. As I recall, her family was afraid she might take her own life, but after only a few weeks here, she improved quite a bit, although not completely."

"Is she capable of hurting someone else?"

"If provoked, perhaps. Any of us would do that and not be judged insane."

This was very true. "So what was the danger of taking her back home if the family wasn't worried about her embarrassing them?"

"There was always the chance that she would fall into despair again. We don't know her circumstances, but whatever her life had been before, it would probably be the same once she returned home. If she wasn't strong enough to cope . . . well, I'm sure you see the problem."

Frank did see the problem. "Might she blame Charles Oakes for sending her back home when she wasn't ready?"

Dr. Dent didn't like this one bit. "I hope you aren't accusing this poor woman of murdering Charles Oakes."

"I'm not accusing anybody of anything, but you're the one who said your patients might hurt somebody else if provoked."

"I said anyone might do that, sane or insane."

"So you're saying Miss Adderly might possibly have been angry with Charles Oakes and been provoked enough to poison him."

"I'm not saying anything of the kind, Mr. Malloy, and now I'm going to have to ask you to leave my office."

8

CATHERINE'S HAPPY SQUEALS TOLD SARAH THAT MALLOY had returned home. She had left Maeve and Mrs. Malloy in charge of the workmen at the new house while she and her mother visited Mrs. Peabody. By the time Sarah returned from the visit, Mrs. Malloy had started supper, so they'd decided to eat together that evening.

Sarah found Malloy and Gino in the front hall being greeted by Catherine and Brian. Maeve, Sarah noticed, was hanging back in the doorway to Mrs. Malloy's parlor, although she was smiling. Gino was smiling back.

"Did you have a productive day?" Sarah asked when the children had been properly greeted.

"We had a busy one, but I don't know how much we learned that will really help us," Malloy said.

"Mother came by earlier and convinced me to go with her

to see a friend of hers, a <u>Mrs. Peabody</u>, who told us some very interesting things about the Oakes family."

Malloy glanced up at the ceiling with a frown. They could hear the muffled sound of hammering from above. "You left them alone?"

"I left Maeve and Catherine in charge."

"I made sure they didn't slack off," Maeve assured him.

"I'm sure you did," Malloy said. He turned to Sarah. "Is your mother still here?"

"No, she and Father had an engagement this evening, so she couldn't stay. She's very anxious to find out how things are going, though, so I'm sure she'll be on my doorstep first thing tomorrow."

"And meanwhile, we need a quiet place to talk," Malloy said, glancing at the ceiling again.

"We put the front parlor to rights this afternoon," Maeve said, pointing to the door across the hall from the rooms that were Mrs. Malloy's. "Mrs. Ellsworth helped me."

"It looks very nice," Sarah confirmed. "They arranged the new furniture and dusted everything."

Malloy glanced meaningfully at the children. Maeve said, "I'll take them. Let's go see what Mrs. Malloy is making for supper," she said, signing to Brian who nodded eagerly in return. He and Catherine darted away, down the hall to the kitchen, but Maeve lingered a moment longer, exchanging another glance with Gino. "You must be thirsty. Should I bring you some lemonade?"

"That would be lovely," Sarah said, then gestured to the parlor door. "Shall we?"

"After you, Mrs. Brandt," Malloy said with a grin.

Sarah led them into the front room that they would use to entertain guests after they were married. Maeve and Mrs. Ellsworth had done a fine job of arranging the new furniture.

A gold velvet sofa and several upholstered chairs were grouped around the fireplace, and several small tables sat conveniently nearby. Lace curtains hung over the windows, filtering the late afternoon sunlight that gave the room a golden glow.

"This is nice," Gino said.

"It is nice," Malloy said, looking around. "I'm starting to think this house might really be livable someday."

"Someday soon, I hope," Sarah said.

Malloy gave a long-suffering sigh, and Sarah bit back a grin.

He joined her on the sofa, leaving Gino his choice of the chairs. "Why don't you tell us what you and your mother found out today?"

"You already knew that Jenny Oakes is originally from Georgia."

"Yes, and that she grew up on a plantation and owned slaves. One of those slaves works in her house."

"Really? I didn't know she brought anyone with her when she came North."

"She didn't. This woman spent the last thirty or so years trying to find her. She finally got to New York a couple years ago, but she still didn't find Jenny until recently."

Sarah frowned. "That's a long time to be looking for someone."

"Yes, it is."

"Was Jenny happy to see her?"

"Not very, but she did tell us about her. Daisy is her name. She's about Jenny's age, so they probably grew up together."

Sarah tried to imagine what that must have been like for both girls, one rich and privileged, the other her property with no rights at all. "Is this Daisy angry that Jenny left her behind all those years ago?"

Malloy glanced at Gino, who said, "She didn't act like it, but maybe that's because she was so scared of me."

"Scared of you?" Sarah scoffed. "What did you do to the poor woman?"

"Nothing. I wasn't even being mean."

"He couldn't be," Malloy said with a grin. "The butler wouldn't leave her alone with him."

"You let the butler stay when you questioned her?" Sarah asked in surprise.

"She was so scared, she was shaking, so Zeller wanted to stay. I figured she'd feel better if he was there, but I didn't realize he's sweet on her."

"Sweet on her," Sarah echoed in delight. "This is very interesting!"

"Yes, it is," Malloy agreed. "Especially when I found out that this Daisy was alone with Charles Oakes the night he died, and she was the one who gave him the poisoned milk."

"Do you think she put the poison in it?"

Malloy turned to Gino. "Tell her what you found out about the milk."

"The milk had been delivered that morning. Several other people drank some of it, both before and after Charles died."

"So the crock wasn't poisoned," Sarah said.

"Right. The cook heated the milk for Charles, then gave it to one of the maids, Patsy, to take upstairs. She said no one else touched it until she handed it to Daisy."

"And nobody else was in the room with her and Charles from then until the poison started to take effect and he got really sick."

"Did the cook or this Patsy have anything against Charles?" Sarah asked.

"According to them and everybody else, they adored him," Gino said.

"So you think Daisy is the one who poisoned him?" Sarah asked.

"Gino doesn't think so," Malloy said.

"She doesn't act like a killer," Gino said. "And besides, they all told us that they don't keep any arsenic in the house."

"Mrs. Oakes, the oldest one, told me the same thing," Malloy confirmed. "She's got this strange fear of poisons and doesn't allow it."

"So someone would've had to get the arsenic deliberately and secretly," Sarah said. "But if nobody had a reason to kill Charles . . ."

"Tell her about Daisy," Malloy said to Gino.

"What about her?" Sarah asked.

"I don't think she told me everything that happened that night."

"He didn't want to push her too hard with Zeller in the room," Malloy said.

"So she's hiding something, and she did have a good reason to kill Charles," Sarah said.

"If she was after revenge, she did," Malloy said. "She didn't have an easy time of it after Jenny left her behind. Maybe she was planning to get even with her old mistress, and she decided that killing her only son would be a good way to do that."

"But wouldn't Jenny have suspected she was out for revenge when she arrived here after all that time?"

"Would you have?" Malloy asked her.

Sarah had to think about that. "I can't speak for Jenny, but I think I would've felt very guilty when Daisy showed up on my doorstep after so many years. I would've tried to make it up to her by giving her a job and a home, just like Jenny did. I think I also would've expected Daisy to be grateful for my kindness. Remember, Daisy was her slave. Why would either of them think Daisy should have gone North with Jenny in the first place or that she deserved the kind of good fortune Jenny had when she married Gerald?"

"But why would she have spent thirty years looking for Jenny if she didn't think Jenny owed her something?" Gino asked.

"Did she really spend thirty years looking for her?" Sarah asked.

"Now that you mention it, I'm not sure she did," Malloy said. "Jenny said Daisy ended up in North Carolina after the war was over. She got married and lived there until her husband died. Then she came to New York to find Jenny."

"So she was only looking for her for a few years. I wonder what took her so long after she got to the city."

"She said she didn't expect it to be so hard to find her. She seemed to think that she could come to New York and ask around and someone would know where Jenny lived," Gino said.

"Oh my, she must have been shocked when she found out how many people live in the city."

"She was, and I gathered that she can't read, so she wouldn't've thought to look in the city directory or anything like that. She said her pastor saw a story in the newspaper about Charles being appointed to his job at the hospital, and he remembered that was the name of the family she'd been looking for."

"How lucky for her."

"And maybe unlucky for Charles," Malloy said.

"But Gino doesn't think she did it, even though she was the only one in the room with him."

"Let's not forget he wasn't in that room alone with her or even in his house the *first two times* he got sick," Gino said.

The parlor door opened, and Maeve came in carrying a tray with four glasses on it. Sarah jumped up to help her. Between the two of them, they served the men and themselves. Sarah didn't remark on the fact that Maeve had brought a glass for herself so she could stay with them.

"Mrs. Malloy is watching the children," she explained before anyone could ask her. "What did I miss?"

Sarah brought her up to date.

"What did you think about Mrs. Peabody's gossip?" Maeve asked the men when Sarah was finished.

"What gossip?" Malloy asked.

"The gossip I was going to tell you when you told me I should start, but then you distracted me by telling me about Daisy."

"Well, tell us now."

Sarah told them what Prudence Oakes had told Mrs. Peabody about her daughter-in-law and her fears that Jenny had tricked Gerald into marriage and that Charles wasn't even Gerald's son.

"What made her think Jenny had lied about her background?" Malloy asked.

"Mrs. Peabody didn't give us any details, but I gathered that Prudence thought Jenny lacked some of the social skills that a young woman with her background should have."

"But didn't she grow up on a farm?" Gino asked.

"A plantation," Malloy said.

"But that's just a big farm, isn't it? Maybe she didn't go to school. Maybe they do things different in the South," he argued.

"That might be true, Gino," Sarah said, "but families who have a lot of money hire tutors for their children if they can't go to school, and I guess manners are the same no matter where you live. But maybe Prudence was so determined to hate Jenny that she exaggerated her faults or made them up entirely. Jenny was very young when she came here and probably terrified. If she was awkward and shy and made mistakes, I don't think anyone could criticize her."

"Her mother-in-law did," Maeve said.

No one had an answer for that.

"What about the story about Charles not being Gerald's son?" Malloy said after a moment. "Do you think there could be any truth to it?"

"Anything is possible, but if Gerald believed he was, that's all that mattered," Sarah said. "Unless you think Gerald poisoned Charles."

"Since Gerald is the one who hired me to find the killer, that doesn't seem likely," Malloy said. "So we're back where we started."

"Oh, I almost forgot," Sarah said. "Charles apparently spent a lot of time at his club, time when other people thought he was at the hospital working."

"Oh yes, we found that out, too," Malloy said. "We went to the hospital this afternoon and talked to the superintendent there, a Dr. Dent. You remember the woman who fainted at the funeral? She was a patient there."

"At the Asylum?" Maeve asked. "I knew there was something funny about her."

"Something more than funny," Malloy said. "It looks like that Adderly fellow, the one who took her away from the funeral, is the one who got Charles his job there. All he wanted in return was for Charles to get her released."

"Why did he want that?" Sarah asked.

"So far, we don't know. She's related to him in some way, too, but I don't know how."

"But if he wanted her released, couldn't he just have asked for them to release her?" Sarah asked.

"I don't know," Malloy said. "Can you do that?"

"I think so. There's probably some kind of legal proceeding, but I'm sure you can," Sarah said. "So why would he go to all that trouble to have Charles do it?"

"Going to court is a lot of trouble, too," Malloy said. "And a lot more public. And wouldn't he have to prove she was sane?"

"I'm not sure, but I'm guessing he wouldn't have been able to prove it."

"No, he wouldn't have."

"All right, I'll agree that Adderly might've had good reasons not to go to court, but how could he be sure Charles would do this favor for him? And how could he be sure he could even get Charles the job in the first place?"

"I guess I'll have to ask Mr. Adderly all those questions when I go to see him tomorrow," Malloy said.

"And what can I do to help?" Sarah asked.

Malloy smiled. "You can visit this Daisy and find out what she's hiding and if she's still mad that Jenny left her behind."

SINCE THE NEXT MORNING WAS SUNDAY, SARAH WAITED until midafternoon to visit the Oakes house again. The maid told her that the family wasn't receiving, but Sarah explained she was there to see Daisy.

"She's not here, miss."

"What do you mean, she's not here?" Servants were virtual prisoners in the houses where they worked, usually getting only one afternoon a month off in addition to being allowed to attend church on Sunday morning.

"I mean she's not back from her church yet."

"But you're back," Sarah pointed out.

"Daisy goes to a different church than the rest of us, and she's not come back yet."

"I see. When do you expect her?"

The girl's face wrinkled in dismay. "I don't rightly know, miss. She's usually back by now, though."

Sarah felt a niggle of unease. They'd suspected that Daisy knew more than she'd admitted about the night Charles had died, and now she'd left the house and hadn't returned when expected. How convenient if she'd killed Charles and now had disappeared. "May I speak to Mr. Zeller, please?"

The girl was only too happy to fetch Mr. Zeller to handle this difficult situation. She left Sarah in the small receiving room just off the foyer, where unexpected guests were asked to wait while the servants found out if they were to be received or turned away.

Sarah was a bit surprised to see that Mr. Zeller was a white man. Not that it was unusual for servants to be white, but somehow she'd expected him to be a Negro after Gino told her he was sweet on Daisy.

"I understand you wanted to speak with Daisy," he said after greeting Sarah.

"Yes, but the girl said she hasn't returned from church yet."

"No, she hasn't, and I confess, I'm a bit worried." He did look worried, and Sarah had no trouble at all believing he cared about Daisy as more than just a fellow staff member. "Of course, Daisy enjoys a bit more freedom than the other maids, because of her place in the household."

"What place is that?"

Zeller shifted uncomfortably. "She's Mrs. Gerald's personal maid. Sometimes she has special permission to do things the other girls do not."

So Jenny allowed Daisy special privileges, Sarah thought. Was this because Daisy was all she had left of her former life or because Daisy had some hold on her? She would dearly love to ask Jenny what other privileges she allowed Daisy and why, but the maid had already told her the family wouldn't see her. She was just about to thank Zeller and take her leave when the maid tapped on the door.

"Excuse me, but Mrs. Gerald would like to see Mrs. Brandt, please," she said.

Zeller bowed slightly, and the girl escorted her upstairs

to the front parlor. Jenny waited for her there, standing erect in her black mourning gown with her hands clutched tightly in front of her.

"I didn't mean to bother you, Mrs. Oakes," Sarah said. "I asked to see Daisy, but they told me she isn't here."

"I know. The girl told me why you'd come. I can't imagine where Daisy has gotten to. I confess, I'm curious about why you're here to see her, though."

"Mr. Malloy asked me to visit her. She was quite terrified by the young man who questioned her yesterday, and he thought she was afraid to tell him everything she knew."

"How odd that Mr. Malloy would involve you in the investigation." Her frown of disapproval told Sarah that she found it far more than odd.

"I've helped Mr. Malloy before. Sometimes a woman can find out things a man can't."

"I see," she said, although she plainly didn't see at all. "Does Mr. Malloy think Daisy had something to do with Charles's death?"

"He thinks she might have some information that would help identify the killer, I believe."

"If she did, I'm sure she would have shared it. Daisy was devastated when Charles died."

"She may not know that what she saw was important. That's why he wanted me to talk to her. Do you have any idea when she might return?"

"I do not. Daisy very much enjoys Sundays with her friends. She had lived in the city for several years before she came to work here, and she was fortunate to have found some people who cared for her. Life can be difficult for Negroes in the city, especially if they don't have any family here."

"You must have been surprised when Daisy reappeared after all those years."

"I see Mr. Malloy has told you I knew Daisy back in Georgia." Jenny didn't look pleased.

"Yes. I can't imagine you were happy to be reminded of that time," Sarah said to see if she could get a reaction out of Jenny.

"On the contrary, I have many happy memories of my old life before the war, and Daisy was part of that."

"But the war did come, didn't it? I imagine Daisy was jealous of you when you married Mr. Oakes and left her behind."

"Again? I thought I'd settled this with Mr. Malloy. Daisy may have been a bit jealous, but she also had no desire to leave the only life she had ever known either. If I tell the truth, I wasn't happy about it myself."

"But the life you had known was over, wasn't it? Your family was gone and your plantation was destroyed."

"Now who is bringing back unhappy memories, Mrs. Brandt?"

"I'm sorry. I didn't mean to be cruel, but we're trying to figure out who might have poisoned your son. It's just hard to believe that Daisy found you again after all those years and why she would have gone to so much trouble—"

"—unless she wanted revenge on me for leaving her behind when I came North, do you mean? Really, Mrs. Brandt, you sound like something out of a dime novel. As I told Mr. Malloy when he suggested this, it's absurd. No one bears a grudge for over thirty years. And if she did, why would she kill Charles instead of me?"

Sarah didn't bother to point out that killing Charles was a way to make Jenny suffer, because that sounded even more like something out of a dime novel. "Then why did Daisy come all the way to New York to seek you out?"

"Because she was hoping I would look after her. She's had

a difficult life, and after her husband died, it got even more difficult. She remembered I had married a wealthy man, and she thought perhaps I would take care of her in her old age, the way the Honeywell family always took care of the people who worked on the plantation."

"She took quite a chance in coming all this way. You might have died in the meantime."

"Or I might not be living in the city anymore. Any number of things might have happened, but they didn't. Daisy also had a difficult time locating me, but when she did, I was happy to offer her a place here."

"That was very kind of you."

"Perhaps I only did it out of guilt, because I did leave her behind when I came North, as you reminded me."

"So you don't think Daisy harbored any ill will toward you?"

"Who's to say? And she would have to be a saint not to have at least been a bit jealous. But I'm certain she wouldn't have taken out her anger on Charles. She was quite fond of him, and he of her."

"That's unusual, isn't it? To become so attached to a servant, especially one who had only been with you such a short time."

"She was a part of my past, and Charles had always been fascinated by the stories of life on the plantation. Daisy had a son who died young, too, so that might have been why she was so fond of Charles. In any case, she wouldn't have poisoned him, no matter what you may think."

"I'm glad to hear it. I would still like to speak with her, though. If we have any hope of finding out who did, we have to figure out how the killer got the poison into Charles, and she was with him that last evening. As I said, she may have seen something and not realized what it meant."

"Very well. I'm sure Daisy will be glad to help if she can.

I'd offer to let you wait until she comes home, but I have no idea how much longer she'll be and I'm afraid I've exhausted my energy for hospitality. Perhaps you could return tomorrow when she's sure to be here."

Left with no other choice, Sarah agreed.

F RANK HAD FOUND AN ADDRESS FOR VIRGIL ADDERLY fairly easily. He was listed in the City Directory, and Frank learned when he arrived at the address that he hadn't moved. Gino had been happy to go along with him, pointing out that even still, Adderly and his two goons would outnumber them. Frank figured Adderly for a reasonable man, however, and he doubted they would come to blows. Still, he was glad to have Gino just in case he was wrong.

Adderly lived in a comfortable house in Lenox Hill. A maid opened the door and left them standing in the foyer while she went to see if Mr. Adderly was in the mood for company. Frank wouldn't have been surprised to be turned away—and he was only too aware that he had no authority to force Adderly to see him—but the maid returned in a few short minutes and escorted them to Adderly's formal parlor.

The room was slightly musty and a bit dark, and Frank guessed Adderly didn't entertain much.

"Mr. Malloy, what a surprise," Adderly said, shaking his hand. His two goons were nowhere in sight. "And who is this with you?"

Frank introduced Gino as his associate.

"Didn't I see you at Charles Oakes's funeral?" Adderly asked.

"Yes, you did." Gino offered nothing else.

"With a young lady, I think," Adderly tried again.

"Who is also one of my associates," Frank said. "Do you have a few minutes? I'd like to ask you some questions."

Adderly's polite smile never wavered. "Questions about what?"

"About what you might know in regards to why someone would want to murder Charles Oakes."

"Murder?" he echoed as if he had never heard the word before. "Really, Mr. Malloy, that's irresponsible of you to be making accusations like that. What makes you think Oakes was murdered?"

"The arsenic that killed him, for one thing," Frank said.

Adderly stiffened in surprise, but whether that was because he hadn't known Oakes had been poisoned or because he didn't know anyone else had figured it out, Frank could only guess. "Maybe we should sit down," Adderly said, indicating the grouping of chairs in the center of the well-furnished room. "Can I get you gentlemen a drink?"

He didn't wait for an answer but moved to the far side of the room where some crystal decanters sat on a sideboard. He returned with three glasses of whiskey. Frank and Gino accepted theirs, although neither of them took more than a sip. Adderly took a long swallow even before he sat down opposite Frank and Gino. Frank found that very interesting.

"Now tell me what you want to know, Mr. Malloy."

"I was wondering why you decided to help Charles Oakes find a job."

"I don't think I *decided* to do it. I heard through some business associates that Gerald Oakes had been asking if anyone knew of something suitable for his son. I found out that Charles was a promising young man from a good family, and after I had confirmed this myself by meeting him, I mentioned his name to some people who were in a position to assist him."

"That's funny," Frank said, although he didn't really think it was funny at all. "The way I heard it, you knew about this

position, and you wanted to fill it with the right person."
This was a lie, of course, but it seemed to hit home.

Adderly's smile had grown a bit strained. "And how would
I have known Charles Oakes was the right person?"

"Because he was someone who needed an income but who
had no desire to exert himself. He was also someone willing
to return the favor when you managed to find a position for
him that perfectly suited his needs."

"You flatter me, Mr. Malloy. I assure you, I couldn't possibly do what you are suggesting."

"Maybe not normally," Frank agreed. "I think that normally, you just introduce people and let them make their
own arrangements, but this time, you were making arrangements for yourself."

"What on earth do you mean?" His surprise seemed
genuine, but Frank wasn't fooled.

"I mean that you needed help getting Ella Adderly out of
the Wards Island Asylum, and Charles was so happy to show
his appreciation for your help in getting him his new position
that he was more than willing to get her released."

Adderly's expression had gone from surprised to furious
in just a few seconds. "I'll thank you not to mention my
cousin's name. You have no right to discuss her private
affairs."

"If they caused Charles Oakes to be murdered, I do."

"They did not, I assure you. If, as you imply, Charles did
a service for Ella, then I had no reason to wish him dead and
every reason to wish him well."

"So he did do a service for Miss Adderly," Frank said.

"And what if he did?"

"We both know he did. He got a doctor to declare her
recovered and release her from the Asylum."

"Please, it's a hospital. And yes, Charles was kind enough to see that my cousin was released from that awful place."

"I was actually surprised to find out that it isn't nearly as awful as I'd imagined. The doctor I talked to said they're very modern in their treatments and that lots of their patients recover and return home."

"And that's exactly what happened with Ella. When I realized she no longer needed to be there, I asked Charles to do the necessary paperwork to have her released."

As if to punctuate his statement, someone upstairs let out a shriek. Frank jumped, and he saw his own surprise reflected on Gino's face. The young man was on his feet before Frank could decide how to react.

"Who was that?" Gino demanded.

Adderly sighed and took another long swallow of his whiskey. "That was Ella, as I'm sure you know. She . . . she often becomes agitated at this time of the day."

The men jumped again at the sound of a loud thump from the floor above.

"Is she all right?" Frank asked in alarm.

Adderly seemed unconcerned. "I have a woman who takes care of her. She can usually control her."

"But not always," Frank guessed. "What happened the day of Charles's funeral?"

"She . . . she'd gotten out somehow in the middle of the night. Judith . . . Mrs. Burgun, I mean, was asleep, and Ella got her keys. We didn't even know she was gone until we got up the next morning. We looked everywhere for her, but she had the whole city to hide in, and she'd had hours to do it."

"But you suspected she was going to attend Charles's funeral," Frank said, motioning to Gino to sit down again now that things had quieted down upstairs.

"I hoped I was wrong, but you were there. You saw what happened."

"She said she was in love with Charles."

"She knew he was the one responsible for getting her out of the Asyl . . . the hospital. She was grateful. Too grateful, I'm afraid. She imagined herself in love with him, and she thought he returned her feelings. Ella never married, you see. Her late parents, my uncle and his wife, kept her very isolated. I suspect they knew early on that she wasn't quite right, and they were trying to protect her from people who might want to take advantage of her."

"How did you get involved with Miss Adderly?"

"Really, Mr. Malloy, this is none of your business. And before you try to argue with me, let me assure you that Ella's situation has nothing to do with Charles. Once she left the hospital, he had nothing more to do with her."

"Do you expect me to believe that? I heard what she said at the funeral."

"Any contact with Charles Oakes was purely in her imagination."

"But you admitted yourself that she got out of the house without your knowledge the day of Charles's funeral," Gino said. "How do you know she didn't get out at other times?"

"I told you, I have a woman who watches her," Adderly snapped.

"And if Miss Adderly got out, do you think this woman would be likely to tell you about it?" Gino asked too politely.

Plainly, Adderly hadn't considered that possibility. "Well, even supposing she did, I don't believe Charles would have met with her. He knew her . . . her condition."

"And yet he agreed to release her from the hospital," Frank said. "And he got a doctor to declare her cured, too. I wonder why you went to all that trouble when she isn't cured at all."

"She's much better off in her own home than surrounded by strangers who also happen to be insane."

"But why did you want to bring her here where she doesn't receive any treatment and where you can't even keep her safely locked up?"

This time Adderly jumped to his feet. "Really, Mr. Malloy, this is too much. I've already told you that Ella's condition is no concern of yours and it certainly has no bearing on Charles Oakes's death, even if he really was murdered, which I doubt."

"I have to admit, I *am* having a hard time figuring out why you'd want to harm him after he did exactly what you wanted him to do. I'm not too sure about Miss Adderly, though. You see, Charles first became ill when he was away from his house. We thought he'd been working at the hospital that day, but we recently learned that he seldom spent any time there. In fact, he hadn't been there since days before he first got sick. So that means he was someplace else, but we don't know where or who he was with. If we knew that, we might be able to figure out who poisoned him."

"I can tell you where he was," a female voice said from the doorway. They looked up to see Ella Adderly standing there, looking exactly the way Frank had always imagined a madwoman would look. "He was with me."

9

ONE GLANCE AT ADDERLY'S FACE TOLD FRANK HOW HOR-
rified he was to see Ella in his parlor. Poor Judith Burgun
was probably going to need a new position very soon, and
she wouldn't be getting a reference from Virgil Adderly.

Before Adderly could take any action to usher Ella out,
Frank was on his feet and striding forward to greet her. "Miss
Adderly, it's so good to see you again."

"I know you," she said, smiling with obvious delight. She
wore a slightly faded housedress, and her hair had been care-
lessly braided and hung down her back. "You were going to
take me to see Charles."

Behind him, Adderly made a strangled sound.

"That's right, I was, but I was told you were indisposed
and couldn't go."

Miss Adderly frowned like a thwarted child. "I wasn't
indisposed. They just say that so they don't have to take me

anyplace. They make me stay home all the time. Sometimes I want to go back to the hospital. At least there we got to walk outside sometimes."

A woman appeared in the doorway behind Ella. She appeared to be in her forties and had the harried look of someone frustrated beyond bearing. Her hair was coming out of its pins and falling into her eyes. She made a futile effort to tuck some of it back into place as her gaze took in the scene. "Miss Ella, you know you aren't supposed to go anyplace without me," she said gently. She smiled uncertainly at Frank. Then she saw Adderly glaring at her and her smile vanished. "I'm so sorry, Mr. Adderly. She pushed me down and by the time I got back on my feet, I didn't know which way she'd gone."

"That's all right, Mrs. Burgun, is it?" Frank asked.

The woman nodded, surprised Frank knew her name.

"I was hoping I'd get to see Miss Adderly while I was here."

"Virgil," Ella said, "did you offer our guests some refreshment?"

"Ella, you need to go back to your room now," he said. "You know how upset you get when we have company."

"I'm not upset. I'm just sad because Charles died and nobody will let me see him. He was my very dear friend," she told Frank, who nodded.

"When was the last time you saw him?" Frank asked.

Adderly groaned, but Ella didn't appear to notice. "Yesterday, I think, or maybe the day before."

She sounded very certain, although Charles Oakes had been safely in his grave well before that. "And where did you see him?"

"Here, of course. He came to call. He was very concerned about me, you know. He knew I didn't belong at the hospital. He told me that. He said he was going to let me go home. All I had to do was talk to the doctor."

"And did you?" Frank asked.

"Yes. He asked me all kinds of silly questions, and he didn't like any of my answers. I could tell by the way he kept wrinkling his forehead. I told him if he didn't like my answers, he should ask different questions, but he said he didn't have any different questions. I thought that was sad, don't you?"

"Yes," Frank said. "It's very sad. Did you ever give Charles some refreshment when he came here to call on you?"

"Malloy, this is ridiculous," Adderly said. "Oakes was never in this house."

"He was, too!" Ella cried. "He came to see me every day."

"He did come one time," Mrs. Burgun said, surprising everyone.

Adderly rose uncertainly from his chair. "He did? Why didn't you tell me?"

"When was this?" Frank asked.

"I don't know," the woman said, her gaze darting uncertainly back and forth between Frank and Adderly.

"Yes, you do," Frank said. "When was he here?"

She glanced warily at Adderly, who was probably glaring at her and wondering how quickly he could find someone to take over watching Ella if he fired her. "I . . . About a week ago, I'd say. One day's much like another here. Sometimes I lose track."

"Do you go to church?"

She seemed startled by the question. "When I can."

"Did you go last week?"

"Yes, I . . . Mr. Adderly watched Miss Ella."

"Was it before or after you went to church that Mr. Oakes came to call?"

She frowned, and for a minute he thought she really wouldn't be able to tell him. Then she said, "It was Saturday a week ago."

The day Charles had first gotten sick. "How did Mr. Oakes look to you?"

"He was beautiful," Ella said. "Such a beautiful man. I told him so and made him blush."

Frank didn't smile. "Besides being beautiful, did he look sick?"

"Not at all," Ella said, but Frank was looking at Mrs. Burgun.

"Not that I noticed. He . . . he said he thought he might've done the wrong thing when he let Miss Ella out of the hospital."

"That's ridiculous," Adderly said, angry again. "Even if he thought so, he wouldn't have confessed it to you."

"He didn't say it to me," Mrs. Burgun said, stiffening defensively. "He said it to Miss Ella."

"He was so kind to me," Ella said. "He thought I was beautiful, too. We were going to get married and move far, far away from here."

"He never said no such thing as that," Mrs. Burgun said, "but he did say he thought Miss Ella should be in the hospital so they could help her."

"Did you offer Mr. Oakes some refreshment?" Frank asked Mrs. Burgun.

"Miss Ella had them make some tea, but I don't think he drank any of it."

Adderly gave a bark of laughter. "Of course he didn't. He never drank anything but the finest whiskey, unless he couldn't get the finest whiskey, and then he'd drink any kind he could find."

Frank glanced at the decanters on the sideboard. "Did he drink any of Mr. Adderly's whiskey?" he asked Mrs. Burgun.

She glanced at Adderly again. "He might have."

"Of course he did," Adderly said with a nasty smile. "That's why the one decanter was almost empty when I got home that night. I thought you'd been sampling it, Judith."

The woman huffed her offense.

"He asked if he could have a drink," Ella said. "He felt a chill coming on, he said, so I gave him a glass of whiskey. He was a guest, Virgil. You can't deny a guest your hospitality."

"Or my whiskey either, I guess."

"Which decanter was it?" Frank asked him.

"What does that matter?" Adderly asked.

"I don't know that it does, but that's the day Charles Oakes first got sick, so that's also the day he first got some arsenic. If he got it here . . ."

Adderly looked over at the sideboard in horror. "I don't know. I don't remember which one it was." Adderly put his hand on his stomach as if checking to make sure all was well.

"Do you remember, Mrs. Burgun?"

"Of course not. They're all just alike."

Adderly looked over at where Gino had set his still-full glass. "That's why you didn't drink any, isn't it? Neither one of you drank any."

"Of course not," Frank said. "I didn't even know Oakes had been here."

"Then why didn't you drink it?" Adderly's voice had grown shrill.

"I don't drink when I'm working. I like to keep my wits about me."

Adderly laughed mirthlessly. "That's rich, Malloy. And you just sat there and let me poison myself."

"Why would you poison yourself, Virgil?" Ella asked.

"He wouldn't," Frank said. "Not on purpose. Miss Adderly, tell me, did you put anything into Charles's drink the other day?"

"I put whiskey in it," she said sweetly. "That's what he said he wanted."

"Can you show me which bottle you poured it from?"

"One of those, I think." She tipped her head from side to side as if trying to get a better view of them. "This one, I think." She walked over and tapped the one from which Adderly had poured their drinks. "It's such a pretty color, isn't it? All golden in the sunlight."

"Adderly, I'd like to take some samples from these bottles and have them tested."

"Of course," he said. He was sweating now, and his face had lost all color. "Judith, get some jars for Mr. Malloy."

She scurried off, leaving the rest of them to stare at each other.

"Miss Adderly, were you angry at Charles Oakes?" Frank asked.

"No, not at all, or . . . Well, at least not very much."

"So you were a little angry at him," Frank said.

"He was so nice to me at the hospital, and I told him he could call on me, but he didn't come, not for ever so long. I was lonely, you see, and he was such a beautiful man. I knew if he came, he'd fall in love with me. I knew he would. It would be just like in the stories Mama used to read to me."

"And when he finally did come, you couldn't help but be mad because he'd taken so long to visit."

"I don't like to say I'm mad," she said solemnly. "It means insane, you know."

"Oh, I'm sorry. I should have said you were angry. Were you angry enough to want to hurt him, Miss Adderly?"

"I wanted him to be sad, the way I'd been sad, waiting for him to come."

"I can understand that."

"What . . . what if she really did poison it?" Adderly asked. "What if she poisoned *me*?"

"If you get sick, call a doctor and tell him you might have

taken arsenic," Frank said. "The good news is that Charles didn't die the first time."

Adderly did not look reassured. He looked a little green, in fact.

"Why did you want Miss Adderly released from the hospital so badly?" Frank asked, since they were still waiting for Mrs. Burgun to return with the jars.

"That's none of your business," he said, but he didn't sound quite so outraged anymore.

"It must involve money," Gino said. "It's always about money, isn't it?"

"Almost always," Frank agreed. He glanced around the room as if trying to judge what the upkeep of a place like that would be. "Maybe there isn't as much money in doing favors for people as I thought."

"What will happen to me if I did get poisoned?" Adderly asked, oblivious to their speculation.

"You'll vomit, I think."

"You'll be very sick," Gino added.

Adderly laid a hand on his stomach again.

"Miss Adderly, is this your house?" Frank asked.

"Of course it is. I live here."

"No, I mean do you own it?"

"My parents own it."

"I thought your parents were dead."

She frowned, confused for a moment. "Oh yes. Sometimes I forget."

"So now you own it."

"I suppose I do. They told me my parents left everything to me."

"Ella, it's vulgar to talk about money." Adderly now looked a little angry in addition to being totally terrified.

"I know. Mother always said so, but we weren't talking

about money. We were talking about the house, I think. Wasn't that what we were talking about, Mr. . . . I'm afraid I don't know your name."

"Malloy."

"Mr. Malloy. You seem like a very nice man. But you aren't beautiful like Charles." She looked over at where Gino stood. "Now he's beautiful and so young."

"He's poor, though," Frank said, trying not to smile at the horrified look on Gino's beautiful face. "He'd have to marry a woman with money of her own."

"I have money of my own. My parents left everything to me. I just told you that."

"How did your parents die, Miss Adderly?" Frank asked.

"They got sick."

"At the same time?"

"Yes. The doctor thought it was something they'd eaten. They were very sick, and then they died."

"But you didn't get sick?"

"No, not at all."

"Were you angry at your parents, Miss Adderly?"

"Stop it, Malloy," Adderly said, although Frank thought maybe Adderly was just afraid to hear the answer.

"I was angry when they died. I was so angry that I had to go to the hospital. But then Virgil came and brought me home again."

Mrs. Burgun came bustling into the room juggling several empty jars. "Here you are," she said, and set them down on the sideboard. Gino went over and began pouring samples from each decanter into separate jars.

"What are you going to do with them?" Adderly asked anxiously.

"I'm taking them to a doctor. He'll test them to see if there's any arsenic."

"And if there is?" Adderly asked in alarm.

"I'll send you word either way." Frank glanced at Ella, who seemed blissfully unaware of her cousin's concerns. "And if you get sick, you'll send me word, won't you?" He pulled out one of the calling cards he'd never thought he'd need and handed it to Adderly.

When Gino had finished, Mrs. Burgun produced a burlap sack into which they put the jars. Then they took their leave.

As they walked down the street in search of a cab, Gino said, "Do you really think she poisoned Charles Oakes?"

"She might have, but it's hard to figure how she could've gotten poison into him two more times after that, especially when one of those times was at his house. I'll be surprised if she did it, but I thought it would be fun to let Adderly think he might've been poisoned, too, at least for a little while."

"Are you really going to get these tested?"

"Oh yes. I think our friend Titus Wesley would be happy to do it for us."

Gino grinned. "I think you're right."

"So we can stop by his shop on the way home and get back in time to get you invited to stay for supper."

"Will . . . Mrs. Brandt be there?"

"Yes, and so will Maeve."

Gino grinned even wider.

SARAH HATED TELLING MALLOY THAT SHE'D FAILED TO question Daisy, but he told her they'd had a little more luck with Adderly, although she'd have to wait until later for the details.

After supper, Malloy and Gino walked Sarah, Maeve, and Catherine down the street to Sarah's house. Gino very gallantly offered to help Maeve put Catherine to bed, leaving Frank and Sarah alone.

As Sarah put some coffee on to boil, Malloy sat at her kitchen table and told her what he'd learned at the Adderly house.

"So you think it's possible that Ella Adderly poisoned Charles?"

"She had just as much of a chance as anyone else the first time, but I just can't figure out how he got poisoned when he was away from his house the second time and then again when he was in it that evening. None of the people who could have done it in one place could have done it in the other. It doesn't make sense."

"It has to make sense, because it happened. We're just missing something."

He sighed. "I'm sure we are."

"I'd completely forgotten to tell you about Charles's drinking. Mrs. Peabody said he often had to be escorted home from his club because he was too drunk to go by himself."

"Lots of young men drink a lot."

"I suppose that's true. Still, you should find Mrs. Peabody's nephew. Maybe he knows where else Charles was on the day he first got poisoned."

"If there's no arsenic in Adderly's liquor, I'll do that. Are you going to go back to see Daisy tomorrow?"

"I might as well, since you're pretty sure they're not going to find arsenic in Adderly's liquor. You've got me curious about Ella Adderly, though. Why do you think her cousin had Charles release her from the hospital?"

"I've been thinking about that," Malloy said. "She inherited a lot of money when her parents died. What would happen to it if she was insane?"

The coffee had started to boil, so Sarah got up and poured

them each a cup. "I'm not sure, but I don't think she'd be allowed to control it if she was judged insane. I think . . . I'm trying to remember if I ever heard about a situation like that. I do know that if the child isn't of age when they inherit, the court would appoint a guardian."

"So Adderly could've gotten himself appointed as her guardian, and that would've given him control of her money."

"Which sounds like the easiest thing," Sarah said, "but maybe he couldn't count on being named her guardian. Maybe there's something in his past or something in his present that made him suspect he wouldn't be chosen."

"So if he couldn't get appointed as her guardian, what else could he do?"

Sarah considered this for a moment. "We know he could have probably gotten her released from the hospital if he'd wanted to go to court, but that wouldn't get her declared sane because anybody who talked to her would know she wasn't. And if she wasn't sane, she'd still need a guardian. So instead he got Charles to say she was cured and release her."

"And now, in the eyes of the law at least, she's not insane anymore."

Sarah could see it all. "But we know she is insane and easily manipulated by her cousin."

"So he can get her to sign everything over to him or at least control of everything over to him, and it would be perfectly legal, since Charles and the doctor said she was sane."

"That's horrible! He's going to take everything she has and leave her with nothing, and then he'll probably put her in some charity hospital and leave her there to rot."

"Unless she poisons him," Malloy said with a grin. "Did I mention that her parents both got very sick at the same time and died?"

"Good heavens!"

"Yes, good heavens. So maybe Adderly is right to be worried. I hope he has a terrible night, at least, wondering if Ella put arsenic in his whiskey."

"Serves him right. But if she didn't poison Charles, can we do something to help protect her from Adderly?"

"I'll look into it . . . *if* she didn't poison Charles."

They sipped their coffee for a moment in silence. Then Sarah said, "Is our house ever going to be finished?"

"Some days I think so, and other days I don't."

"Don't say that! It has to be finished soon."

"We could get married anyway," he pointed out hopefully. "We're going all the way to Europe on our honeymoon. Maybe it'll be finished by the time we get back."

"And would you leave Maeve and your mother in charge of the work while we're gone?"

He sighed in defeat. "I'll speak to the workmen tomorrow."

SARAH AND THE GIRLS WERE CLEANING UP THE BREAK-fast dishes when their neighbor Mrs. Ellsworth knocked on the door. She had brought them some muffins as an excuse to check on the progress with the new house. Mrs. Ellsworth had always found that minding other people's business was much more interesting than minding her own.

"Oh, Mrs. Brandt, you mustn't give up hope," she said after Sarah had given her the discouraging report Malloy had delivered last night. "I broke a needle last night when I was mending Nelson's shirt. That always means a wedding will happen very soon."

"You've been seeing wedding omens for years," Maeve reminded her.

"Well, some of them I made up," Mrs. Ellsworth said without the slightest hint of guilt, "but this one is genuine."

"Maybe the wedding will be Nelson's," Sarah suggested. Mrs. Ellsworth's son had been keeping company with a young lady for several months.

"I keep hoping, but Nelson doesn't want to rush things, while I'm sure Mr. Malloy would be happy to."

Sarah thought so, too, but she said, "The girls and I can't move in until the house is ready. It's bad enough the poor Malloy family has to put up with the mess."

"Then you must hurry the workmen along, because September is the best month for you to marry, unless you want to wait until November."

"Why is that, Mrs. Ellsworth?" Maeve asked with feigned innocence, knowing how much Sarah hated for her to encourage their neighbor's superstitions.

"Because, as the rhyme says, 'Married in September's golden glow, smooth and serene your life will go. Married when leaves in October thin, toil and hardship for you begin.'"

"Oh my, I had no idea," Maeve said, ignoring Sarah's frown. "But maybe they want to wait for November for better fortune. What does that bring?"

"'Married in veils of November mist, fortune your wedding ring has kissed.'"

"And what about December—" Maeve started, but Sarah interrupted her.

"We aren't waiting until December. Now I'm sorry, but I have an errand to run. I'll probably be back by noon, but if Malloy needs someone to watch the house before I get back, I know I can trust you to do that."

"Oh yes, we'd be happy to," Mrs. Ellsworth said. "The parlor looks very nice, doesn't it?"

"Yes, it does," Sarah said. "Thank you so much for helping Maeve. Maybe we should put you in charge of the workmen."

Mrs. Ellsworth smiled. "I'm always happy to help."

THE MAID AT THE OAKES HOUSE WAS EXPECTING HER. "Mrs. Gerald told me to take you right up as soon as you arrived, Mrs. Brandt."

Sarah frowned. She hoped Jenny didn't intend to monitor her conversation with Daisy or, worse yet, refuse to allow her to speak with her at all.

The maid took her to the rear parlor, the room the family used as the center of their activities. Jenny waited there for her, standing in the middle of the room, her hands clutched tightly in front of her. She didn't smile or offer a single word of greeting, and as soon as the maid closed the door behind her, she said, "Daisy didn't come home last night."

"Not at all?" Sarah asked stupidly, too stunned to really comprehend.

"I've sent Zeller out to see if he can find her."

"Just this morning? Weren't you worried when she didn't come back yesterday?"

"Not particularly. She knew I wouldn't mind if she was late yesterday. She was very upset about Charles's death, and she was looking forward to seeing her minister. I thought . . . Well, it doesn't matter what I thought."

"But surely you were concerned when she didn't come in by evening."

Jenny turned away and walked to the window, although Sarah didn't think she was even aware of it. "I'm not concerned about her safety, if that's what you're asking."

Sarah needed a minute to figure out what she was saying. "You think she's run away."

"Zeller said she was very frightened when that young man questioned her."

"But she doesn't have anything to worry about if she's innocent."

Jenny gave her a pitying look. "If you're colored, you always have something to be worried about. Whether you're innocent or not, you'll probably be blamed."

"Did she think she'd be blamed for Charles's death?"

"Of course she did. She was alone with him for several hours right before he died and she's colored. Who else would be blamed?"

"The real killer, of course."

Jenny laughed mirthlessly. "Nothing in Daisy's experience would lead her to believe that, Mrs. Brandt. In this city, the police routinely beat and arrest young colored men for the crime of being jobless and having nothing better to do than sit on their own front stoops. Any colored woman walking on a city street is assumed to be a prostitute and may be arrested on the spot. Add to all that the fact that Charles's wife has told everyone who will listen that Daisy poisoned him, and Daisy has every reason to expect that your Mr. Malloy will take her away in chains."

"Did she tell you this?"

"Of course not, but when she didn't come back, I wasn't surprised."

"But you've sent someone to look for her."

"I have to find out what's become of her. She's my . . . Well, she doesn't belong to me, but I still feel responsible for her."

Sarah wondered if all slave owners had felt the same sense of responsibility for their slaves. Surely not, but it was nice that Jenny did, at least.

"If your man finds her, what are you going to do?"

"What do you mean?"

"Do you plan to bring her back?"

"Force her, you mean? She's not a slave anymore. She's free to leave here if she wants."

"If she's innocent."

Sarah watched the color drain from Jenny's face. "Do you really think she killed Charles?"

"I don't know, but running away makes her look guilty, doesn't it?"

Jenny had no answer for that.

They stared at each other for a long moment, neither willing to discuss the suspicion Sarah had raised. Then someone knocked on the parlor door.

"Come," Jenny called.

Zeller stepped into the room. He was ashen, and he looked somehow shrunken since the last time Sarah had seen him just the day before.

Jenny hurried to him. "Zeller, what is it?"

"It's Daisy, ma'am," he said, his voice oddly hoarse.

"What is it? What's happened?"

"She . . . she's dead."

"WE'RE WORKING AS FAST AS WE CAN, MR. MALLOY, BUT you know the trouble we had with the bathtub, and then there was the paneling that Mrs. Brandt wanted that didn't come, and now—"

"I know all that," Frank said, "but you must be almost finished by now."

"I wouldn't like to promise anything. We're still waiting for some things to come in, and one of the men hurt his back and . . ."

Frank didn't really listen to the rest. He knew exactly how to get a criminal to confess, and how to encourage him if he hesitated with a touch of the third degree, but he had no idea how to put the fear of God into these workmen. They knew he was rich, thanks to the newspaper stories about him, so they were probably stretching the job out so they could charge him more. He was pretty sure rich people didn't use the third degree on people who worked for them, though.

Finally, someone knocked on the front door, so Frank had an excuse to send him back to work while he dealt with his visitor. Only when he heard the knock again did he remember he'd meant to mention the doorbell again.

Gino greeted him much too happily for so early in the morning. "Where are we going today?"

"I've got to sit here and make sure the workmen keep working."

Gino could obviously tell from Frank's expression that he didn't think this was at all funny, so he didn't make a joke. "Well, I can do something. Will Wesley have finished the tests on the liquor, do you think?"

"We should give him until this afternoon, at least."

Gino sighed. "Who else would you like to talk to? Or is there anything you need to find out?"

"Are you hungry?"

Gino blinked in confusion. "What?"

"Are you hungry? There's biscuits left from breakfast, and most of a cake that Mrs. Ellsworth and the girls baked."

"The one we had last night?" Gino asked hopefully.

"Yes." Frank led him into the kitchen. Eating would give him something to do. Frank cut him a large slice of the cake and poured him what was left of the breakfast coffee.

For a few blissful minutes, he didn't ask Frank a single question. Then he finished the cake. "I was thinking we should find this Mrs. Peabody's nephew. That Percy fellow, what's his name? He's probably at the club where Charles was a member. He might know where Charles was when he got sick."

"That's a good idea. How are you going to get into the club?"

"I'll knock on the door and they'll open it."

"Are you a member?"

"Of course not."

"Then they won't let you in. That's the whole purpose of these clubs, to keep out the riffraff."

"But they'll have to let me in."

"Why?"

Gino opened his mouth, probably to remind Frank that they wouldn't dare defy the New York City Police, but no words came out because before he could speak, he had obviously remembered that neither one of them worked for the New York City Police anymore. He closed his mouth with a snap. "Do we know where Percy lives?"

"I'm sure we can find out. His aunt might even tell us. In the meantime, we can wait until Mrs. Brandt gets back from seeing Daisy."

"I shouldn't've let Zeller stay in the room when I questioned her," Gino said.

"It probably doesn't matter. She was too scared to talk to you no matter who was in the room."

"But I could've been rougher with her if he wasn't there."

"And made her cry? Or faint? Then Zeller would've had your head. I just wonder if there's something between him and Daisy or if it's just him."

"I don't know. That's where it would've been good to have Mrs. Brandt there, too. Zeller is sweet on her. I'd bet a month's pay on that."

"How did she act with him, though?"

"She . . . I don't know. Not like she was sweet on him

back, I don't think. At least, that's not how I'd want a woman to act if she had feelings for me. I think she was afraid of him, too."

"Afraid?"

"Not scared, like she was of me, but afraid she'd do something wrong in front of him. It was the way people act when their boss is watching and maybe looking to fire them. She was trying to be careful because he was there, but she was scared out of her wits not to answer me, too."

"And even still, you think she lied."

"Not lied, exactly, but she didn't tell me everything she knew. She didn't want one of us to know whatever it was, but maybe it was Zeller she was hiding something from."

"Maybe it was. And maybe it was both of you."

"Is that somebody knocking on the door?" Gino asked.

Frank hadn't been paying attention because he was always hearing pounding noises coming from somewhere in the house. This was more insistent, though. He really needed to get the doorbell fixed. He made his way to the front door, and when he opened it, he found Judith Burgun standing on the porch.

She looked harried and desperate, and she held Frank's calling card tightly in one hand. "Oh, Mr. Malloy, thank heaven. I was about to give up!"

"What are you doing here?"

"It's Mr. Adderly. He's been poisoned!"

10

"DEAD?" JENNY ECHOED STUPIDLY. "HOW CAN DAISY BE dead?"

Sarah had rushed to Zeller, and she took his arm. "You need to sit down."

"Oh no, I couldn't possibly," he said, because the butler never sat down in the presence of the family, but Jenny took his other arm.

"Of course you can," she said, and between the two of them, they got him down onto one of the chairs. The fact that he allowed this proved how distraught he was. "Now tell me what happened."

"I went to the church, like you told me to," he said. "It's just a storefront," he added to Sarah, who nodded her encouragement. The poor man looked poleaxed.

"Does the minister still live upstairs?" Jenny asked.

"Yes, he . . . he and his family. They were . . . When I got there, though, everybody was sick."

"What do you mean, sick?" Sarah asked.

"Sick like Mr. Charles was," he said, and a chill ran down Sarah's back. "There were so many people there helping that at first nobody even noticed I'd come in. I had to grab one woman by the arm to stop her when she went hurrying past. I nearly scared her to death. She wanted to know why I was there and what did I want and was I a doctor? I told her I was looking for Daisy, and her face got all funny and she shouted out for the minister. Mr. Nicely is his name. He wasn't sick, at least. He was in his shirtsleeves with the cuffs rolled up, and he looked like he'd been up all night."

Zeller covered his face with both hands.

"It's all right," Sarah said. "Take your time."

He lowered his hands and looked up at Sarah with haunted eyes. "It's not all right, Mrs. Brandt. He told me . . . I asked him where was Daisy and was she still there, and he shook his head, but he says, 'She's here, but . . .' and he can't say any more because he's crying. That's when I got really scared, and one of the women, she says, 'Who are you?' so I told her my name and that I worked at the same house as Daisy, and I'd come to fetch her home. Then somebody called for Mr. Nicely to go back into the other room and he went. He didn't even excuse himself. I asked the women what was going on, and one of them tells me that Mrs. Nicely was took sick yesterday and her daughter, too, and their friend Daisy."

"So Daisy is only sick," Jenny said, as if this was good news. "We'll bring her straight home and get the doctor in to see her and . . ." Her voice trailed off when Zeller met her gaze.

"I told them I wanted to see Daisy, and they didn't want me to, but I told them I'd come to take her home, so they took me back. The rooms they live in, there was the main room and Mr. Nicely and his wife had another, and their daughter had the other one. They took me in there. The daughter, she was in the bed, moaning, so I knew she was alive. Daisy was on the floor. They'd put some blankets down for her to lay on, and I thought she was asleep, she was so still. And then I saw how pale she was, and how her face was all twisted, like she was in pain except it didn't move, not a bit. That's when they told me she was dead."

Jenny made a startled sound, almost like someone had stuck her with something sharp. She wrapped her arms around herself and swayed. Sarah grabbed her to keep her from falling and lowered her into another chair.

"You're sure she was dead?" Sarah said to Zeller.

He nodded.

"What about the others?" she asked. "Mrs. Nicely and her daughter?"

"They were very sick but still alive when I left."

"Had they called for a doctor?"

"I asked them that," Zeller said, the color coming back into his face at the memory. "I wanted to know did they have a doctor for Daisy, but they said doctors won't go to Coontown."

Sarah felt the molten fury rising up in her. "Can you take me there? I'm a nurse. Maybe I can help."

Zeller glanced at Jenny, who had yet to say a single thing after hearing Daisy was really dead. She still had her arms wrapped tightly, as if she were holding herself together by her own strength, and she rocked herself back and forth, as if hearing some secret lullaby. "Mrs. Gerald?" he said softly.

"Yes, go," she said raggedly. "And bring Daisy back. Don't leave her there."

"Who should I call for you?" Sarah asked. "Your mother-in-law?"

"No!" she said sharply. "Gerald."

Sarah went to the bellpull and yanked it sharply while Zeller pushed himself out of the chair and onto his feet. Then they waited for someone to come.

"WHAT DO YOU MEAN HE'S BEEN POISONED?" FRANK asked.

"He's been deathly sick all night long," Mrs. Burgun said. "It started right after you left yesterday. I sent for the doctor, and he's still with him, but Mr. Adderly, he told me to fetch you. He said you'd know what to do about Miss Adderly."

Gino had joined them, and they exchanged a glance.

"I could get Dr. Wesley," Gino said.

"Have him do the tests first, if he hasn't done them already," Frank said. "I'll go back with Mrs. Burgun. But stop at Mrs. Brandt's house on the way and ask Maeve to come over to sit with the workmen."

Mrs. Burgun had a cab waiting for her, so they climbed in for the ride up to Lenox Hill.

"What did the doctor say about Adderly's illness?" he asked her when the cab had lurched into motion.

"He didn't say much to me, I'm sure, but Mr. Adderly told him right away that Miss Adderly had put arsenic in his liquor bottles. The doctor gave him a purgative, which seemed odd to me since Mr. Adderly had been purging his bowels long before the doctor even got there. Then he did something to his stomach to wash it out, which also seemed odd because he'd been vomiting so much already."

"Where's Miss Adderly?"

"I had to lock her in her room. She got real upset when Mr. Adderly accused her of poisoning him, but by this morning, she was fine again. I wanted one of the maids to stay with her, but they're all scared of her now. They think she's going to kill them, too."

"Adderly isn't dead yet," Frank reminded her.

"They think he will be, though, and of course they know that Mr. Oakes is already dead. They won't be able to keep servants at all now."

"What about you, Mrs. Burgun?" Frank asked. "Will you stay now that you know Miss Adderly is a murderer?"

"I don't know no such thing, but I think Mr. Adderly will send her back to the Asylum now, so I'll have to find myself some other work."

"Do you know why Adderly brought his cousin home from the Asylum in the first place?"

Mrs. Burgun stiffened and turned away, as if she'd developed a sudden interest in the people they were passing on the sidewalk.

Frank waited, knowing how much people hated silence. They would often blurt out the most incriminating things just to fill it. He had just started to think he had finally met the one person in the city who could outwait him when she turned back to him.

"She's not cured, you know."

"I know."

"I don't care what those people at the Asylum said. Mr. Adderly told me a doctor examined her. Well, he might've looked in her throat and listened to her heart, but he never talked to her, or if he did, he lied. Mr. Adderly must've paid him a lot of money to say she was cured to get her out of that place."

"He probably just thought she'd be happier at home. Nobody wants somebody they love in a place like that."

Mrs. Burgun sniffed derisively. "Mr. Adderly don't love Miss Adderly. He don't care a fig about her. In fact, if you was to tell me one of them would poison the other one, I'd've said it would be the other way around."

"You think Adderly wants to kill his cousin?"

"I wouldn't go that far, but I don't think he'd mourn too long if she was to die."

"And yet he brought her home and hired you to take care of her."

She sniffed again. "She's got a lot of money. Did you know?"

"She told me."

"She tells me all the time. She owns the house, too. She owns everything."

"But Adderly is her guardian."

"Oh no. Some lawyer uptown is her guardian. Or was. I guess she don't need one now that she's sane," she added with a touch of sarcasm.

"Why wasn't Adderly her guardian?"

"Nobody tells me anything, you understand, but the servants talk. I don't have time to sit with them of an evening, but I still hear things."

"And what did you hear about Adderly?"

"I heard he's been in some trouble. He got out of it somehow, but he didn't want to get involved with judges and lawyers anymore. At least that's what he says to his friends when they visit. So that's why he didn't ask the judge to make him Miss Adderly's guardian. If you want to know what I think, I think he didn't want some judge looking at him too close and deciding he shouldn't be living in the house with her."

"Do you think he might harm her?"

Mrs. Burgun gave him a pitying look. "You don't kill the goose what lays the golden eggs, now, do you?"

"Not unless you're going to inherit her eggs if she dies."

"I don't know, but I think if that's the case, she'd be dead by now."

Ah, so either someone else had a prior claim or Miss Adderly had a will that named someone else as her heir. That would narrow Adderly's options. "Does Miss Adderly have any other family?"

"Not that I know of, but she doesn't always talk sense, if you know what I mean, and Mr. Adderly doesn't confide in me."

"And yet you do know an awful lot about them."

She shrugged.

Frank sighed and wondered what she didn't know that he needed to find out. She might know one more thing that could help, though. "What's the name of that lawyer who used to be her guardian?"

JENNY OAKES MADE THEM TAKE HER CARRIAGE, AL-though Sarah felt sure she could have traveled more quickly if she'd taken the elevated train. They had to stop off at Bank Street so she could get her bag and some medical supplies. She also needed to check her late husband's medical books for the treatments for arsenic poisoning. Maeve and Catherine weren't at home, and Mrs. Ellsworth helpfully came over to tell her Malloy had asked them to go sit with the workmen while he and Mr. Donatelli went back to see Mr. Adderly.

Then Sarah and Zeller were on their way again to the small and ever-shrinking pocket of the city where Negroes were permitted to live. The landlords charged their unfortunate tenants exorbitant rents because, unlike their white neighbors, they couldn't move to another part of the city to find cheaper lodgings. The landlords also let the buildings fall into disrepair because they knew colored people wouldn't

complain about living in squalor because they had no other
choice.

Sarah had often found it ironic that the Negroes lived in
the worst buildings in the city and yet their homes were as
neat and clean and well furnished as they could possibly
make them. The Nicelys' home was no exception. As Zeller
had explained, the minister's family lived on the second floor
over an ordinary storefront. The only indication that it was
any different from the other shops on the street was a hand-
painted sign displaying a large yellow cross and the words
HOLY REDEEMER CHURCH. A glance through the front window showed her rows of crudely made benches where the
faithful would gather to worship.

A flight of rickety wooden stairs clung to the side of the
building, and Zeller followed her up, carrying Sarah's bag
for her. The door stood open, probably to help disperse the
terrible sickroom smells that assaulted her the instant she
stepped inside.

"Hello?" she called into the eerie stillness. Zeller had
found the rooms full of helpers earlier. The front room stood
empty now.

After a moment, a woman stepped out of one of the back
rooms, eyeing her warily. "Who are you?"

"I'm Sarah Brandt. I'm a nurse. I came to see if I could help."

For a second, the woman looked as if she might object,
but then she caught sight of Zeller. "You brought her, then?"

He nodded.

The woman sighed. "Not much you can do now. Miss
Rose, she gone."

"What about . . . ?" Sarah realized she didn't know the
names of either woman.

"Isabel. She . . . Mr. Nicely's with her now." She nodded
toward the room she'd come from.

Sarah took her bag from Zeller. "See if you can get some milk."

"What do you need milk for?" the woman asked.

"It coats the stomach and binds the arsenic," Sarah said. At least Tom's medical book had indicated that it might, although it hadn't worked for Charles Oakes.

"*Arsenic?*" the woman echoed in horror. "What's this about arsenic?"

"We think . . ." Oh dear, how could she explain that they suspected the women had been poisoned? It sounded far-fetched even to her. "It's possible they accidentally . . ."

She cast Zeller a desperate glance.

"The man Daisy worked for died of arsenic poisoning," he said, which sounded even less convincing.

"Milk won't hurt in any case," Sarah finished lamely and walked around the woman to get to the sickroom.

The room smelled of vomit and feces, although Sarah could see the basin by the bed had been emptied. A young woman lay motionless in a narrow bed against one wall. An older man sat on a wooden chair beside the bed, holding one of her hands in both of his. His face looked ravaged, and he didn't even seem aware of Sarah's presence.

"Reverend Nicely?" Sarah said.

He looked up at last, his eyes full of pain. "Yes?"

"I'm Sarah Brandt. I'm a nurse. Mrs. Gerald Oakes sent me to see if I could help."

"It's too late, I'm afraid," he said. "My wife . . . My wife is gone. And Sister Daisy, too."

"Is this your daughter?" she asked, setting her bag down on the floor.

He nodded. He still held her hand.

Sarah could see the girl's chest rising and falling, however slightly. "May I examine her? I might be able to help."

"Help?"

"I'm a nurse," she reminded him. "I think I know what made her sick. Please."

With obvious reluctance, he released the girl's hand and rose from his chair, stepping back to make room.

Sarah picked up her bag and set it on the now-empty chair. Rummaging through it, she pulled out the stethoscope and listened to the girl's heart and lungs, then checked her pulse and looked in her eyes and mouth. The symptoms of arsenic poisoning were difficult to distinguish from many other ailments, and they could be completely wrong about what had afflicted these women, but the similarities of their illness with Charles Oakes's was simply too much of a coincidence.

"Reverend Nicely, are you ill, too?"

The poor man was so haggard, he might well be. "Me? No, not at all."

"Can you tell me how your wife and daughter and Daisy first became ill, then?"

"Not really, no. Everyone was fine after the church service. Rose, my wife, she had made Sunday dinner, and we invited Sister Daisy to join us. We hadn't seen much of her since she moved uptown, and she was mourning the death of a young man she'd grown very fond of."

"Charles Oakes."

He seemed surprised she knew his name. "Yes, that's right."

"So you all had dinner together. Did you eat the same things everyone else did?"

"Yes, of course. My wife is a very good cook . . . I mean, she was . . ." His eyes filled with tears.

Sarah had to keep him on track. "Are you sure? You ate everything that was served?"

"Yes, I told you."

"And how long after you ate did they become ill?"

"I . . . I don't know. One of my parishioners is dying, and her family sent for me. They thought the end was very near, and she was asking for me."

"How long were you gone?"

"Several hours, I think. I don't know. I didn't pay any attention, but when I got home, they were all three very sick. I gathered that Sister Daisy was the first to fall ill, but I didn't . . . I couldn't ask them many questions by then. I asked one of the neighbor ladies to help, and when the word spread, several of our parishioners came. They did all they could, but . . ." His voice broke and he began to sob.

Sarah put her arm around him and led him back to the front room. An overstuffed chair held a place of honor by the front window, and she took him to it and sat him down. Zeller and the woman were gone. Sarah hoped they were getting her some milk, for what little good that might do for poor Isabel Nicely. "I'll do what I can for Isabel," she said.

"I'll pray for her," he said, pulling out a well-used handkerchief to wipe his face.

"Pray for me, too," she said.

Mrs. Burgun had a key to the house, so they didn't have to wait for someone to answer their knock. The house seemed very quiet as she led Frank upstairs to the bedrooms.

"This is his room," she told him when they stopped outside one of the doors. "I'll check on Miss Adderly."

Frank knocked and a strange man opened the door. "Are you the doctor?"

"Yes, and you must be Mr. Malloy. Mr. Adderly's been asking for you."

Frank stepped into the room and wrinkled his nose at the stale odor of vomit. The well-furnished room appeared to have been the master's, full of heavy mahogany pieces and papered in a dark maroon. Obviously, Adderly had chosen the best room in the house for himself. He lay in the imposing four-poster bed, looking awful.

"You're still alive," Frank observed.

"Just barely. Thank God Dr. Younger came when he did."

Frank turned to the doctor. "Did he tell you he'd been poisoned with arsenic?"

"Yes. He claimed his cousin put it in his whiskey. I understand she's not entirely herself."

"She's not entirely anything," Frank said, "although Adderly here went to great pains to get her declared sane so she'd be released from the Asylum."

"It's a hospital," Adderly said weakly.

Frank ignored him. "What have you done for him?"

"There's not much you can do for arsenic once it takes hold. I pumped his stomach and gave him a purgative, in hopes of ridding his body of as much of it as possible."

Frank saw an empty glass on the bedside table with white residue at the bottom. "What's that?"

"Milk."

Frank thought of Charles and the milk he'd drunk the night he died. "What does the milk do?"

"We think it binds the arsenic, and it does soothe the throat and stomach."

"Do you think it was really arsenic?"

The doctor shrugged. "It could be that or gastric fever or any number of other things."

"And if it really was arsenic?"

"I don't have a lot of experience with arsenic. Not many people get poisoned, at least not that I've seen."

Frank had to agree. Most people avoided eating arsenic.

It was the sensible thing to do. "I guess it's promising that he's still alive."

"Malloy," Adderly said, "you have to do something about Ella."

"What would you like me to do?"

"I . . . She tried to kill me."

"Are you sure? Because I thought she put the arsenic in the whiskey to kill Charles Oakes."

"Who is Charles Oakes?" the doctor asked.

"A fellow who died from arsenic poisoning the other day," Frank said.

"Oh my."

"Yes, well, he'd just visited Ella and drank some of Adderly's whiskey, and Ella was mad at him."

"Angry," Adderly said.

"Oh yes, sorry. She was angry. She doesn't like to use the word *mad* because that also means *crazy*."

"I see," said the doctor, although he didn't seem to.

"So we suspected she might have put arsenic in the whiskey that Charles Oakes drank."

"And then Mr. Adderly drank some of the whiskey, too," Dr. Younger guessed.

"Yes, he did," Frank said.

"You have to do something, Malloy," Adderly said.

Frank wasn't too sure about that. "What do you want me to do? Take Ella back to the Asylum?"

"No!" Adderly cried, confirming Frank's suspicions.

"But what if she really tried to kill you?" Frank asked as innocently as he could manage. "She's dangerous. She might go after Mrs. Burgun or one of the servants next."

"I'm sure it was an accident that I drank the whiskey. She's not violent," Adderly insisted. "She's just . . ."

"Dangerous," Frank repeated. "Is there some reason you don't want to take her back to the . . . uh . . . hospital?"

"I can't put her back in that horrible place," Adderly said.

"But she'd be safe there," Frank said. "*You'd* be safe, too."

Adderly moaned.

"I think my patient needs to rest now," Dr. Younger said.

"I had the whiskey tested," Frank told the doctor. "I'll be waiting downstairs for the results, if you need me."

Frank wandered around the house until he located a maid who showed him to the front parlor. Then he sent her in search of Mrs. Burgun.

She arrived a few minutes later with the doctor in tow.

"How is Miss Adderly doing?" Frank asked her.

"She's quiet, but she usually is this time of day. I didn't tell her Mr. Adderly is sick."

"Didn't she already know?"

"She forgets things."

"So, Doc, what do you think?" Frank asked.

"What do I think about what?"

"Do you think Adderly will live? Do you think he was really poisoned?"

"Like I said, there's really no way to tell for sure unless Miss Adderly admits she put arsenic in his whiskey. Did she actually say that?"

Frank glanced at Mrs. Burgun, who shook her head. "I guess not. I know a fellow who can test the stomach of a dead person to find out."

"I can't imagine Mr. Adderly would allow you to do that test on him," Dr. Younger said with some amusement.

"I think you're probably right."

"Do you suppose we could have something to eat?" the doctor asked Mrs. Burgun. "I never had any breakfast."

"Of course," she said. "I'll go speak to the cook."

"And in the meantime," Dr. Younger said to Frank, "you can tell me about this fellow Charles who got himself poisoned."

Isabel Nicely was barely conscious, so Sarah could only get a few drops of milk into her at a time. It certainly wouldn't do to try to pour it down her throat and end up drowning her instead. She had, at least, stopped vomiting. Her poor body was exhausted, though, and Sarah didn't know if she was resting and on her way to recovery or simply in the last stages of a coma before death. All she could do was keep trying to get her to swallow some milk, so that's what she did.

Isabel looked to be about sixteen, with perfect skin the color of coffee with cream. Under other circumstances, she was probably lovely. She had her whole life ahead of her, and Sarah was furious at whoever or whatever had tried to cut that life short.

When she had finally succeeded in getting the entire glass of milk into the girl, she stepped back out into the front room to see how the Reverend Nicely was doing. He still sat in the chair where she'd placed him. Zeller sat at the kitchen table, his head in his hands. Both men scrambled to their feet when they saw her.

"Isabel?" Nicely asked, fear and hope warring in his bloodshot eyes.

"She's resting."

"There's some coffee if you'd like," Zeller said.

"Thank you." She glanced at the kitchen area of the room.

"I'll get it," Zeller said, hurrying to serve her. He was probably grateful for something to do.

Sarah sat down at the table, and Nicely sank back down into his chair.

"I've been trying to think what they could've eaten to

make them sick," he said, looking around the room. "But there's nothing here that hasn't been here all along."

"And nobody's visited you recently?" Sarah asked.

"No one in the past few days except Sister Daisy."

That was it, then. "She must have brought something with her." It was the only explanation that made sense. If someone wanted to poison Daisy . . . But why would anyone want to do that? Revenge for Charles, if Daisy had indeed poisoned him? Or something else? And how had they done it? "Did she bring something for your dinner? Or a gift perhaps?"

"No . . . Oh, wait, a gift, yes! There was something! Now I remember. She said she had a treat for us."

"What kind of treat?"

"She didn't say. She just said it was for later, after we ate."

"And she didn't give it to you?"

"Not while I was here."

But she must have given it to the women after he left. Sarah tried to think what it could have been. Mrs. Ellsworth was always bringing her something, usually a pie or a cake, which would be a traditional offering if one were invited to dinner. But Daisy didn't have access to the kitchen at the Oakes house. She couldn't have brought them something she'd made herself. Had she purchased something? But what? And where would she have gotten it? And how would she have carried it here without Mr. Nicely noticing? And who would have poisoned it? And when and how? Too many questions and not a single answer.

Zeller set a cup of coffee down in front of her. She thanked him. "What was Daisy carrying when she came?"

"I didn't pay any attention."

Sarah glanced around. "Do you see anything that you don't recognize that might have been hers?"

The Reverend Nicely glanced around. He could easily see

every corner of the room from where he sat, and after a moment he said, "There, by the door."

A worn carpetbag sat forgotten against the wall. Zeller snatched it up. "Yes, this was hers. Mrs. Gerald gave it to her."

"What's in it?" Sarah asked. Zeller brought it to her and gently laid it on the table, making her remember that he had cared for Daisy. Sarah opened it with the same gentle care and rummaged through it, finding nothing but a few odds and ends, a bit of knitting, and a handkerchief. If she'd carried something with her that had brought death to her and her friend, no trace of it remained. "It must be here someplace, though," Sarah said. "Reverend Nicely, can you help me look?"

They made short work of the front room. The kitchen area provided the only storage space, and they found nothing but the remains from the dinner Mrs. Nicely had cooked herself and the Reverend Nicely had obligingly eaten of without any ill effects. Mrs. Nicely's and Daisy's bodies were in the Nicelys' bedroom. They'd moved Daisy in there after Mrs. Nicely passed, he explained. They searched in silence out of respect for the dead, but found nothing.

Nicely stopped by his wife's body, which lay on the bed, wrapped in a sheet, and touched her head tenderly. "I guess I should call the undertaker," he said after a moment. "I just hate to let her go."

"Mrs. Gerald will take care of Daisy," Zeller said from the doorway. "She told me specially to bring her home." His voice broke on the last word, and he turned away.

"That's kind of her," Nicely said. "But I suppose it's only right, since they were sisters."

FRANK HAD LONG SINCE FINISHED TELLING DR. YOUNGER all he knew about Charles Oakes and his mysterious death, but the good doctor was still trying to puzzle out what could have happened. They agreed Ella Adderly could have poisoned him the first time with her cousin's whiskey, but how could she have managed it the second time, and it was impossible for her to have given him a third dose that evening at his home.

Tired of discussing it, Frank decided to change the subject. "Doc, what do you know about insanity?"

"About as much as anyone knows, I guess."

"Do you see a lot of it?"

"More than I'd like. Melancholia mostly."

"What's that?"

"The patient falls into a depressive state and is unable to bring himself out of it. He takes no pleasure in anything, even things that would normally bring him pleasure. He often will take to his bed and be unable to eat or even rise and dress himself. I say 'him,' but it's mostly females who are prone to this malady, I'm afraid. It seems more prevalent among the poor, too, although they often have good reason to be depressed."

"And when you have a patient like this, what do you do with them?"

"There's not much I can do. In particularly severe cases, people sometimes take their own lives, but usually, if they are able to rest and have someone to look after them, they eventually come out of it."

"I guess poor people don't have the chance to rest, though."

"Not usually, no."

"Do you ever send someone to the Asylum?"

"I thought it was a hospital," Dr. Younger said with a small smile.

"I guess they changed the name of it, didn't they? Hospital sounds much nicer."

"Yes, it does. I've only sent someone there a time or two,

when I felt they were a danger to others or they had no one to care for them."

"Are you the one who sent Miss Adderly there?"

He frowned. "I'm afraid I had to. After her parents died, she suffered a complete breakdown, and she had no one here to look after her."

"I guess you were glad to hear she was released, then."

"Yes, I was, but . . ."

"But what?"

"Mr. Malloy, you're a man of the world, so I know it won't shock you when I say that I don't believe Miss Adderly should ever have been released."

Before Frank could respond, the parlor door opened, startling them both. Mrs. Burgun came in. "That young man is here," she told Frank.

The young man in question hadn't waited to be announced. Gino followed her in and brought Titus Wesley with him. Frank introduced them to Dr. Younger.

"Are you the one who can find out if someone was poisoned by looking in their stomach?" Younger asked.

"Yes, I am. I can also tell if somebody put poison in your whiskey."

"And did they?" Frank asked.

"No," Wesley said with a satisfied smile. "There wasn't a speck of arsenic in any of the whiskey you brought me."

II

"SISTERS?" SARAH ECHOED. "WHAT DO YOU MEAN, THEY were sisters?"

Nicely snatched his hand away from his wife's body and stared back at Sarah guiltily. "I shouldn't have said that. I'm sorry."

"Were Daisy and Jenny Oakes sisters?" she asked again, turning to Zeller to see his reaction. Oddly enough, he also looked guilty, and not a bit surprised. "You knew, too, didn't you?"

"It doesn't matter now," Zeller said.

Sarah returned to the front room where Zeller stood. Nicely followed her.

"You have to understand," Nicely said. "Things in the South were different when they had slavery. The women had no choice."

Sarah had heard stories, of course, and everyone knew why

some Negroes had lighter skin than others. She hadn't met Daisy, but maybe if she had, she might have guessed the truth herself.

"Daisy's mother was a house servant," Zeller said. "Apparently, it was quite common for the master to have his way with the servant girls."

And that would explain why Jenny and Daisy were together when they fled the plantation, and why Daisy had sought Jenny out after so many years, certain Jenny would take her in. "Then Charles was her nephew."

"Mr. Charles didn't know, of course," Zeller said. "Daisy would never tell him such a thing, but she said he reminded her so much of her own son who died."

"Then she really cared for him?" Sarah asked.

"Oh yes. She blamed herself when he died, too. Thought she should've done more, although I guess there was nothing anybody could've done."

But she also might have harbored a grudge against Jenny for all those thirty years while Jenny lived in luxury after leaving her poor sister behind to fend for herself. But if so, and if she'd killed Charles in revenge, who had killed her?

Someone who wanted revenge of her own, of course.

Sarah didn't have time to think about it now, though. "I should check on Isabel."

She found the girl much the same, although Sarah thought her breathing might be a bit easier. Sarah sent up a silent prayer for her. Not only did she want the girl to live for her own sake but because she was the only one who might give them a clue as to who had caused all this death and destruction.

"YOU DIDN'T FIND ANY POISON AT ALL?" FRANK ASKED Wesley.

"Not a bit. And if you don't mind, I'll keep what's left of the whiskey. It's fine stuff. There was bourbon and Scotch and—"

"Then what's wrong with Adderly?" Frank asked the doctor.

"I told you, it could be anything. It could even be . . ."

"What?"

The doctor shrugged apologetically. "It could even be that he made himself sick just thinking he'd been poisoned."

"Is that possible?" Gino asked.

"It sure is," Titus Wesley said with a grin.

"How would we know?" Frank asked.

"Why don't we tell him there wasn't any poison in his whiskey and see what happens?" Wesley said.

Frank thought that was a brilliant idea, so he and Dr. Younger went upstairs and did just that.

"Then what made me sick?" Adderly demanded when he'd heard them out.

"It could've been anything," Dr. Younger said. "Sometimes people get sick like that just because they're frightened."

Adderly laid a hand on his abdomen. "I've always had a nervous stomach."

"How do you feel now?" Younger asked.

"I . . . Better, I think. It's like the sickness just suddenly went away. A pain I had right here"—he pointed to the center of his chest—"is gone."

The doctor gave Frank a knowing smile.

"What do you want me to do with Miss Adderly?" Frank asked.

"Why, nothing," Adderly said cheerfully. "If she didn't poison me, she probably didn't poison Charles Oakes either. I should've known that."

"I guess you should've. And I guess you'll let me know if I can be of any more service to you," Frank said.

"Yes, of course, although I can't imagine what that might be. I owe you a debt, though, Malloy, so if there's anything I can ever do for you, just let me know."

Frank couldn't imagine ever needing help from the likes of Adderly either. Besides, when he was finished dealing with him, Frank doubted Adderly would be quite as anxious to assist him.

SARAH HAD BEGUN TO WONDER IF SHE SHOULD SEND Zeller to find Malloy. He needed to know where she was and what had happened to Daisy. Maybe he could help her figure out what had happened here, too. Then she heard a familiar voice outside. She went to the still-open front door and looked down to see Malloy and Gino Donatelli standing in the street and looking around.

Gino saw her first. "Mrs. Brandt!" he called. "There she is."

Malloy turned and saw her, then came bounding up the steps.

"How did you find me?" she asked when he reached the top.

"When we got home, Mrs. Ellsworth came over to tell me where you'd gone. It took us a while to find the church, and we had to stop on the way to get Wesley."

"Who?"

"The undertaker who was testing Adderly's whiskey. Too bad we didn't know we'd need him again so soon. We'd just dropped him off at his shop on our way back from Adderly's and had to go back and get him again." Malloy stepped inside and stopped when he saw the Reverend Nicely.

Sarah introduced them. "And you already know Mr. Zeller. Reverend Nicely's wife and Daisy have both passed away."

"I'm sorry," Malloy said. "This is a terrible thing. Your family shouldn't've been harmed by it."

Nicely nodded, but his expression was still wary. He'd been through so much, and now this strange white man had barged into his house.

"You weren't poisoned, too?" Malloy asked him.

"No," Sarah said, saving him from having to explain. "He wasn't here, but his daughter Isabel was also poisoned. I've been doing what I can for her, but I haven't been able to wake her up yet."

"Maybe Wesley can do something," Malloy said. "He's a doctor," he added to Nicely. "I'll get him."

Malloy went back down the stairs, and a few minutes later a tall, thin young man appeared in the doorway. His long face was suitably solemn, but his suit was a bit the worse for wear, and he carried no medical bag.

Sarah introduced herself and the others. "Mr. Malloy thought you might be able to help Miss Nicely."

"I don't know that I can do much," he said, speaking to the Reverend Nicely. "By now the arsenic will have taken hold. Sometimes people recover and sometimes they don't, and even if she survives, your daughter may have lingering effects from the damage the arsenic does to the body."

The Reverend Nicely winced, but he said, "Anything you can do."

Wesley nodded, and Sarah took him back to the room where the girl still lay, motionless. Using Sarah's stethoscope, he listened to her chest and checked her pulse, eyes, and throat, as Sarah had done.

"We don't really know why arsenic kills," he said. "If we did, maybe we could figure out how to treat it. It's funny how it works. If people are exposed to it over a long period of time, at less than a fatal dose, they can develop a tolerance for it. I had a patient once, his wife had been giving him arsenic for months in his morning coffee. He'd been really sick the whole time, too, but it wasn't until I finally noticed his fingernails . . ."

"Fingernails?"

"Yes, long-term exposure to arsenic can cause white lines in the fingernails. As soon as I saw that, I knew what it was. He figured out it was his wife who was trying to kill him and had her arrested. When he wasn't being poisoned anymore, he made a complete recovery. But another time, a young woman tried to kill herself, so she took a lot, all at once. Her family found her almost immediately, so I irrigated her stomach and even though she got really sick, she didn't die. But she was never the same. Her hands and feet lost all feeling, and her heart was damaged. She only lived a few years after that."

"So if Isabel survives, she might be damaged."

"I'm afraid so, although that's no reason to let her die."

"Is there anything else I can do for her?"

"Arsenic causes dehydration, so keep trying to get her to swallow some liquids."

"Milk? I read that binds the arsenic."

"Nobody knows if that's true or not, but it does soothe the throat and stomach, at least."

"I'm going to stay with her, at least until I know if she's going to survive. Besides, she's the only one who could tell us what happened and how they got poisoned in the first place."

"You don't know?"

"No, Reverend Nicely wasn't here when the women ate or drank whatever it was in, and we haven't found anything that it could have been. I guess we're really just assuming it was arsenic, since we can't even know that for sure."

"Well, then, I wish you luck."

Malloy was waiting in the front room when they came out.

"Mrs. Brandt is doing all the right things," Wesley told

the Reverend Nicely. "But there really isn't much we can do now except wait."

"And pray," the Reverend Nicely said.

"That's probably the best thing you can do," Wesley said.

"Dr. Wesley is also a coroner," Malloy said to Zeller. "He has a wagon downstairs, and he can take Daisy's body."

"She's colored," Zeller said, obviously well aware that not all coroners were willing to bury Negroes.

"That's all right," Wesley said. He turned to the Reverend Nicely. "I can take your wife as well, Reverend Nicely, or if you've got someone you'd rather send her to, I can take her there."

Nicely shook his head. "Thank you, sir, but I don't know when I'd be able to pay you."

"Don't worry about that," Malloy said. "The Oakes family will take care of it."

Sarah doubted the truth of that. More likely, Malloy would take care of it, but she didn't say a word.

Wesley gave the Reverend Nicely his card and told him to let him know when he wanted to have the funeral.

Gino helped Wesley with the grim task of carrying the two women's bodies down the narrow stairs. When they were finished, Malloy told Zeller to return home. Now that Daisy's body was gone, he had nothing else to keep him there, so he gratefully accepted the suggestion. Then Malloy sent Gino back to Bank Street.

"Let Maeve and my mother know that we'll be staying here, at least for a while."

"What should I do then?"

"Go back to Amsterdam Avenue and start visiting all the druggists to see if anybody from the Oakes house bought any arsenic in the past month or so."

"Will they remember something like that?"

"No, but when you buy a poison, you have to sign a book. Just check the books for familiar names. Start with the shops closest to the house and work your way out."

"How far should I go?"

"Until you run out of time or you find something. If it was a servant or one of the women, they probably walked. A servant would have to, and the family wouldn't want anyone else to know where they'd gone, so I'm thinking they didn't go far."

"And what about tomorrow?"

"Come to my house in the morning, and if I'm back by then, we'll figure out what to do next. If I'm not back, come here to find me."

When Gino and Zeller were gone, Malloy turned to Nicely. "Sir, why don't you try to get some rest. Mrs. Brandt will look after your daughter, and I'll be here if she needs anything. You won't be any good to your daughter if you get sick yourself."

He argued a bit, but he was too exhausted to put up much of a fight. Sarah was sorry she had to send him to the bed where his wife had died, but if that thought occurred to him, he didn't mention it. After she'd spent a few minutes with Isabel, trying with some success to get her to swallow some more milk, she came back out into the front room, leaving the door ajar in case Isabel stirred.

Malloy met her halfway across the room and enfolded her in his arms. She hugged him back, savoring the feel of his strength surrounding her. She'd seen too much death today.

"How are you doing?" he asked into her hair, not letting her go.

"I'm fine now. I just needed this."

He kissed her and then led her over to the table where he'd set out a cup for her. Then he poured the fresh coffee that he'd made.

When he'd taken a seat, she asked, "What were you doing today?"

"Virgil Adderly sent me word that he'd been sick all night, just like Charles. I sent Gino to find out if Wesley had checked the whiskey for arsenic yet, and I went to the Adderly house to see what was going on."

"Had he really been poisoned?"

"No."

Sarah almost laughed out loud. "But you said he was sick."

"Apparently, he got so scared when he thought Ella had poisoned him that he made himself sick. As soon as Wesley told him there was nothing in the whiskey, he made a complete recovery."

"Does this mean that Ella Adderly didn't poison Charles either?"

"It's seeming much less likely. She still could have, of course, if she only put it in the glass he drank out of that day, but there's still no explanation for how she could've poisoned him a second and third time."

"That really does seem impossible, so we still don't know who poisoned Charles, and now we have the question of who poisoned Daisy and the Nicely women."

"How did it happen?"

Sarah told him what she knew.

Malloy sipped his coffee and considered what she'd told him. "They ate or drank something that Daisy had brought with her then."

"They must have. There's no other explanation. It must have been something the killer had given her, probably intending that she'd be the only one who ate or drank it. At least I'd like to think so."

"Who would want to poison Daisy, though?"

"And most of all, *why?*" Sarah added.

"Maybe Daisy knew who had poisoned Charles."

"Why didn't she just tell someone then? Gino gave her every opportunity."

"Maybe because it's someone she wants to protect."

"Like her sister."

Malloy straightened in surprise. "What sister?"

"Jenny Oakes is Daisy's sister, or was, I mean."

"Who told you that?"

"Reverend Nicely. When she first came to New York, Daisy told him she was trying to find her sister. Well, her half sister, I guess. It seems some slave owners fathered children with their slaves as well as with their lawful wives."

"So Jenny was his daughter by his wife, and Daisy was his daughter by a slave."

"Which would make them half sisters."

"And when Jenny married Gerald Oakes, she left her sister behind." Malloy shook his head in wonder.

"We already suspected Daisy was bitter about being left when we thought she was just Jenny's servant. But if they were sisters . . ."

"She must've been really angry about that."

"I don't know if she was or not. Would a slave expect her mistress to take her North with her, even if they were related? She was apparently very certain Jenny would take her in when she got to New York, though."

"And she was right about that. But could she really forgive Jenny for leaving her behind?"

Sarah sighed. "I don't think I could, especially if my own sister did it, and if she still hated Jenny, Daisy had a good reason for killing Charles."

"But who had a good reason for killing Daisy?"

Sarah had to think about this for a minute. "We're back to the same old theory: Maybe Jenny figured out what she'd done to Charles and took some revenge of her own."

"But why not just turn Daisy over to the police for killing Charles?"

Sarah instantly knew the answer to that. "Because a case like this would be a sensational story for the newspapers, and she didn't want people to find out that she had a colored half sister."

"If Daisy killed Charles, that explains why she was so scared when Gino questioned her, too."

"Yes, it does." Sarah sipped her coffee and considered all the facts again. "Except . . ."

"Except what?"

"Except how did she poison Charles the first two times, when he was away from home?"

This time Malloy considered. "Maybe she gave him something to eat that he took with him when he left the house."

"The same thing Daisy brought with her today?"

Malloy frowned. "That doesn't make sense, does it? Unless Daisy wanted to commit suicide."

"And even if she did, why would she poison her friends, too?"

"You're right, that doesn't make sense. But maybe somebody figured out how Daisy had poisoned Charles and played the same trick on Daisy."

"That seems possible," Sarah agreed. "Maybe someone at the Oakes house will know what Charles was likely to have taken with him."

"Of course, we're just assuming that Daisy and the Nicely women were poisoned with arsenic."

"Can we find out for sure?"

"Yes, we can. That's the main reason I brought Wesley

here. He's going to check Daisy's body for evidence of arsenic poisoning."

Sarah glanced at the door behind which the Reverend Nicely slept and lowered her voice. "What about Mrs. Nicely?"

"He'll check her body, too. I told him the Oakes family wanted Daisy embalmed, so he'll do the same for Mrs. Nicely."

"Did the Oakes family really say they'd pay for Mrs. Nicely's funeral?"

"No, but I'll put it on their bill."

Sarah thought that was probably fair. Mrs. Nicely wouldn't have died if someone hadn't killed Charles in the first place. "How on earth are we going to figure out who is responsible for all of this?"

"One way is to find out how Daisy and the Nicely women were poisoned. Could someone else have visited the Nicelys while Reverend Nicely was out?"

"I don't know. They do have a lot of friends. Mr. Zeller said the house was full of women helping when he got here this morning. All but one of them had left by the time I arrived, though."

"If there were a lot of women here, then that explains it."

"Explains what?"

"What happened to the poison or whatever the poison was in. The one thing women can't resist doing is cleaning up."

"Oh my, I didn't think of that! Of course. They would have washed up any dishes and cleared away any trash."

"Can we find out who was here? Somebody will remember."

Sarah glanced at the bedroom door again. "Reverend Nicely probably could, but I couldn't bear to disturb him."

"I suppose it can wait until he wakes up."

Sarah went back in to tend to Isabel, and when she was

finished, she found Malloy facing off three women. One of them was the woman who had been there earlier when Sarah had first arrived. She recognized Sarah, and nodded. They were all carrying plates covered with cloths, obviously supper for the Reverend Nicely.

"She's a nurse," the woman she recognized said to the others, nodding to indicate Sarah. "Where's Reverend Nicely?"

"He's resting," Sarah said.

"Who's he?" one of them asked, nodding at Malloy.

"This is Mr. Malloy, my fiancé," Sarah said.

"He looks like police," the woman said.

"I'm not with the police," he assured them. They didn't look like they believed him.

"How's Isabel doing?" the first woman asked.

"She's still unconscious, but I've been giving her milk. The doctor was here, and he said it's important to give her liquids."

"We can do that now. You don't need to stay."

The message was plain. Sarah and Malloy were unwelcome here. Or perhaps they were simply not trusted. No one in this neighborhood had any reason to trust white people, least of all one who looked like he might be with the police.

"May I show you how to give Isabel the liquids without choking her?" Sarah asked.

The three women exchanged glances and some silent communication, and then the first woman said, "I suppose that'd be all right."

"I'll wait outside," Malloy said, and Sarah bit back a smile at his cowardice.

Sarah gave the woman a quick lesson, then collected her things. The women had already set out the supper they had prepared for the Reverend Nicely. She only hoped they wouldn't wake him up to feed him. She was at the door before she remembered what she and Frank had wanted to know. "Were any of you ladies here earlier, helping out?"

None of them answered. Their dark eyes simply stared at her suspiciously.

She tried again. "We were wondering if anyone noticed anything strange, something that didn't belong here." The question sounded odd even to Sarah, and the women acted like they hadn't even heard it. She gave up and said, "Please tell Reverend Nicely to send for me if he needs anything." She offered her calling card to the women, but none of them would accept it, so she left it lying on the table.

Malloy was waiting for her at the bottom of the stairs. He took her medical bag, gave her his arm, and they started down the street. They were the only white people visible in any direction. People stared at them from windows and doorways, and children stopped their play to watch them walk by. Malloy waited until they were a block away from the church building before he asked, "Why do people always think I'm a policeman?"

"They don't always think that."

"Yes, they do, even when I'm wearing a tailor-made suit. Do you know how much this suit cost?"

"I'm sure it's just your imposing manner."

Malloy made a rude noise and let the subject drop. "Did you find out anything from those women?"

"I asked if they were here earlier and if they'd noticed anything out of the ordinary, but they didn't even reply. This is going to be much more difficult than I expected."

"I could have told you that. Colored people in this city learn pretty quickly that the best way to stay out of trouble is to keep quiet, and even that doesn't always work."

"But we're trying to help."

"They don't know that. They probably think you want to blame one of them for making those women sick."

"That's what Jenny Oakes warned me about. She said Daisy would think she was being blamed for Charles's death, no matter what we told her. If only I'd gotten to talk to her."

"She probably wouldn't have told you any more than she told Gino."

"We'll never know now, will we?"

He sighed. "No, we won't."

THE NEXT MORNING, SARAH SET MAEVE AND CATHERINE to the task of packing a basket of food for the Reverend Nicely. As she'd lain awake last night, too distraught over the tragedy she'd seen at the Nicely house to sleep, she'd decided she had to go back this morning. She would check on Isabel and enlist the Reverend Nicely's help in questioning the women who had been at his house on Sunday to care for the sick women. He was probably the only one who could discover what they knew, since she was sure none of those women would speak to her, and they certainly wouldn't tell Malloy anything either.

Malloy would probably want to go with her, but she would have to go alone if she had any hope of finding out the truth.

"I could go with you," Maeve said as they were wrapping food for the basket. "So you wouldn't be alone and Mr. Malloy could stay with the workmen."

"Who would look after Catherine?" Sarah asked.

Catherine grinned. "Mrs. Ellsworth."

"Did you two already discuss this?" Sarah asked.

Maeve smiled innocently. "Of course not, but when I go someplace, Mrs. Ellsworth always watches Catherine."

"She gives me cookies," Catherine said.

"We'll see," Sarah said, thinking she'd keep it as an option if Malloy simply refused to let her go alone.

FRANK AND GINO WERE IN THE KITCHEN DISCUSSING Gino's fruitless visits to the various pharmacies yesterday and making their plans for the day when Frank heard the oddest sound. "What was that?"

"It sounded like a doorbell," Gino said.

Frank made his way down the hall toward the front door, and sure enough, he heard it again. It really was a doorbell. He threw the door open to find Sarah, Maeve, and Catherine on the stoop.

"The doorbell works," he said.

"Yes," Maeve said. "I had one of the workmen fix it yesterday. And did you know they finished the bathroom? It just needs a good cleaning now."

Frank stood back while the females entered. He felt a little stunned.

Gino greeted Catherine warmly, Sarah politely, and Maeve shyly.

"Did Brian already go to school?" Catherine asked him.

"I'm afraid so. What are you going to do today?"

"Eat cookies with Mrs. Ellsworth."

Frank gave Sarah a questioning look.

"I need to go see Reverend Nicely and check on Isabel," she said. "Maeve said she'd go with me, so you don't have to leave the house."

"Gino and I were going to find Mrs. Peabody's nephew to see if we can figure out all the places Charles Oakes was the day he first got poisoned. I was going to ask if you could stay here with the workmen, but now . . ." He eyed Maeve, sure he'd never really seen her clearly before.

"Why are you looking at me like that?" she asked.

"Because I don't think I ever really appreciated your talents, Maeve. You're going to stay here with the workmen today, and maybe we can get them to finish with the house before New Year's."

Maeve started to protest, but Catherine beat her to it. "I wanted to eat cookies with Mrs. Ellsworth."

"I'm sure Mrs. Ellsworth can bring cookies over here," Frank said. He turned to Sarah. "As for you going to see Reverend Nicely—"

"I can go alone," she said. "I'll be less intimidating that way."

"Gino can go with you," he said, not liking the idea of her going off to that part of town by herself.

"Don't be silly. Gino looks as much like a policeman as you do. Nobody will tell me a thing if he's with me. The person who killed those women won't be down there today, I promise you. I'll be perfectly safe."

Frank tried pointing out that no one in New York City was ever perfectly safe, and Sarah pointed out that she wouldn't be in any more danger today than she was on any other day, and in the end, he had to admit she should probably go by herself.

Maeve and Catherine stayed behind to supervise the workmen, although they were both pouting. Frank and Gino went in search of Percy, and Sarah set out for the Reverend Nicely's house.

WHEN SARAH ARRIVED AT THE CHURCH AND CLIMBED the outside staircase, she found the door still standing open to the warm breeze. She knocked on the doorjamb. "Hello?"

A woman came out of Isabel's room. It was the woman she had first met yesterday. She didn't look happy to see Sarah. "What do you want?"

"I brought some food," Sarah said, holding up her basket

to prove it, "and I thought I'd check on Isabel. How is she doing?"

"She's doing just fine. We don't need your help anymore."

"Did she wake up?"

Plainly, the woman didn't want to give her any information at all, but she said, "She asked for her mama."

How horrible, Sarah thought. "May I come in and examine her?"

"I don't know what Reverend Nicely would say about that," the woman said.

"Where is he? Can we ask him?"

"He's right here," the Reverend Nicely said, coming out of the other room. He was just shrugging into his suit coat. "It's nice of you to come, Mrs. Brandt. Sister Mary, why don't you take that basket from Mrs. Brandt and get her a cup of coffee?"

Mary accepted the basket Sarah handed her, although she made sure Sarah knew how much it offended her.

"I just heard Isabel woke up," Sarah said.

"I don't know about that," Nicely said with a sad frown. "She was asking for her mother, but I'm not sure she was really awake."

"Would you mind if I examined her?"

"Please do." The Reverend Nicely let her into Isabel's room. "The ladies have been looking after her faithfully. They said you told them to give her milk, and when they ran out of milk, they started giving her water."

"That was exactly the right thing to do," Sarah said. She opened her medical bag, took out her stethoscope, and examined the girl. Her heartbeat seemed stronger than it had yesterday, and her lungs were still clear. She tried shaking her gently. "Isabel? Can you hear me?"

The girl moaned.

"Reverend Nicely, why don't you try? She may respond to a familiar voice."

He stepped forward eagerly. "Isabel, dear, wake up now. It's time to wake up." When he tried to shake her shoulder, she shrugged away.

"Look, she's responding," Sarah said. "Shake her again."

He did, and he called her name and told her to wake up over and over until her eyes fluttered open. "Papa," she said hoarsely, "I'm tired."

"Praise God," he cried, his eyes welling with tears. "Isabel, my sweet, sweet girl."

"Let me sleep," she whispered, but he sank down beside her on the bed and took her in his arms, praising God for a miracle.

Sarah wasn't sure it was a miracle yet, but at least she'd come out of her coma. If they could get her to eat, and if the poison hadn't damaged her body too much . . . Too many ifs for Sarah to rejoice just yet, but it was the first good news poor Reverend Nicely had gotten in almost two days, so Sarah let him enjoy it.

Mary came to the door, and when she saw Isabel was awake, she also started praising God. "I'll go spread the word, Reverend Nicely," she told him. "Everybody'll want to know right away."

Sarah went to the kitchen and sorted through the various foodstuffs that the Reverend Nicely's parishioners had brought. She found a jar of soup, so she poured a bit of it into a cup and snatched up a spoon. She'd try to get some of this into Isabel before she fell asleep again.

Isabel hadn't wanted to stay awake, but her father helped Sarah keep her roused until she'd swallowed at least a few spoonfuls of the rich broth. When she'd drifted off again, exhausted from the effort, Sarah made herself useful by unpacking the basket she had brought while the Reverend Nicely sat beside Isabel's bed, talking to her even though she gave no indication that she could hear him.

Sarah had imagined that she would ask him to go with her to visit the women from his congregation so they could question them about what they'd found in the Nicelys' house that might have contained the poison. Seeing him now, she realized it would be cruel to ask him to leave Isabel's side just yet. At least he could tell her the names of the women who had been there, or maybe she could convince Sister Mary to give her the names. Maybe Sister Mary would even go with her and introduce her to the women so Sarah could ask her questions herself. No sooner had she thought of this idea than she discarded it. Sister Mary wasn't going to help Sarah do anything. And the other women wouldn't tell her anything, she was sure. She tried to think of some other way to find out what they needed to know, but she couldn't come up with a single thing.

She was starting to wonder if she should just give up and head back home when she heard someone running up the stairs outside. She was on her feet when Sister Mary burst in, breathless and panicked.

She froze when she saw Sarah, and for a moment Sarah thought the woman was going to order her to leave again. Instead she said, "Thank heaven you're still here. My girl's sick just like Sister Rose and Sister Isabel. Real sick. Can you come?"

12

"I THOUGHT YOU SAID THESE FELLOWS SPEND ALL THEIR time at their clubs," Gino said as they made their way to Sixth Avenue to catch the elevated train uptown. "What makes you think we'll find him at home?"

"Because it's morning. These rich boys who don't have anything useful to do spend their nights drinking and their mornings sleeping."

"And you're sure he still lives in his mother's house?"

Looking up Mrs. Peabody's sister in the City Directory had been the easy part of this. "No, but if he doesn't, we can probably get somebody there to tell us where he does live."

The maid who answered the door at the Littlefield house looked confused when Frank asked for Percy Littlefield, but not because she didn't know where he was. "He . . . He don't get up until past noon usually."

Frank gave Gino a smug glance. "I'm afraid you'll have

to wake him. I have some very urgent news for him about one of his friends."

"I don't know," she said, plainly concerned she would get in trouble if she disturbed young Percy.

"He won't thank you for turning us away, I guarantee. He'll want to hear this news immediately," Frank lied.

She looked both of them over with a disapproving eye. She was probably wondering what an Irishman and an Italian wanted with the young master. "I'll ask his valet, but I can't promise he'll come down to see you."

She let them in the front hall and left them standing there. The Littlefield house wasn't large enough to have a receiving room, but the neighborhood was fashionable and the house expensively furnished and well kept. Left alone, Percy would probably run through the family fortune in a few years, but for now, his mother seemed to be in control.

The maid was gone a long time, and she didn't look happy when she finally returned. "Come with me, please," she said, and led them upstairs to a room that had probably been young Percy's father's study. Several overstuffed chairs were grouped around the hearth, and the air smelled faintly of cigar smoke and dust. After another long wait, Percy Littlefield finally made his appearance. He glared at them through red-rimmed eyes, his face chalky white above his hastily donned suit. He hadn't bothered with a necktie and his vest was buttoned crooked, but his shoes seemed to be on the right feet. He'd wet his blond hair and combed it down, but one spot on the side of his head where he had slept on it wrong had refused to be tamed. It was gradually springing back up in defiance.

"Who are you and what do you want?" Percy demanded when he saw them. He was a stocky young man with a florid complexion and obvious bad manners.

Frank introduced himself and Gino. "We need to ask you some questions about Charles Oakes."

"Charles? Is that the friend you were supposed to tell me about?"

"Yes."

"But he's dead, and I already knew that. And what could you possibly want to know about him?"

"Who poisoned him, for one thing."

Percy blinked several times, as if trying to bring Frank and Gino into focus. "What do you mean, *poisoned*?"

"Somebody poisoned him with arsenic. Didn't you wonder why he died so suddenly?"

Percy scratched his head. "It did seem strange."

"Maybe you should sit down, Mr. Littlefield," Frank said.

"I could use a drink first," he said.

"I'll get you one." Gino scrambled to do so, having already located the decanters on a sideboard.

"Help yourself to one, too," Percy said as he sank down unceremoniously into one of the chairs. His manners were improving slightly.

Gino brought him a glass with a generous quantity of amber liquid in it. Percy gratefully took a gulp.

"Who told you Charles was poisoned?" he asked while he waited for the whiskey to do its work.

"The coroner. It seems somebody was giving him arsenic for several days. The first time was the Saturday before he died. Did you see him that day?"

He needed a moment to remember. "I think so. He was at the club."

"What club is that?"

"The Devil's Dogs."

"Interesting name," Frank said.

"It's all in fun," Percy said.

Frank could imagine. "So you saw Charles Oakes that Saturday?"

"Yes, he came in and we were playing cards for a while, but he left early. He felt sick."

"Did you see if he had anything to eat while he was there?"

He gave Frank a withering look. "We don't go to the club to eat."

"I see. I guess he was drinking, though."

"We were all drinking."

"Were you all drinking the same thing?"

"I don't know. The waiters were serving us."

For a second Frank thought maybe a waiter, angry at some slight, could have slipped something into Charles's glass, but then he remembered Charles had gotten his fatal dose at home. No waiter could have given him that one. "Do you know where Charles had been that day, before he came to the club?"

"No, I don't." He rubbed his forehead and took another sip of whiskey. "What are you getting at? Do you think somebody at the club poisoned poor Oakes?"

"It's possible."

"No, it isn't. Everybody liked him, and he owed everybody money. Why would anybody want to kill him?"

A good question, Frank thought. "That's what I'm trying to find out. Can you think of any reason why somebody would want to harm him?"

Percy sipped his whiskey and considered. "He's been . . . I don't know how to say it, but he's seemed kind of sad lately."

"Sad? What do you mean?"

"I said I don't know. He just . . . Well, he was worried, I think."

"About what?"

Percy shrugged, obviously uncomfortable. "Trouble with the wife, seemed like."

"What kind of trouble?" Frank asked, remembering that Charles had recently started sleeping in his dressing room.

"I don't know and I didn't ask. It's none of my business, is it?"

He was right, of course, but Frank couldn't help wishing he'd been nosier. "What did he do that made you think he was sad?"

Percy grinned without humor. "You know what they say about drowning your sorrows."

"So he was drinking heavily?" Frank remembered what Sarah had reported Mrs. Peabody saying about Charles's drinking habits.

"He always drank. We all do. But lately there's been more . . . I guess you'd say *purpose* to it. He even took to carrying a flask, so he could have a nip when we were on our way to the theater or something."

Was his marriage enough to worry him that much? What else could have been bothering him? Frank remembered he'd regretted releasing Ella Adderly from the Asylum. "Was he worried about anything to do with his job at the hospital?"

"I told you, I don't know." Percy's patience was running low.

"Who *would* know?"

Percy glared up at him. "Charles would know. Ask him."

SARAH COULD HARDLY BELIEVE WHAT SHE WAS HEARING. "What do you mean, she's sick?"

"Sick like Sister Rose and Isabel," Mary repeated desperately. "She told me she's been throwing up and having the runs all morning. Please, will you come?"

"Of course," Sarah said, hurrying to fetch her medical bag from Isabel's room.

She almost collided with the Reverend Nicely, who had

obviously heard Mary's plea and was coming out of his daughter's room. "Sister Mary, what's this about Letty?"

"I went to tell some of the ladies that Isabel woke up. Then I stopped by my place to tell Letty, and she's been taken real bad, Reverend Nicely."

"Mrs. Brandt will help her. I'll be praying for her."

Sarah had fetched her bag, and she emerged from Isabel's bedroom. Mary was already out the door. Sarah had to rush to keep up.

Mary was almost running now, elbowing people aside as she made her way down the crowded sidewalks. Sarah was having a difficult time keeping her in sight, even though the people on the sidewalk made way for her, a white woman in a colored neighborhood. She wondered if they were being polite or if they just wanted to get a better look at her.

Only moments after Sarah realized she'd lost Mary in the crowd, the woman came stumbling back, having realized that she had left Sarah too far behind. "Please hurry," Mary begged her. "I'm so sorry I was mean to you. You won't hold that against my girl, will you?"

"Of course not. Tell me, did your daughter say anything about not feeling well before you left her this morning?"

"No, she was fine. She's a good girl, Mrs. Brandt. She don't deserve nothing bad to happen to her."

Sarah figured Isabel was a good girl, too, but she didn't say that. Instead she tried to figure out how on earth Mary's daughter could have been poisoned. Of course, they hadn't heard back from Dr. Wesley yet. Maybe Rose and Daisy hadn't been poisoned either. Maybe this was some malady that was just beginning to strike the city, hitting the poorest and most vulnerable people first. That would be even worse than if someone had poisoned them, because there would be no end to it.

Mary lived on the third floor of a dilapidated tenement

building two blocks away. Even though the landlord obviously hadn't done any work on the building in years, the hallway and stairs were immaculate, swept clean by the residents. Sarah rarely saw that in other neighborhoods. Mary's tiny flat was sparsely furnished, but she'd made every effort she could to make it beautiful. She'd hung curtains over the open shelves in the kitchen where she stored her dishes and made a skirt for the kitchen sink. Back in the windowless bedroom, the bed had been covered by a colorful quilt that had been pushed to the foot in a tangle. A picture of a lovely garden hung on the wall. It looked as if it had been torn from a magazine and carefully framed.

On the bed lay a girl who looked about ten years old. She was curled into a fetal position, and she gazed up at Sarah in absolute terror. A basin full of vomit sat on the floor, and the chamber pot in the corner was overflowing. The stench was overpowering in the small space.

"This here's Mrs. Brandt, Letty," Mary said. "She's one of them nurses. She's come to help you."

The girl shuddered, and Sarah couldn't tell if it was the sickness or fear of her.

"Maybe you could empty these," Sarah suggested to Mary, indicating the basin and the chamber pot.

Mary hastened to do just that, while Sarah pulled out her stethoscope. The girl cringed when Sarah sat down on the edge of the bed.

"I'm not going to hurt you, Letty. Like your mama said, I'm a nurse. Can you tell me when you first felt sick?"

"Answer her," Mary called from the kitchen when the girl did not reply.

"I . . . This morning."

"After your mother left?"

She nodded.

"What did you have for breakfast?"

The girl's eyes widened in renewed terror. "Bread."

"Did you have anything on it? Butter or jam?"

The girl shook her head. Of course not. Butter and jam would be a luxury here. "What did you drink?"

"Water."

"And that's all you had to eat?"

Mary brought the empty basin back, and Sarah saw the anxious glance the girl gave her mother before she said, "Yes, ma'am."

She was lying, but she wasn't going to admit it, at least not in front of her mother.

"I'll be right back," Mary said. "I got to go empty the pot."

Sarah pretended to examine the girl, looking in her throat and listening to her heart until she heard the door close behind Mary and enough time had passed for her to be well out of earshot.

"What did you eat that made you sick, Letty?"

The girl shook her head frantically in denial.

"Letty, somebody poisoned Mrs. Nicely and Isabel. That's what made them sick."

"Poison?"

"Yes, somebody put arsenic in something they ate. It's the poison people use to kill rats."

"Sister Honeywell?"

"Who?"

"Miss Daisy Honeywell. Is she the one who done it?"

"No, she was poisoned, too. We think she brought something with her that had the poison in it. I need to know if you ate some of it, too."

Tears flooded her dark eyes. "I didn't mean to steal it!"

"What was it, Letty? What did you take?"

"I'm going to die now and go to hell!"

"People don't go to hell for stealing one thing," Sarah assured her.

"Reverend Nicely, he say they do!"

"But you can ask forgiveness. Tell me what you took, and I'll forgive you, and God will, too. What was it, Letty?"

"I didn't mean to take it, but it was so pretty."

"What was?"

"The box. I never saw a box so pretty."

"Where was it?"

"On the floor. It got knocked off the table, I guess. Nobody noticed it. They was all looking after Mrs. Nicely and Isabel and Miss Honeywell."

"So nobody saw you take it."

"God saw me." The tears were coursing down her face now. "Oh, miss, I'm so sorry! I never meant to do it. I would've give it back, but then Mrs. Nicely, she died, and I didn't know who to give it back to."

"Where is it?" Sarah asked, looking around frantically.

Before she could speak, Letty started to retch, and Sarah got her the basin just in time. When she was finished, she was too exhausted to speak. Sarah realized she needed to irrigate the girl's stomach immediately if she had any hope at all of helping her. It was probably already too late, but she would do whatever she could.

When Mary returned, she helped, and when they were done, they let Letty sleep. At least Sarah hoped she was only sleeping and not slipping into a coma.

"Do you have any milk?" Sarah asked Mary, knowing it was a silly question.

"No."

Sarah pulled a few coins out of her pocket. "Would you get me some, please?"

Mary didn't reach for the money. Sarah was sure she

couldn't afford to buy it herself, but she wasn't going to take charity either.

"Please," Sarah said. "It's for Letty. It might save her life."

Mary took the coins and hurried out.

While she was gone, Sarah made a quick search of the flat. She found the box wrapped carefully in a shift at the bottom of the wooden crate that held Letty's meager wardrobe. It was heart shaped, no more than six inches across, and decorated with rows of lace and ribbon surrounding a small, perfect artificial rose in the very center. Just the right size to have fit easily into Daisy's carpetbag, too. It had probably been a Valentine's gift to someone, months earlier. It was empty now, but it had once held candy, chocolates probably.

Chocolates someone had undoubtedly laced with arsenic.

Daisy must have been so delighted to receive it from her killer. She'd probably never owned anything half as beautiful, nor would she have ever received a gift of chocolate candy either. She'd wanted to share her good fortune with people who had shown her kindness and befriended her in this unfriendly city. The tragedy of it all broke Sarah's heart, but it also infuriated her. Whoever had committed this horrible crime must be punished.

Sarah stuck the box in her medical bag so Mary wouldn't see it. Letty would probably rather die than have her mother know she was a thief. Sarah might not be able to save her life, but she could keep her secret.

Now they'd need to find out who had owned this box, who had received it as a gift, or who had found it discarded someplace and ultimately given it to Daisy. Sarah was sure of at least one thing, however. That person lived in Charles Oakes's house.

When Mary returned with the milk, Sarah roused Letty so she could drink some. She managed quite a bit, and when her mother left the room for a moment, Sarah whispered, "How many candies did you eat?"

The girl's eyes widened in shock.

"I found the box. It had candy in it, didn't it?"

Letty nodded.

"How many of them were left? How many did you eat?"

She held up one finger.

Sarah sighed with relief. She could imagine the scene around the Nicelys' kitchen table. Daisy so happy to share the treat with them and urging them to eat as many as they liked. But they'd saved the last one for the Reverend Nicely. So if two or three was a fatal dose, then perhaps only one would not be for Letty.

"Where are we going now?" Gino asked, matching Frank stride for stride as he hurried away from Percy Littleton's house.

"Back to the Oakes house."

"To find that flask?"

"Right."

Frank decided they would get there faster if they walked. Traffic clogging the city streets could grind to a standstill for hours.

"It explains everything, doesn't it?" Gino asked after they'd dodged a carriage to cross the street.

"Mostly. We've been trying to figure out how he could've gotten poisoned when he was away from the house and inside it both. If the killer put arsenic in his flask, then he probably drank it for the first time sometime on Saturday."

"According to Wesley, it takes a while for the arsenic to start working, so he wouldn't have realized it was the liquor in the flask that made him sick."

"And he was at his club, drinking other liquor when he started feeling bad," Frank said.

"Why did he get better on Sunday, though?"

"Maybe he didn't drink anything that day. He'd been sick the day before, so maybe he was being careful."

"Did you ever know a drunk to be careful?"

"We don't know he was a drunk."

Gino gave him a look.

"We know he drank a lot, especially lately," Frank conceded. "So maybe he did drink that day, but he wouldn't need his flask if he was at home. He'd drink his father's liquor."

"And the killer would have the chance to refill his flask with more poison."

"He felt better by Monday, so he went out again."

"With his refilled flask," Gino said.

"And he poisoned himself all over again."

"But how did he get the final dose that evening? If he wanted a drink, he could've used his father's liquor like he did the day before."

Frank considered. "It's still possible Daisy poisoned him. If she was the one, she could've put it in the milk the way she put it in his flask."

"But who killed her?"

"Someone who wanted revenge on her for killing Charles."

"But why not just have her arrested?"

"Mrs. Brandt thinks Jenny Oakes might not want it to come out that Daisy was her sister."

"How could they be sisters? Jenny's white and Daisy is colored. I mean, she had light skin, but . . ."

Frank explained it.

"Oh. I guess things aren't so different in the North, are they? I mean, rich men get their maids with child sometimes, too."

"Yes, and neither the Northerners or the Southerners have to claim the children."

"So Mrs. Oakes and Daisy were sisters, and Daisy might've killed Charles to make her suffer, and Mrs. Oakes might've killed Daisy to get revenge. Who else could've done it?"

"Anybody in the house could've put arsenic in the flask. Let's not forget his wife wasn't too happy about being married to him, and maybe somebody else we haven't thought of wanted him dead. The question is, who could've given it to him the night he died?" Frank asked.

They walked for a while in silence while they considered.

At last Gino said, "Maybe Daisy or the other maid were lying about who carried the milk up to him. Daisy was lying about something, I'm sure."

"We know Charles was probably too sick to get up and get anything for himself, so somebody had to bring it to him."

"Where were his clothes?" Gino asked, startling Frank.

"What do you mean?"

"I mean he'd come home wearing the clothes he'd worn all day with the flask in the pocket. We're pretty sure he drank out of it that day because he'd gotten sick again, so he must've been carrying it with him."

"And they took him to one of the spare bedrooms when he got sick, not his own room."

"They probably undressed him, and the flask was in his pocket."

"So if they left his clothes in the room, his flask would've been handy if he wanted a drink," Frank concluded.

"From what we've heard, he always wanted a drink, too. So Daisy might've used the poisoned whiskey in the flask and mixed it into the milk. But why wouldn't she say so when I asked if he'd had anything besides the milk?"

"Maybe because she put the arsenic in the flask in the first place," Frank said. "Or if she wasn't the killer, maybe because she didn't want us to think he was a drunk or something."

"Or maybe she'd figured out the poison was in the flask, and she thought she'd be blamed for killing him even though she didn't. But if she didn't poison him, the killer would be afraid that sooner or later she'd tell someone about the flask, and maybe it would come back to him."

"Or her," Frank said. "Poison is a woman's weapon, and there aren't a lot of men living in that house."

"And then we're back to why would somebody kill him? It looks like Daisy is the only one who had a reason."

"A reason that we know of. First we need to find the flask and have Wesley test it to see if it had arsenic in it."

"We could also find out if anybody knows what he was sad about and if it was more than just his marriage."

Frank didn't think Wesley had a test for that.

Gerald Oakes had them brought up to the library. "Have you found out anything?" he asked by way of a greeting as soon as the maid closed the door behind them.

"We found out a lot of things, but nothing that makes much sense yet. Did Charles have a flask?"

"A flask? Of course he did. Every man has a flask."

Frank didn't bother to mention that he didn't have one. "Do you know where it is?"

"I have no idea. Why do you want to know?"

"Because we think that's where the killer put the poison."

"Dear God. I'll get Zeller in here. He'll know."

He rang for the maid, and she went to fetch Zeller.

"What makes you think the poison was in his flask?" Oakes asked.

Frank told him their theory.

"That explains a lot, I guess, but who would've done it?"

"And who would've wanted to kill Daisy?" Frank asked.

"You can't think the two are connected."

"Why wouldn't they be?" Frank asked.

Oakes had no answer for that. A knock on the door announced Zeller's arrival. He came in, moving very slowly. His face was drawn, and he looked as if he hadn't slept much lately. "You sent for me, sir?"

"Yes, Mr. Malloy has some questions for you," Oakes told him.

"Are you feeling all right, Zeller?" Frank asked.

"I'm a little peaked today, sir."

"Since when?"

"Since sometime in the night. I'll be all right."

Frank had a horrifying thought. "Did you drink out of Charles's flask, by any chance?"

Zeller's face lost whatever little color it had. "Of course not."

"We think the killer put the arsenic that killed him in the flask," Frank told him, watching him closely. "Maybe you found the flask when you were going through his things and thought a little nip would do you good."

"I . . . I wouldn't . . ." he tried.

"Zeller, tell them the truth," Oakes said. "Don't die because you're embarrassed!"

"There was only a swallow left," he said, his desperate gaze darting between Oakes and Frank. "Am I poisoned?"

"We should get a doctor here to look at you," Frank said. "Gino—"

"I'll get Wesley," Gino said, already heading for the door.

"Who's Wesley?" Gerald asked.

"He's . . . an expert on arsenic poisoning," Frank hedged, not wanting to frighten them with the word *coroner*. "You might want to send for your own doctor in case Wesley isn't around," Frank told Oakes. "Zeller, where is the flask now?"

"I put it away, in Mr. Charles's dressing room with the rest of his things."

"Please tell me you didn't wash it out."

"No, I—"

"Good. Take me there."

Zeller hesitated. "Mrs. Charles is in her room," he said to Oakes.

"She'll just have to go out for a few minutes while Mr. Malloy does his work." Oakes turned to Frank. "Hannah is packing. When she heard that Daisy had died, she . . . Well, it frightened her, I guess. She's moving back to her parents' house."

From his tone, Frank suspected they'd be happy to see the last of her. Frank couldn't blame them.

"This way, sir," Zeller said.

The butler moved carefully, probably trying not to be sick, and he struggled on the stairs, having to pause more than once to rest for a moment.

"Where is your room, Zeller?" Frank asked when they'd reached the next floor.

"In the servants' hall, sir."

"Upstairs?"

"Yes."

"After we're finished, you'd better go on up and get in bed until the doctor gets here."

Zeller didn't reply. They reached a doorway where the open door revealed a bedroom. A large trunk sat in the middle of the floor. For some reason, Frank had expected to see Hannah packing, but instead, she was lounging in a chair giving orders as her maid actually did the work.

"No, not that old rag. I can't wear colors for a year, and by then it'll be hopelessly out of fashion. And not that. It has a stain. Yes, the rose is fine. Careful, don't crease it!" she cried shrilly.

Zeller tapped on the doorjamb. "Excuse me, Mrs. Charles, but Mr. Malloy and I need to get something from Mr. Charles's dressing room."

"Can't you see I'm busy?" she snapped. "You can come back later, when I'm finished."

"We can't wait," Frank said.

Hannah jumped to her feet. "Zeller, I can't believe you've brought a strange man to my bedchamber. Does Mr. Gerald know about this?"

"He sent us, ma'am."

"He did, did he? How dare he? I suppose since I'm leaving, he's decided my feelings don't matter anymore. Well, he'll hear about this from me. You can be sure of that!" She headed purposefully toward the doorway where Zeller and Frank stood. For one second, Frank wondered what she would do if they didn't step aside, but of course they did, and she stormed off down the hallway, probably to give Gerald Oakes a piece of her mind.

The maid and Zeller exchanged an exasperated look, and he led Frank into the lavishly furnished bedroom and through a door into another room about half the size. Shelves and drawers and cabinets covered one wall, where Charles Oakes's clothes and other belongings were stored. A narrow bed sat along the opposite wall. Not a cheerful place for the heir to spend his nights, particularly when his bride slept in luxury only a few feet away. But maybe moving in here had been his idea. Frank could easily imagine wanting to be as far away from Hannah Oakes as possible.

Zeller pulled open one of the drawers and removed a silver flask.

"That's odd," he said, frowning.

"What's odd?"

"These spots."

Frank had to look closely to see what he meant. Faint white spots dotted the silver surface.

"They're water spots. I would never have put it away without wiping it dry and polishing it."

"I thought you said you didn't wash it out."

"I didn't, although perhaps I should have."

He stared at it for a long moment, as if trying to remember something. Then he tried to unscrew the top. For a moment, Frank was fascinated. He'd never seen a flask with a screw-on top. It must have been very expensive. Then he realized Zeller was having trouble.

"Is something wrong?"

"The top is screwed on crooked. There," he said, finally working it free. "The threads are very fine, so it's tricky, but I would never have done that either." He lifted the flask to his nose and sniffed. Then he held it out for Frank to sniff.

"Soap?"

Zeller nodded. "Someone washed it out."

13

SARAH HAD NEVER BEEN SO TORN ABOUT WHAT HER REAL duty must be. She needed to stay with Letty and make sure she was going to be all right. She needed to check on Isabel and see how she was doing. And she needed to find Malloy and tell him what she'd learned so no one else got poisoned.

Of course, Letty's poisoning was an accident, as was Isabel's, and Isabel's mother's as well. Surely, no one else would become an accidental victim, but if Charles's killer felt it necessary to kill Daisy, who knew what other horrors he might consider necessary. Or she. Sarah didn't want to think a woman had caused all this, but the evidence was mounting. Could Jenny Oakes really have destroyed so many people just to protect her secret? It wasn't as if she was in any way responsible for having a Negro half sister. Yes, it would be delicious gossip for a while, but Jenny didn't strike Sarah as the kind of person who would care so very much about what people said.

"Are you going to tell my mama?" Letty asked Sarah after she'd succeeded in getting the girl to drink some broth. Mary had gone to report to the Reverend Nicely that Letty was feeling much better.

"I'm not going to tell anyone," Sarah said. "The only person you harmed was yourself."

"I thought the box was empty or I never would've taken it," she said, tears welling again. "I took it and ran all the way home and hid it. I didn't look at it again until this morning, and when I saw the candy, I . . . It looked so delicious. And it *was* delicious. I never tasted chocolate before."

"I hope you taste it again someday without the bad effects. Tell me, what was inside the chocolate?"

"Some kind of white cream. It was so sweet, it melted on my tongue."

"Did it look like the candy had been tampered with?"

Letty's puzzled frown told her the girl had no idea what she was talking about. Letty had probably never seen a chocolate candy, at least not up close, so how would she know what they were supposed to look like and how it would look if someone had tampered with it? "Never mind. The important thing is I don't think you got enough of the poison to truly harm you." Sarah prayed she was right about that, at least.

"And I'll never steal anything again so long as I live," Letty promised fervently.

When Mary came back, the Reverend Nicely was with her.

"Several ladies came to help when they heard Letty had gotten sick, too, so I felt I could leave Isabel for a few minutes to pray over you, young lady," he told the girl.

Letty started to cry again, probably thinking she didn't deserve that, being a thief, but her mother hugged her for a while, until she stopped. Then the Reverend Nicely sat with Letty for a few minutes and prayed over her. When he was finished, he and Mary took Sarah out into the hall where Letty couldn't overhear them.

"Reverend Nicely told me you think Sister Rose and Sister Daisy were poisoned," Mary said, horrified at the thought. "Do you think Letty was, too?"

"It's possible," Sarah said, having already decided what she would say to them. "We think Daisy may have brought something with her from the house where she worked that had the poison in it. I asked Letty if she'd eaten anything at your house, Reverend Nicely, but if she did, she doesn't remember. She may have picked up something without thinking, but I suspect she probably just got sick the way children do, and it doesn't have anything to do with your family."

"Then you don't think she's going to die?" Mary asked.

"She's already getting better," Sarah said. "It was probably just a case of summer complaint."

"Thank heaven," Mary said, making it a prayer.

"Praise God," the Reverend Nicely said.

"If Letty's going to be fine, you should go back to Isabel, Mrs. Brandt," Mary said. "I thank you for looking after my Letty."

"I was glad to do it." Sarah gave her instructions for caring for Letty. "Send for me if she gets bad again, though," she added, giving Mary her card. This time she took it eagerly.

The Reverend Nicely walked Sarah back to his church. "Isabel woke up again," he told her. "She was asking for her Mama. I don't know what to tell her." He pulled out a handkerchief and wiped his eyes.

"You're right not to tell her until she's stronger."

"Who could have done this?" he asked. "And why? What is more important than a human life?"

"Nothing, to a normal person. Whoever did this isn't normal, though. I promise you we'll find out who did it."

She wished she could promise the killer would be punished, too, but that would depend on who it was and who wanted to protect that person. But no matter what happened, they would never be able to bring back the people who had died.

Sᴀʀᴀʜ ᴡᴀꜱ ᴊᴜꜱᴛ ᴛʜɪɴᴋɪɴɢ ᴛʜᴀᴛ ꜱʜᴇ'ᴅ ᴅᴏɴᴇ ᴀʟʟ ꜱʜᴇ could for Isabel Nicely, who did seem to be doing better now. She was taking nourishment and seemed aware when she was awake. All they could do now was wait to see if the arsenic had caused her any permanent damage. She really hated to leave the Reverend Nicely alone, but the ladies from his church seemed more than capable of looking after them, and they'd brought more food than he could hope to eat in a week.

When Gino Donatelli appeared at the door, she knew she must go.

"What is it?" she asked, alarmed to think he had come all this way to find her.

"The butler this time, but it was an accident," he said softly so no one else would overhear. "He's going to be all right, but Mr. Malloy wanted me to find you. He wants you there when he questions Mrs. Oakes."

Sarah gathered her things and took her leave of the Reverend Nicely and the ladies who were helping. She accepted his thanks and urged him to send for her again if he needed her.

Gino carried her bag as they made their way through the crowded streets to the elevated train station. As they walked, he told her how Zeller had gotten himself poisoned.

"I went and got Dr. Wesley to come take a look at Zeller.

He told us he'd checked Daisy's and Mrs. Nicely's bodies, and they both had arsenic in their stomachs."

"I know how they got it, too," Sarah said and told him about the candy box and how Letty had taken it that first day.

"Is the little girl going to be all right?"

"I hope so. She only had one piece of the candy. That's all that was left in the box. If she was telling the truth about that, then she didn't get much of the poison, and she may recover completely."

"Who do you think did this, Mrs. Brandt?"

"Someone in the Oakes household, and it must be a female," Sarah said. "We know it wasn't Mr. Oakes, because he's the one who asked us to find out who killed his son. The only other man left in that house is Zeller, and I can't imagine he'd poison himself just to throw off suspicion."

"Besides, he was pretty fond of Daisy."

"That might not matter much if he was trying to protect himself from discovery."

"He didn't have a reason to kill Charles Oakes, though, or none that we know of," Gino reminded her.

"But *nobody* had a reason to kill Charles Oakes," Sarah reminded him right back. "Did you find out anything from Percy Littleton?"

Gino related their conversation with the young man.

"If Charles was sad enough for his friends to notice, it must have been something serious," Sarah said. "And Percy thought it had something to do with his wife?"

"That's what he thought, but I don't think he was sure. We do know they were having trouble, though."

"But we don't know why. Maybe that would give us a clue. We need to talk to Hannah."

"We'll have to hurry then, because she's moving out."

"What do you mean, moving out?"

"When she heard Daisy had died, she told Mr. Oakes she was too scared to stay there anymore, so she's going back to live with her parents."

"I guess I can't blame her, but you're right, we need to talk with her before she leaves. I'm guessing she'll never agree to see us once she's with her parents."

When they reached the El station, they climbed the long stairway up to the platform along the tracks that ran two stories above the street. While they waited for the train, Gino said, "Mrs. Brandt, do you think a woman could really kill her own son?"

"People do terrible things, Gino, and their reasons hardly ever make sense to other people."

AFTER SPENDING SO MUCH TIME IN THE OAKES HOUSE, Frank was starting to understand why Gerald and Charles drank so much. He needed all his willpower not to take Sarah in his arms when she finally came through the parlor door with Gino. He couldn't remember ever being quite this glad to see her.

"How is Zeller doing?" she asked.

"Wesley said he'll probably be fine, although Gerald Oakes called his own doctor, and he's still clucking around upstairs. I think he just wants the family to think he's being thorough. How is the Nicely girl doing?"

Sarah told him and explained what had happened with Letty. She pulled the candy box out of her medical bag.

"No wonder she took it," Gino said. "I never saw anything so fancy."

"I doubt anybody in that neighborhood ever did either," Sarah said, "which makes the trick that much more cruel. Is Hannah still here?"

"Yes. I asked Gerald to keep her here as long as he could, so he told her she can't have the carriage until tomorrow."

The parlor door opened, and Jenny Oakes came in. The two men jumped to their feet and so did Sarah. "They told me you'd arrived, Sarah. I've been worried about the minister's daughter. I hope she's better." Her face was pinched and pale, and dark circles shadowed her eyes.

"She seems to be, but we can't be sure for several more days, at least."

"That poor girl. That poor family. I hope you told them they could call on us if they need anything. They were very kind to Daisy, I understand."

"I believe Mr. Malloy told them you'd pay for Mrs. Nicely's funeral," Sarah said.

"Of course," she agreed without batting an eye. "It's the least we can do for them. What's that?" she asked, noticing the heart-shaped box Sarah still held.

Malloy gave Sarah a questioning look, and she nodded. They needed to know the truth. Jenny Oakes might never admit anything at all, but she certainly wouldn't say anything incriminating in front of Malloy and Gino.

"Gino," he said. "Let's leave these ladies alone so they can talk."

When the men were gone, Jenny gave her an arch look. "Should I be worried that they've left us alone?"

"Not at all. I just need to ask you about something. Please, sit down."

Jenny came over and joined her on the sofa, her expression wary. "I guess this has something to do with that candy box."

"Have you ever seen it before?"

"That particular box? I couldn't say. I've seen boxes like it."

"Where?"

"Gerald gave me one for Valentine's Day, I think. They're very fashionable now."

"Was it like this one?"

"Yes, very like this one. They're all like that, done up with ribbons and lace. Are you asking me if this is exactly like the one he gave me?"

"Yes, I am."

"Then I have no idea. I'd have to see the two together."

"Do you still have yours?"

"I'm sure I do. One doesn't just discard something so beautiful."

"May I see it?"

"Why? What's this all about?"

"Let me see the candy box, and I'll tell you."

She wasn't acting like a woman who had poisoned her son and her sister, Sarah thought as Jenny rose and pulled the bell cord for the maid. When the girl came, Jenny instructed her where to find the box.

When Jenny sat down again, she looked at the box and then at Sarah. "Can't you at least tell me if this has something to do with Charles's death?"

"Not Charles's, but it might have something to do with Daisy's."

Jenny's eyes widened. "Someone gave her poisoned candy?"

"And she shared it with Mrs. Nicely and her daughter."

Sarah waited, watching her closely, but her face was like a mask, betraying nothing. Was she surprised because she hadn't known about the candy or because Sarah had figured it out? But would Jenny have chosen to poison Daisy in a way that was bound to lead right back to her own door? Daisy would never have been able to buy a box of candy like that, nor would she have been likely to receive it as a gift from anyone except the people in this house.

The minutes ticked by and Jenny sat perfectly still, as if bracing herself for a blow. Finally, the maid tapped on the door and when she entered, she carried a heart-shaped box all done up with red and white lace and ribbons.

"Is this what you were looking for, Mrs. Gerald?" the girl asked.

"Yes, thank you, Patsy." She waited until the maid had gone, then put the box next to the one Sarah still held. They weren't identical, but close enough. Then she said, "Did Charles get poisoned candy, too?"

"We think it was in his flask."

She stiffened slightly. "Of course. That makes perfect sense." She drew a deep breath. For a second she looked as if she might weep, but she blinked it away. She certainly wasn't acting like a killer.

"Mrs. Oakes, Charles's friends mentioned that he seemed sad about something, or troubled, maybe. Do you know what was bothering him?"

"No," she said, and Sarah was sure she was lying. She rose. "I hope you'll excuse me, Sarah. I'm not feeling well."

For a moment, Sarah wondered if she'd been poisoned as well, but then she realized Jenny was simply making a polite excuse to leave an uncomfortable conversation.

"I'd like to speak with Hannah, if I may."

"That's Hannah's decision. Do you know she's leaving us?"

"Yes. It . . . it must be difficult for her here."

"It's difficult having her here. I'll be glad to see her gone." Jenny went to the door. When she opened it, she saw Patsy still waiting outside. "Mrs. Brandt would like to see Mrs. Charles, please. I'll be in my room."

Sarah frowned. Could she have been wrong? They'd been so sure that Daisy had killed Charles for revenge and Jenny had avenged his death by killing her. Now she wasn't sure of anything. She'd also been sure the candy box was Jenny's, but now . . .

Malloy came in and closed the door behind him. "What did she say?"

"The candy box wasn't hers. Gerald gave her one almost like it for Valentine's Day, and she showed it to me."

"I know. I saw the maid bringing it in. I was positive Jenny had killed Daisy in revenge for killing Charles, but now . . ."

"I know. Maybe we've been looking at the wrong person. Charles and Hannah weren't happily married. Even his friends noticed how unhappy he was."

"And his flask would have been in his bedroom, where Hannah would've had access to it. What about the candy box?"

"If Gerald gave Jenny one, maybe Charles gave Hannah one, too."

The parlor door opened, and Hannah stepped in. "I don't know why you want to see me. I already told you everything I know about what happened to Charles, and I certainly don't know what happened to that colored woman."

Sarah smiled as graciously as she could manage. "Thank you for coming. I know you don't know anything about the deaths, but would you mind answering a few questions about Charles himself? You're the one who knew him best, after all."

She preened a little at that. "Well, I suppose I did."

"I'd be very grateful," Sarah said.

Hannah gave Malloy a sharp glance that made him back up a step. "If you'll excuse me," he said and made a hasty exit.

"Please, come sit here by me." Sarah patted the sofa.

Hannah strolled over, as if it were her own idea, and took her seat. "Oh, how pretty," she said, noticing the candy box in Sarah's lap. "Is it your birthday or something?"

"This? No, it's . . . I thought it might be yours."

"No, I don't think so. Oh, wait, I think Charles gave me one like that on Valentine's Day, but that was months ago."

"Didn't you keep it?"

"Whatever for? Once the candy was gone, what good is it?"

What good, indeed? Sarah studied Hannah's lovely face and saw no indication she was lying or even feeling the least bit guilty.

"Charles's friends said that he was very upset lately."

"Upset about what?"

"They thought he was upset because he was having trouble with his marriage."

She gave a ladylike snort. "I don't know what he would have to be upset about."

"Maybe the fact that he was sleeping in his dressing room," Sarah tried.

This shocked her, as Sarah had intended. "Who told you that?"

"Everyone," she said, only exaggerating a little. "Were you quarreling?"

"Not at all. There was nothing to quarrel about."

"Then why was he sleeping in the dressing room?"

"Not that it's any of your business, but the fact is that I had decided I didn't want to have any children."

"Oh," was all Sarah could manage.

"Don't look at me like that. A woman should be able to decide whether she wants to have children or not, shouldn't she?"

In a perfect world, she should, Sarah supposed, but they didn't live in a perfect world. "No wonder Charles was upset."

"Don't take his part."

"I wasn't. I just—"

"Don't lie to me. I can see it on your face. You think I'm

a terrible wife, not fulfilling my wifely duties and driving my husband from the marriage bed."

Plainly, someone had already expressed these sentiments to her. "I don't—"

"But what can a female do when she's been tricked and cheated? My whole life was ruined."

"Did Charles cheat on you?"

"Don't be ridiculous. Of course he didn't cheat *on* me. I told you, he cheated me and tricked me. He'd misrepresented himself and there was nothing I could do about it."

Sarah tried to remember what she knew about Hannah and what she'd been unhappy about. "It must have been a disappointment to discover that the Oakes family wasn't as wealthy as you'd thought."

"It was horrible, but I could have lived with that. My father would have helped us. He was already helping us, so I don't know why Charles had to get that awful job at that awful hospital with the crazy people."

"So it wasn't money you were angry about?"

She lifted her chin. "What kind of a woman do you take me for?"

Sarah wondered if she'd practiced that expression in front of a mirror. "I'm sorry. I should have known better."

"Yes, you should. A lady never discusses money."

A lady wasn't supposed to denigrate her husband in public either, but that wasn't stopping Hannah. "I'm a midwife," she said in case Hannah had forgotten. "I can certainly understand that you might be afraid of childbirth."

"I'm not afraid of anything," she snapped.

"But you said you didn't want to have children . . ."

"I didn't want to have *Charles's* children!"

"Then you're not afraid?"

"I told you, I'm not afraid of anything! I'd have a dozen children by a white man!"

Sarah stared at her for a moment in stunned silence. Surely, she'd misheard her. "Did you say . . . ?"

But Hannah had already clapped a hand over her mouth, because she really had said "white man."

"Charles was a white man," Sarah said.

"Of course he was," Hannah said too quickly. "I don't know what made me say that. I've just been so upset since he died, I don't know what I'm saying half the time."

Sarah's mind was racing. Could Hannah have heard the story of Daisy and Jenny and misunderstood? "Daisy and Jenny were half sisters, but Jenny was white. Their father owned the plantation, and Daisy's mother was a slave."

"Is that what they told you? Oh, of course it is. That's the story she wanted people to believe, but it's not true. They tricked me, and then I was trapped. I couldn't even get a divorce because divorced women aren't accepted in society. What was I supposed to do?"

"What are you talking about?" Sarah asked, hopelessly confused.

"I'm talking about how Jenny Oakes lied about where she came from. Oh, her father did own the plantation, and she and Daisy were sisters, but not because they had the same father. They were sisters because they had the same mother, and she was a slave!"

FRANK HAD SENT GINO HOME. THERE WAS NO USE IN both of them sitting around feeling useless. Gino hadn't wanted to leave until Frank told him he should stop by the house to make sure Maeve was handling the workmen all right. Then he rushed right out.

Now all Frank had to do was wait for Sarah to finish with Hannah so they could decide if she's the one who killed Charles and Daisy. Frank should have considered her more seriously before now. She'd sent her husband to sleep in his dressing room, after all. Although, now that Frank thought about it, that was more of a reason for him to murder her.

This case was one of the most baffling he'd ever worked on, and certainly one of the messiest. He couldn't remember a killer so sloppy that innocent bystanders got killed or at least sickened by accident.

"Mr. Malloy?"

Frank looked up. He hadn't noticed the maid approaching him. "Yes?"

"Mr. Oakes would like to see you in his study."

She led him, although Frank knew perfectly well where Oakes's study was by now. She opened the door for him and closed it behind him.

Gerald Oakes looked like he hadn't moved from his chair all day, but Frank knew that couldn't be true. He'd certainly gotten up at least a dozen times to refill his glass.

"What's going on, Malloy? Patsy tells me my wife has gone to her room to lie down. Don't tell me she's been poisoned, too."

"Not that I know of."

"Should I get the doctor back here for her, do you think?"

"I'm sure she'll let you know if she needs him."

"And what's this about a candy box?"

"I understand you gave your wife one of those fancy, heart-shaped boxes of candy on Valentine's Day."

Gerald frowned, as if he needed to concentrate to remember something as far back as February. Frank realized he must be incredibly drunk, yet he showed no outward signs except for the rosy glow of his cheeks. "What on God's earth does candy have to do with any of this?"

"Mrs. Brandt has discovered that Daisy was poisoned with candy."

"How would they get poison in candy?"

"I don't know that, and the victims ate all of the candy, so we don't have any to look at."

"And you think it was the candy I gave Jenny for Valentine's Day?"

"No, we don't think that."

"I should hope not. Jenny would've died months ago if that was the case."

Frank was starting to wonder if Gerald was drunk or just stupid. "I guess Charles gave Hannah a box of candy, too."

Gerald waved away such a notion. "The boy never thought a breath of it. I got one for her and let him take the credit. Not that it did him much good. She just complained that she didn't like the candy. Nothing is ever good enough for that girl."

"Do you know why they stopped sleeping together?"

Some emotion flickered across Gerald's florid face, but he said, "No idea at all. Probably just a lover's quarrel. They would've been back together in another week or two, I'm sure."

"Too bad they'll never have the chance to make up now."

Gerald didn't respond to that. He didn't even seem to have heard it. "Can I get you a drink?" he asked, getting up to get another one for himself.

"No, thanks."

Watching Gerald fill his glass reminded Frank of Charles and his drinking habits. "Did Charles have a favorite brand of whiskey?"

Gerald looked up in surprise. "I doubt it. He usually drank whatever was here."

"So he did drink from the same decanters that you did?"

"Of course. Why do you ask?"

"Because we think the poison was put into his flask."

Gerald nearly dropped the glass he'd just picked up. "His flask? Are you sure?"

"He was in several different places the day he first got sick, but we couldn't find any other way he could've gotten it without others getting poisoned as well. His friend told us he'd started carrying the flask with him lately and sipping from it when he wasn't in a place where he could get a drink."

"He got the flask for his birthday, less than a month ago." Gerald made his way carefully back to his chair and lowered himself slowly. The hand that raised the glass to his lips was not quite steady, and he wasn't looking at Frank anymore.

"Did you know he'd started drinking pretty heavily?" Frank asked when Gerald made no comment.

"Young men drink."

"Charles's friends said he was unhappy."

This made Gerald angry or at least annoyed him enough that he frowned again. "Who are these friends you keep quoting?"

"Percy Littleton, for one." The only one, Frank thought, but Gerald didn't need to know that.

"Percy Littleton is an idiot. I wouldn't put much stock in anything he had to say."

"Then you don't think Charles was carrying his flask and drinking out of it from time to time?"

Gerald ran a hand over his face. "I can't speak to that. He probably was. Young men carry flasks, and they do drink from them, after all."

Frank waited, giving Gerald a chance to think and possibly say more. Like most people, he grew uncomfortable as the silence stretched.

"My mother gave him that flask," he said at last, tears welling in his eyes. "For God's sake, don't tell her. She'd never be able to bear it."

Frank thought the senior Mrs. Oakes could bear just about anything, but he wasn't going to give an old woman that awful knowledge if he could avoid it.

"Does Jenny know?" Gerald asked after another moment.

Frank figured Sarah would have mentioned it. "I think she might."

"No wonder she took to her bed. I didn't know it would hurt so much."

"What would?"

"Finding out how Charles died. I thought having him die at all was the worst pain I would ever feel, but now, knowing someone did that to him on purpose . . . It was someone close to him, wasn't it?"

"It almost always is," Frank said. "Murder is a very personal crime. Maybe you don't really want to know any more about it."

A tear slid down Gerald's face. "I don't. The very idea terrifies me, but now I have to know. How can I live the rest of my life in this house, suspecting everyone who lives here, and never knowing the truth?"

He was right, of course.

Someone tapped on the door, and the maid stuck her head in. "Mr. Malloy? Mrs. Brandt said to tell you she's ready to leave."

That was odd. Or maybe not. If Sarah had discovered something important, maybe she just didn't want to talk about it in the house where they might be overheard.

"Does this mean you don't know anything yet?" Gerald asked with something that sounded like relief.

"Yes, but as soon as we do, we'll tell you."

Gerald nodded and looked down at his now-empty glass,

as if it might hold some secret. Frank left him, feeling a relief of his own. Whatever Sarah did or didn't find out, they wouldn't have to confront the killer today.

He found her in the foyer, slapping her gloves against her skirt impatiently, and wearing an expression he couldn't read. The maid handed him his hat and held the door for them as they took their leave.

"We need to find a cab," she said before he could ask her anything. "We can't talk about this on the El."

They walked over to Broadway, where Frank hailed a cab, and when they were inside and making their way at a snail's pace down the boulevard, he turned to her and said, "Well?"

"I don't know what to tell you. I mean I know what to tell you, and it's quite a story, but I still don't have any idea who killed Charles and the rest of them, or why."

"Tell me the story, then."

"You know how Jenny was raised on a plantation and how Gerald found her there and married her and sent her home?"

"Yes. Isn't it true?"

"It's true as far as it goes, but . . . According to Hannah, Jenny wasn't who she claimed to be. Hannah said that Jenny's father was the owner of the plantation but that her mother was a slave."

"What? How could that be?"

"I thought at first that she was just confused. Daisy told the Nicelys that she and Jenny were half sisters. I'm not sure exactly what she told them, but they apparently assumed that Jenny was the daughter of the house and Daisy was a child Jenny's father had by a slave woman."

"And that's what we thought, too."

"Because that's what Jenny let us believe, but Hannah told me it isn't true and that Jenny was actually a slave herself."

"That's ridiculous. How could she have passed herself off as a rich white girl? And look at her. She's as white as you are."

"I'm not saying Hannah was right. I'm just telling you what she said, and if a story like that ever got out, even if it wasn't true, imagine the scandal!"

Frank could easily imagine. "But where did she get a story like that?" Knowing what little he did about Hannah, he wouldn't be surprised if she'd made it up herself.

"That's the very worst part. She said Charles told her."

Jenny
⑤ Hanna

14

"AT LEAST THAT WOULD EXPLAIN WHY CHARLES WAS SAD and drinking so much," Maeve said several hours later as they sat around Sarah's kitchen table.

"Yes, it would," Sarah said with a sigh. When they'd arrived back at Malloy's house, they'd had to have supper with the children, and then Maeve had to put Catherine to bed at Sarah's house before they could really talk. Sarah had made Malloy and Gino wait until Maeve came back downstairs before they discussed the case. Then Malloy and Sarah had told Maeve and Gino what they'd learned that day.

"It gives Hannah a good reason to kill Charles, too," Gino said.

"Yes, it does," Sarah said. "She actually mentioned that a divorce would have made her unacceptable in polite society, which is apparently all she cares about in life."

"But Mrs. Belmont is divorced," Maeve said, naming the

former Mrs. William Vanderbilt who was still a leading socialite.

"Mrs. Belmont has more money than God," Malloy said. "She could divorce a dozen husbands and still be acceptable."

"Really?" Gino asked.

"He's exaggerating a bit," Sarah said. "Hannah was probably right about herself, though. A divorced woman who has no family connections and who divorced the son of one of the old Knickerbocker families wouldn't be welcome anywhere."

"Not even if she divorced him because he was the son of a slave?" Maeve asked.

Sarah shook her head. "Probably not even then, because she'd also be tarnished by the scandal the same way the rest of the family was."

"So it was in Hannah's best interest to keep the secret," Malloy said.

"But she wasn't going to have a child by him, which is why she made him sleep in the dressing room," Sarah said.

"And if she couldn't divorce him, and she couldn't stay married to him," Maeve said, "her only choice was to murder him."

They all sat silent for a long moment. Sarah saw her own doubts reflected on their faces. "But she doesn't act like a killer."

"How does a killer act?" Maeve asked.

"Guilty, if you're lucky," Malloy said. "Or nervous or maybe they're too helpful."

"And they usually don't ask questions about what happened because they already know," Gino told her with the gentle patience of a young man trying to impress a girl without making her feel stupid.

"Did Hannah ask questions?" Maeve asked Sarah.

"Yes, she did. Not as many as I expected, but I think she just didn't really care about all the details. Charles was dead and she was a respectable widow, which is all that mattered to her."

"Maybe she's one of those people who don't feel any guilt," Malloy said.

"That might be true. She's not a very nice person," Sarah said. "I'm sure of that, at least, and I have to admit, I'd really like for her to be the killer."

"And if she isn't, who is?" Gino asked no one in particular.

No one in particular had an answer for him.

"I was sure it was Daisy who killed Charles," Malloy said. "Even before we heard the story about her being a slave."

"She still could be the killer," Sarah conceded. "And if the story about Jenny is true, then Daisy had an even better reason to want revenge for being left behind."

"That's right," Maeve said. "If Jenny really had been her mistress, then Daisy wouldn't expect Jenny to take her North, but if Jenny was a slave girl, too, and they'd somehow passed her off as white . . ."

"Exactly," Sarah said. "And Daisy could have been furious all these years and finally gotten her revenge on her sister."

"And then Jenny would have killed her in a revenge of her own," Malloy said.

Sarah sighed. "I told you I didn't think Jenny was the killer, but I could be wrong. It's happened before."

"How did she act that made you think she was innocent, Mrs. Brandt?" Gino asked.

"She asked questions. She . . ."

"What is it?" Malloy asked when she didn't finish her thought.

"I just realized her reactions were a little odd. She didn't act guilty, which is why I didn't think about it before, but now that I look back, she was acting like she . . . like she knew something I didn't."

Malloy frowned. "What does that mean?"

"I'm not sure. She didn't seem upset or angry or even horrified when I told her about the poisoned candy. And I'd swear that she had no idea the candy box she saw me with had any connection at all to the killings until I told her."

"And if she did, why would she admit that she had one like it?" Gino asked.

"Because her husband might've told someone he gave her one," Maeve said, not nearly as kind about contradicting Gino as he'd been about explaining to her. "And if she poisoned the candy, she would never have used her own candy box for it, which is why she admitted she had one and got it to show Mrs. Brandt. That could be her way of proving she had nothing to do with it."

"So you think Jenny used Hannah's candy box?" Sarah asked.

"Wouldn't you?"

"Hannah said she'd thrown her box away," Sarah said.

Maeve shook her head. "If it was as pretty as you say, somebody would've saved it, one of the servants maybe, and Jenny could've found it."

"You're all forgetting one thing, though," Malloy said. "If Jenny killed Daisy, it was because she thought Daisy killed Charles, but if Daisy killed Charles, who washed out his flask to hide the evidence?"

That stumped them all for a few seconds.

"If only you could've found out who bought the arsenic," Maeve said to Gino.

"I can keep looking, but none of the druggists within two miles of the house have any record of it," Gino said with a sigh.

"Zeller must have been the one who washed out the flask," Sarah said, trying to get them back on track. "He just forgot he did it."

"I don't think so," Malloy said. "He was much too disturbed by the water spots."

"What water spots?" Sarah asked.

"Whoever washed the flask didn't dry it properly and polish it up, the way Zeller would have done. It left spots on the silver. That person also put the cap back on crooked, so Zeller could hardly get it off again without ruining the threads."

"It had a screw-on top?" Gino asked, obviously impressed.

"And it was engraved with Charles's monogram. Gerald said his grandmother gave it to him for his birthday."

"That's terrible," Sarah said. "Imagine knowing that someone used your gift to kill your grandson."

"Gerald asked me not to tell her."

"I just hope we can keep it a secret," Sarah said.

"But we still don't know who washed it out," Maeve reminded them.

"The killer," Gino said. "It had to be."

"And it still could have been Daisy," Sarah said. "Charles died Monday evening, and Daisy didn't die until Sunday afternoon, almost a week later."

"That was plenty of time to wash it," Maeve said. "She knew exactly where it was, too, because she'd used it the night Charles died."

Malloy shook his head. "Zeller drank out of it yesterday, and he was sick overnight. So he probably drank what was left of the whiskey that poisoned Charles. He said just a mouthful was left, and he swears he didn't wash it out after he'd drunk out of it either. He figured if someone else wanted to use it sometime, they'd just put whiskey in it again, so why bother?"

"That's a man for you," Maeve said to Sarah, earning a grin.

"But it was probably a woman who washed out the flask," Gino said.

"Yes, either Jenny or Hannah," Sarah agreed. "But why wait until now to do it? The earliest they could have done it was . . . When did Zeller say he'd drunk out of the flask?"

"Yesterday afternoon."

"Where had it been all this time?"

"In the pocket of Charles's jacket, I guess."

"And where had the jacket been?"

"I didn't ask Zeller that."

"That's a man for you," Maeve said again, earning a glare from Malloy and another grin from Sarah.

"We need to find out," Sarah said. "And find out who knew Zeller had found the flask and put it away."

"Hannah would've known," Maeve said. "It was practically in her bedroom, and surely she knew Zeller had been in there. Then the next day she decides to move back into her parents' house. That sounds suspicious to me."

"So we're back to Hannah," Frank said.

"Jenny could have known, too," Gino said. "Maybe Zeller told her he'd put Charles's things away."

"And it's her house. Nobody would've wondered why she was messing with Charles's things," Maeve said. "Maybe she just went looking for it and found it after Zeller put it away."

"So we have to go back there tomorrow and talk to Zeller," Malloy said. "We need to get there early, before Hannah has a chance to get away."

"Yes," Sarah said. "I think if we can get the answers to our questions, we'll know who the killer is."

"What will you do then?" Maeve asked Malloy.

"Just what I promised Gerald Oakes I would do. I'm going

to tell him. Then he'll have to decide if he wants to destroy what's left of his family."

MAEVE AND GINO HAD ARGUED LONG AND HARD FOR the right to accompany Frank and Sarah the next morning, but in the end, they'd stayed behind. Maeve had grudgingly agreed to supervise the workmen again, while Gino headed back out to revisit the druggists he'd already seen and ask them new questions.

Frank and Sarah had ridden the crowed El uptown and been admitted to the Oakes home by a grim-faced Patsy.

"Who would you like to see this morning, sir?" she asked Frank.

"Is something wrong?" he asked.

"Mrs. Charles is leaving us."

"And that makes you sad?" Sarah asked. Frank thought she sounded a little skeptical.

"Oh no, ma'am, but it . . . Well, it reminds me that Mr. Charles is never coming back. That makes me sad to think on."

"Of course it does," Sarah said. "Is she leaving right now?"

"Oh no, ma'am. She's not even up yet. None of the family is. Maybe you could come back later."

"That's all right. We wanted to talk to Zeller first anyway," Frank said. "I assume he's up."

"Yes, sir, although he's still feeling a little poorly."

"I can go up to his room if that's easier for him."

"Oh no, sir, he wouldn't think that was proper at all, I'm sure. I'll take you to the parlor and he'll come down to you."

Frank wandered around the parlor while they waited, examining all the bric-a-brac that covered every square inch of every tabletop in the room. "Where do people get all this stuff?"

Sarah smiled at him from where she sat on the sofa. "They collect it. We'll do that when we're on our honeymoon."

"We will?"

"Yes, Europe is full of things for Americans to buy and ship back home. Really rich Americans have had whole castles dismantled and brought to America."

"That's insane."

Sarah's smile told him she thought so, too, which was one reason why he loved her. "But we'll probably find some furniture we like, and some artwork."

"Can't we buy furniture here?"

"Yes, but it would be American furniture."

Frank wasn't sure he'd know the difference. "Do we really need artwork?"

"I'm afraid we do. Our heirs will cherish it."

"Catherine and Brian?" he asked doubtfully.

"You might be surprised."

He would be very surprised, he thought, gazing up at a piece of artwork hanging on the wall. Why did anyone need a picture of people from ancient Rome in their parlor? People they didn't even know.

A tap on the door told them Zeller had arrived. He stepped into the room and gave them a curt nod before closing the door behind him.

"Good morning, Mrs. Brandt, Mr. Malloy."

"How are you feeling this morning?" Sarah asked

Frank knew it wasn't just a courtesy. The man looked awful, pale and haggard, as if he'd been up all night. Maybe he had.

"I'm better, thank you. Patsy said you wanted to speak with me."

"Yes," Frank said. "Please, sit down."

"Oh, I couldn't do that, sir." He stiffened his spine and

lifted his chin, as if he could defy his illness by force of will. Maybe he could.

"We'll be as quick as we can then," Frank said, glancing at Sarah. She nodded. "Zeller, you said you put Charles's flask away in his dressing room the day before yesterday."

"Yes, sir, that is correct."

"Where had it been in the meantime?"

Zeller frowned. "I'm not sure I understand your question."

"We've figured out that whoever poisoned Charles put the arsenic in his flask. He'd drunk out of it on Monday while he was away from home, which is what made him sick again that day. Daisy was looking after him, and she must have given him another drink from his flask—"

"—or poured some in the milk Patsy had brought up for him," Sarah added.

"And that's what finally killed him."

Zeller flinched at that, and whatever color had remained in his face drained completely away. Frank caught him when he swayed and led him over to a chair.

"This is most improper," he protested when Frank made him sit down.

"It's more proper than falling on your face," Frank said.

Sarah was already up and she poured a small amount of whiskey into a glass for him. He protested that, too, but Sarah pressed it to his lips and made him drink it. Then he tried to rise again, but Frank clapped a hand on his shoulder and held him in place.

He looked up at them with pain-filled eyes. "Daisy didn't do it on purpose. She couldn't have known about the poison."

"We don't think she did," Sarah said, which wasn't exactly the truth.

"Now where was the flask from the night Charles died until you put it away?" Frank asked.

"In Daisy's room."

Frank exchanged a puzzled look with Sarah.

"Why was the flask in her room?" she asked.

"It wasn't. I mean . . . It was in the pocket of Mr. Charles's suit jacket. After she . . . Well, I didn't trust the other girls to go through her things, so I did that myself. I found the jacket there. I couldn't imagine why she'd taken it to her room, but then I noticed one of the buttons was loose. She'd probably taken it to mend, and then . . . Well, I can't know for certain, of course, but I imagine she realized there was no reason to mend it with him dead, so . . . You have to understand how much she loved him."

"*Loved* him?" Frank echoed incredulously.

"He was her nephew, you understand. She'd lost everyone she'd ever loved, so when she found him and he was such a kind young man . . ."

Frank glanced at Sarah and saw his own confusion mirrored on her face.

"Zeller," she said gently, "Was Daisy bitter about the way her sister had left her behind all those years ago?"

"I . . . I'm not sure you'd say she was bitter. They were both so young, and from what Daisy told me, Mrs. Gerald had promised to send for her. Neither one of them knew how hard that would be, with the war and then after, with things so unsettled. Daisy had gone with the Union army, and Mrs. Gerald wouldn't've had any idea where to look for her after the war was over. Then when Daisy came to the city and she had so much trouble finding Mrs. Gerald . . . Well, I think she understood."

"Was Mrs. Gerald happy to see her?" Sarah asked.

"I think she was," Zeller said. "I'll never forget that first day Daisy came here, asking to see Mrs. Oakes. Patsy came to get me, to ask if she really should tell Mrs. Gerald that some colored woman was here claiming to know her from back in Georgia. Mrs. Gerald was surprised, as you can imagine, but when she saw Daisy, she threw her arms around her, and they both started crying. She sent me out right away, but they sat together for hours. When she finally rang for me again, she told me Daisy would be staying and she'd be Mrs. Gerald's personal maid."

Just because Jenny was glad to see Daisy didn't mean Daisy didn't want revenge, Frank thought, but he could see this cleared both women in Sarah's mind. They hadn't gotten all the information they needed from Zeller, though.

"So when you found the suit jacket in Daisy's room, with the flask in the pocket . . . ?"

"Yes. That's when I was feeling so low, thinking about Mr. Charles and now Daisy, and when I found the flask, I thought I'd drink a little toast to them or something."

"You're lucky there was only a little bit left."

Zeller nodded forlornly.

"Zeller," Sarah said, "who knew you'd found Charles's flask?"

"What do you mean, who knew?"

"Someone washed it out after you'd put it back in his dressing room," Frank said. "Probably the same person who put the poison in it in the first place."

"And the killer wouldn't have known where it was from the night Charles died until you found it in Daisy's room," Sarah said, her arched eyebrow silently reminding him that if Daisy had been the killer, she would have washed the flask out at once since she was the only one who knew where it was. "Who knew you'd found it?"

"I . . . I don't know. I don't remember mentioning it to anyone. Who would care?"

"The killer," Frank said. "Was Mrs. Charles in her bedroom when you put the jacket away?"

"No, of course not. I would never have disturbed her."

"And you didn't mention that you'd been in there?"

"No, although . . . I did ask Mr. Gerald if I should see about packing away Mr. Charles's things. I didn't know Mrs. Charles would be leaving, you see, and I thought it might distress her to see them still there."

"What did he say?" Sarah asked.

"He said to wait awhile. He said Mrs. Gerald might want to go through his things, and she wasn't ready to do that just yet."

"Did any of the servants know you'd put the flask back in his room?" Sarah asked. Frank could hear the urgency in her tone. Someone must have known because the killer found out somehow.

"I don't know why they would, but maybe . . . I'll ask them."

Frank was thinking he'd ask them himself when the parlor door opened and Gerald Oakes walked in. He seemed older than he had yesterday, as if his son's death was aging him years with each day that passed.

Zeller jumped to his feet, horrified at being caught sitting in the presence of guests. He started sputtering an apology, but Gerald waved it away. "Do you have any news for me, Malloy?"

"Not yet," Frank said. He didn't add that the more information they collected, the farther from a solution they seemed to get.

"How is your wife doing?" Sarah asked.

"I have no idea. She retired to her room last evening, and I haven't seen her since."

Another rich couple with separate bedrooms. Frank would never understand it.

"I may have upset her by talking about Charles yesterday," Sarah said.

"Jenny isn't usually prone to the vapors, though," Gerald said, walking over to the sideboard where the liquor decanters sat.

Zeller cleared his throat. "If you're finished with me, Mr. Malloy, I have work to do."

"Yes, thank you, Zeller. If you think of anything else, please let me know."

He nodded and hurried out.

"May I get you something? Coffee or tea?" Gerald asked, returning with a glass of amber liquid in his hand.

"No, thank you," Sarah said. Frank caught her frowning her disapproval, although Gerald didn't seem to notice. "I understand Hannah is still here."

"Yes, she ranted and wept, but I told her I wasn't going to get the carriage out for her until this morning. Do you think she's the one who killed Charles?" He looked almost hopeful.

"We don't know yet," Frank said.

"Mr. Oakes," Sarah said, "did you know that Daisy had been a slave on Jenny's plantation?"

"What?" Gerald seemed genuinely confused, and Frank wondered if he could be drunk already.

"Jenny and Daisy grew up on the plantation together." Frank noticed Sarah wasn't mentioning the possibility that they were sisters. "In fact, Daisy had come to New York looking for Jenny. She thought Jenny would take care of her, I think."

Gerald seemed to be giving the matter some thought, and Sarah let him think. "Now that you say it, I do remember Jenny mentioning that one of her father's slaves had shown up looking for a place. And you say that was Daisy? The one who just died?"

Frank remembered Jenny's claim that Gerald couldn't even tell the Negro maids apart. What would he do if he found out Jenny was a Negro, too?

"That's right," Sarah said.

"Do you think that had something to do with Charles's death? But how could it?"

A tap on the door saved them from replying. Zeller stepped in. "I'm sorry to interrupt, sir, but I thought you'd want to know. Mrs. Gerald seems to be missing."

"Jenny?" Gerald asked in that puzzled way that made Frank sure he was drunk. "What do you mean, she's missing?"

"Patsy went into her room to wake her, but she wasn't there, and her bed hasn't been slept in."

"That's impossible. She must be here somewhere."

"Patsy and the other girls have looked all over the house, but they haven't found her."

Frank exchanged a glance with Sarah. Could they have been wrong about her? Could Jenny have killed Daisy after all? Had she run away to escape punishment?

"Could she have gone out somewhere?" Sarah asked.

"Not this early," Zeller said.

"But you said her bed hadn't been slept in. Maybe she went out last night."

"Surely someone would have seen her."

"And where could she have been all night?" Gerald asked with growing alarm.

"Can you take me to her room?" Sarah asked.

"I'll have one of the maids show you up," Zeller said, stepping out to fetch one.

Frank pulled her aside. "What are you thinking?"

"I'll check to see if she took anything with her or packed

a bag, but I can't imagine she'd run away. Even if she did kill Daisy, it was because Daisy had killed Charles, and Gerald would never allow her to be punished for it."

"You're right, but where could she be?" Society matrons didn't just vanish.

Patsy came in and escorted Sarah upstairs. Jenny's bedroom door stood open, and Zeller was right, her bed was still neatly made. She checked the dressing room and found it just as tidy. "Is anything missing?" she asked Patsy.

"What do you mean?"

"A suitcase or some kind of bag? Any of her clothes?"

"Do you think she went on a trip someplace without telling anybody?" she asked doubtfully.

"I'm just trying to think of any possible explanation."

But when Patsy finished her search, she said, "Nothing's missing except the clothes she was wearing yesterday."

"When you say you looked all over the house, did you check the servants' rooms?"

"Why would she be up there?"

"I don't know, but she's not anyplace she's supposed to be, so it won't hurt to look, will it?"

"No, ma'am."

Sarah followed Patsy upstairs and they peered into every one of the rooms. Sarah had harbored some hope that they might find her in Daisy's old room. Maybe she'd gone there to mourn her sister and fallen asleep, but that room stood empty, the bed stripped and the mattress rolled up. Jenny wasn't in any of the other rooms either.

"Did you check with Mrs. Charles? Maybe she knows something."

Patsy's eyes widened in alarm. "We don't disturb Mrs. Charles until she rings for us, ma'am."

So Hannah was truly the harridan she appeared to be.

"I'm not afraid to disturb her. Maybe Mrs. Gerald went to help her pack."

Patsy's horrified expression told Sarah she didn't believe that for a moment, and of course Sarah didn't believe it either, but if Jenny had thought Hannah killed Charles, she might have gone to her room last night and taken some vengeance. Since they had exhausted all the logical explanations for Jenny's disappearance, the real reason must be something they would never have considered.

Patsy took Sarah to the door of Hannah's bedroom, but she stopped there.

"I wouldn't want to be the one to wake her," Patsy whispered.

"Then walk down the hallway, out of sight. I'll go in by myself," Sarah said.

She waited until Patsy was gone. Then she tapped on the door and opened it without waiting for a reply. Hannah was sleeping soundly and hadn't even moved. Sarah made a quick sweep of the room, then checked the two adjoining dressing rooms without success. When Hannah still hadn't stirred, Sarah crept over to make sure she was breathing.

She was. She also looked absolutely lovely with her face relaxed in sleep. No wonder Charles had married her. Sarah fervently hoped she'd marry some wastrel who would make her as miserable as she made other people.

As soon as Sarah closed the door behind her, Patsy reappeared and hurried toward her.

"Is there any place you haven't looked? Anyone you haven't asked besides Mrs. Charles?"

Patsy shrugged. "Old Mrs. Oakes. I didn't want to bother her, and what would Mrs. Gerald be doing in her room anyway?"

What, indeed, but it wouldn't hurt to look. "Which room is it?"

Patsy led her down the hallway to the very end. She apparently wasn't as terrified of the old woman as she was of Hannah. She knocked loudly. "Mrs. Oakes? Are you awake?"

They waited, but heard nothing.

"She's a little hard of hearing," Patsy explained. She tried again, and when she still got no reply, she smiled apologetically and tried the door. "That's funny," she said when it didn't open. "She never locks it."

Sarah stepped up and pounded much more loudly. "Mrs. Oakes, are you in there? Are you all right?"

They still heard nothing, but Sarah had noticed a familiar odor. Just a whiff, probably coming from under the door, but she knew only too well what it meant. "Do you have a key?"

"Mr. Zeller does."

"Go get him."

FRANK PACED THE PARLOR WHILE GERALD SIPPED HIS morning whiskey, as if fortifying himself for some dreadful news. Frank figured he was wise to do so. Whatever they found out this morning was going to be awful.

A tap on the door announced Zeller's return. "Mr. Malloy, that young man—" he began, but Gino pushed his way into the room before he could finish.

"Mr. Malloy, I found out who bought the arsenic. You won't believe it when I tell you!"

"Who was it?" Frank asked.

Gino opened his mouth, but before he could speak, Patsy rushed in behind him. "Mr. Zeller, come quick. We can't rouse Mrs. Oakes and her door is locked."

Zeller gave Oakes a questioning glance, but Gerald waved him on. "Go with her."

Zeller hurried out behind her, and Malloy followed with Gino behind him and Gerald trailing them all.

AFTER PATSY LEFT, SARAH KEPT KNOCKING AND CALLING, until Hannah came stumbling out of her room, still tying the sash of her robe.

"What on earth is going on?" she demanded. "Mrs. Brandt, is that you?"

"I'm sorry I woke you," Sarah lied. "But Mrs. Oakes isn't answering and her door is locked."

"She's nearly deaf," Hannah said. "She probably can't hear you."

Sarah knew the old woman wasn't that deaf. She knocked again, even though she was sure by now that she would receive no response.

After what seemed an hour but was probably only minutes, Patsy and Zeller came running up the stairs and down the hallway, with Malloy and Gino and Gerald Oakes right behind.

Gino? Where had he come from?

Zeller had a ring of keys, and he nearly dropped them as he struggled to find the right one.

"She never locks her door," Gerald was saying. "None of us lock doors. Why would we?"

No one answered him.

Finally, Zeller found the right key, fitted it into the hole, and turned it. "There," he said and stood back, obviously unwilling to be the one to open the door.

Perhaps he smelled it, too, the stench of sickness and death. Sarah reached out and turned the knob and threw the door open.

"What's that smell?" Gerald gasped.

Sarah remembered that he hadn't visited his son's sickroom the night he died. She hadn't either, but she'd been at the Nicelys' home and in Letty's room, so she knew it well.

She stepped into the room. The draperies were drawn so she needed a moment to adjust to the dimness. The old woman lay on the bed, still and white.

Jenny Oakes sat in a chair by the fireplace looking as composed as she always did. She looked up at Sarah, smiled slightly, and said, "She's dead."

15

SARAH HAD TO CHECK, OF COURSE. PRUDENCE OAKES truly was dead. She lay as her daughter-in-law had left her, in her own vomit and waste. A small silver tray sat on her bedside table. On it was a cup and saucer. The cup had once contained something that looked like hot chocolate. Sarah was fairly certain it had also contained arsenic.

For some reason, no one else had entered the room behind her. She saw Gerald Oakes had come to the doorway, his puzzled gaze darting between his mother and his wife, but he couldn't seem to bring himself to cross the threshold. "What happened here, Jenny?" he asked.

"She killed Charles. And Daisy. She confessed it all to me, at the end."

"That's what I was going to tell you," Sarah heard Gino say to Malloy. "It was the druggist on the next street. He told me an old woman bought the arsenic. She gave another name, but he recognized her as Mrs. Oakes."

Sarah pulled the coverlet over Mrs. Oakes's face. Then she went to Jenny and put her arm around her. "Jenny, come with me."

For a moment, Sarah was afraid she wouldn't obey, but then she slowly rose and allowed Sarah to lead her from the room. The crowd that had gathered around the door parted for them to pass.

Gerald reached out to his wife, but Malloy stopped him.

"Let them go," Malloy said. "Mrs. Brandt will sort it out."

Sarah didn't think anyone could sort this out, but she might finally be able to make some sense of it, at least. Jenny went meekly, allowing Sarah to escort her into her bedroom. Sarah closed the door behind them and led Jenny to one of the two slipper chairs that sat beside the cold fireplace.

"Can I get you anything?" Sarah asked.

She shook her head, but Sarah saw a carafe of water on the bedside table and poured her a glass. She drank it gratefully. Sarah noticed her hands were perfectly steady.

"Did you poison her?" Sarah asked.

"Of course. It was pathetically easy. She always has a cup of hot chocolate at bedtime. I'd found the arsenic hidden in her room while she was downstairs at supper, so I mixed it in her regular chocolate. I had Patsy bring it to her so she wouldn't suspect."

"How did you know she'd done it?"

"When you told me about the flask, that's when I knew. And the candy. Gerald gave his mother a box of the candy, too."

"And she'd given Charles the flask for his birthday."

"She'd planned it all, for weeks. She didn't know Daisy

would be the one taking care of Charles, but when she did, she realized she had to kill Daisy, too."

"Do you know why she did it?"

Jenny's head jerked up and her eyes were cold. "No."

"I think you do. I think I do, too. It was because you and Daisy were sisters."

Something flickered in Jenny's eyes, but she never even blinked. Sarah realized she would keep her secret until the day she died.

"Let me tell you what I know," Sarah said. "You and Daisy were sisters, but not the usual way that white children would have a Negro half sibling. Your mother was a slave and your father owned the plantation. When the Union soldiers came, you somehow passed yourself off as the only surviving member of the family. Then you married Gerald and he brought you here, and you kept your secret all these years, until Daisy showed up. You must have been horrified to see her after all those years, the one person who could ruin the life you'd built here."

"No!" she cried, and Sarah watched transfixed as Jenny's icy calm disintegrated. Her eyes filled with tears and she began to tremble. "No, it wasn't like that!"

Jenny wrapped her arms around herself and began to sob. Sarah hurried over to the door and was not surprised to find Patsy waiting outside. "Bring us some tea and some brandy. Hurry!"

Then she returned to Jenny. She knelt beside her chair and put her arms around her, offering her what comfort she could as she wept scalding tears that seemed to come from her very soul.

By the time the tea tray arrived, Jenny was calmer, and Sarah mixed a liberal dose of brandy into the tea she urged her to drink. When the cup was empty, Jenny looked up again, her eyes red-rimmed and still full of pain.

"You don't understand at all. I was happy to see Daisy. So very happy."

Sarah sat down in the other chair and leaned forward to encourage her. "Tell me. Why were you so happy?"

"Because I finally had someone I could talk to. Someone who knew who I was and loved me anyway."

"Who are you, Jenny?"

Her smile was achingly sad. "I'm not Jenny. Jenny was *her* child."

"Whose?"

"The mistress. Jenny was my other sister. Half sister. She was born a month after me, and my mother nursed us both together. We grew up together and did everything together all our lives, up until the day she died."

"You were raised as sisters?" Sarah asked.

"Oh no, not sisters. I was her slave. We slept in the same room, but she slept in the big bed, and I slept in the trundle. And when we got older, I learned how to comb her hair and dress her. That was our life until the war came."

"And then she died?"

"They all died. The master and Jenny's older brother, they died in the war. The mistress and the younger boy, they got sick, and my mother was supposed to take care of them. I sometimes wonder if she really did or if she just let them die, but I never asked. Then Jenny got sick, too. We'd just buried her when we heard the Yankees were coming. We didn't know what they'd do to us, but my mother got the idea that they'd treat us better if one of the family was still there, so she dressed me up in one of Miss Jenny's dresses.

"I'll never forget. 'Lily,' she said. That's my real name, Lily. 'You can talk just like Miss Jenny. I've heard you mimic her a thousand times. You tell them your family is dead and you need their protection.'"

It was, Sarah had to admit, a brilliant plan. "And you fooled them."

"I fooled them all. The captain offered to take me to a neighbor's, but they would've known I wasn't really Jenny, so I asked them to take us with them instead. They already had a whole bunch of runaway slaves following the army, so we joined them. The captain, he didn't like the idea of a white girl going in with all those slaves, though, so he kept me close and found a tent for me to sleep in. I kept my mama and Daisy with me. For protection, I said. Gerald was his lieutenant, and he was assigned to look after me."

"And you fell in love," Sarah said.

"He fell in love. My mama told me what to do to get him to love me. After, I cried and told him I was ruined, and he'd have to marry me. I didn't really think he would, but my mama did, and she was right."

Not exactly the romantic story Sarah's mother had heard. "So you had to leave Daisy and your mother behind."

"My mama was an octoroon, but she couldn't pass for white, and Daisy's father was one of the slaves. She was younger than me, and darker. I didn't want to leave them, but Mama said I should go because this was my only chance. She said I could send for them later."

"So you really were going to do that?"

"I thought so. She must've known I'd never be able to find them, but she couldn't tell me that, or I never would have gone. As it was, it about broke my heart. I'd never been so scared in my life, before or since."

"And you fooled everyone."

"Not everyone. Not completely," she said, her expression hardening again. "I never fooled the old woman. She knew something was wrong, even though she never knew what until Daisy came."

"How did she figure it out?"

"She didn't. Oh, she sensed that I was hiding something all those years, but she always believed Charles wasn't Gerald's son. She thought that was my terrible secret, but she never dared accuse me to my face or to Gerald."

"How on earth did you manage to make people believe you were Jenny?"

"I learned early on to keep my mouth shut and just watch how everyone else behaved. When I made a mistake, I'd just tell them we did things differently in the South."

"If she never figured it out, why did she . . . ?"

"She didn't figure it out, but Charles did. He . . . There was some kind of instant bond between him and Daisy. It was as if he'd been waiting for her all these years, too. She had a son who died young, only fourteen, and she doted on Charles. If only . . ." She squeezed her eyes shut and two tears ran down her face.

Sarah waited for her to regain her composure. "Did Charles tell his grandmother?"

"Oh no, but he did tell Hannah. He never saw her for who she truly is, you see, and he thought she loved him as much as he loved her."

Just as Gerald thought Jenny had loved him, Sarah thought, but she didn't say it.

"He was upset," Jenny continued. "He didn't know how to feel about this knowledge, and he didn't know who to tell. He thought he could trust his wife, so he told her."

"And that's when she refused to share her bed with him anymore," Sarah said.

"She wanted to leave him, but what reason could she give? She was afraid if she revealed our secret, she would be tainted as well. She'd married a Negro, after all, the son of a slave."

"Who told your mother-in-law then?"

"I'm not sure. She may have just pieced it together. Charles and Hannah were quarreling, and she probably offered each of them a sympathetic ear until she'd gotten all the information she needed."

Sarah could just imagine the old woman asking probing questions while sympathizing with the young people. "But why on earth would she poison Charles?"

"Instead of me, you mean?" Jenny asked. "Because she wanted to protect her precious family name, and she knew I was never going to tell anyone my secret. She couldn't trust Charles, though. He'd already told his idiot wife. Hannah wasn't going to speak of it outside the family, of course. She was too afraid of ruining her social standing. But there was no telling who Charles might tell next. One of his friends at his club, perhaps, when he was too drunk to be careful."

"And I understand he was drinking very heavily."

"Like his father," Jenny said bitterly.

"But to kill her own grandson," Sarah said.

"I told you, she never believed he *was* her grandson. Never mind that he looked just like Gerald or that they were too much alike not to be father and son. She also knew how much losing Charles would hurt me, every day for the rest of my life. Killing me, too, would be a mercy, and she had no mercy."

"And Daisy?"

"She was merely protecting herself. Daisy might have figured out that the poison was in the flask and told someone. Besides, she couldn't trust Daisy not to tell anyone about us either. With Daisy dead, she thought she had eliminated everyone who might reveal my secret."

"And killing Daisy was another way to hurt you."

Jenny smiled mirthlessly. "That would never have occurred to her. She could never have understood that I loved a slave woman. She probably believed killing Daisy was no different than killing a dog or a cat."

"Do you know how she did it? I mean, we think she put the poison into some candy, but—"

"Oh, she thought that was so clever. She could have bought a fancy candy box, but she wasn't going to waste that on a darkie, she told me. Oh no, she bought some cheap candy and cut it open and mixed the cream filling with arsenic, and then stuck the pieces back together and put them in the empty box. It wasn't neatly done, but she was sure someone like Daisy wouldn't know the difference, and of course she didn't."

Sarah found she had no more questions, and she was glad of it. The answers were too painful to hear.

"What are you going to do with me now?" Jenny asked.

"We aren't going to do anything. We aren't the police. Your husband hired Malloy to find out who killed Charles. It's up to him to decide what he wants to do with the information."

"I wonder what he'll do with me when he finds out I was a slave. He already knows I killed his mother."

"He knows you killed his mother, and he knows you did it because she killed Charles, but no one is going to tell him your secret unless you decide to tell him yourself."

"Are you serious?"

"Of course I am. Right now, I'm the only one who knows for sure, so I can promise you that."

"Hannah knows."

"Then be sure she understands that you have no intention of ruining her reputation either. She'll keep your secret to protect herself."

Jenny leaned her head back against the chair and closed her eyes. Sarah realized she must have sat up all night watching her mother-in-law dying and making sure she couldn't call for help. Sarah wondered how she herself would have reacted if she found out someone had murdered her child.

She didn't think she could have done what Jenny had, but she could also understand why Jenny had done it.

"Would you like to rest now?" Sarah asked.

"I need to speak with Gerald. I need to tell him what she did."

Sarah nodded and stepped out into the empty hallway. She found Malloy and Gino downstairs in the parlor with Gerald. Gerald jumped to his feet when he saw her.

"How is she?"

"She's very upset, as you can imagine, but she'd like to speak with you."

Gerald hesitated. Then he glanced at Malloy, as if seeking approval. Malloy nodded and Gerald hurried out.

Sarah closed the door behind him.

"Did the old woman really kill them all?" Gino asked.

"Yes, just like we thought. She put the arsenic in Charles's flask."

"The one she gave him," Malloy said grimly.

"Yes. Jenny thinks she planned it that way. I guess everyone knows he drank too much, and if he had a fancy flask, he was bound to carry it around and use it from time to time."

"What about the candy?" Malloy asked.

"Gerald had given his mother a box of Valentine candy, too, so she used the empty box. Mrs. Oakes bought some chocolates and cut them open and mixed the arsenic with the filling. She thought Daisy might figure out that the poison was in the flask and guess she was behind it."

"But why did she kill Charles in the first place?" Gino asked.

What could she tell him that would make sense? "After Daisy came, Charles figured out that she and his mother were half sisters. He told Hannah, which is why she moved him to the dressing room. Old Mrs. Oakes found out, probably from Hannah, and she decided to kill Charles so he wouldn't tell anyone else. I guess she didn't want her society friends to find out."

"Would people have really cared?" Gino asked.

"Many of them would," Sarah said. "I guess she didn't want to take the chance."

"Her own grandson? Just to keep a secret like that?" Gino asked incredulously.

"She never believed Charles was really her grandson," Sarah said. "I think . . . She must have been getting senile or something. I don't think we'll ever be able to understand why she did it."

Malloy came over and put his arm around her. "Are you all right?"

Sarah shuddered. "I will be. What is Gerald going to do?"

"He told the maids to wash the old woman and burn the bedclothes. They're going to put her in her clean bed and say they found her like that and she must've died in her sleep."

"I can't believe it!"

"Someone in this house killed three people to prevent a scandal and almost killed a few more. Why wouldn't they burn a couple sheets to prevent one now?"

"Can he really forgive Jenny for killing his mother?"

"The woman killed his son," Malloy said.

Suddenly, Sarah felt unutterably weary. "Can we go home?"

"We certainly can."

"What about Gerald and Jenny?"

"If they need us, they know where to find us. Let's go."

SARAH'S MOTHER HAD SHOWN UP ON HER DOORSTEP early that evening. Word of Mrs. Oakes's sudden death had reached her, and she couldn't wait until morning for the details.

"Why couldn't you have told me yourself," her mother scolded her as they sat at her kitchen table. "I had to hear it from strangers!"

"Did an actual *stranger* tell you Mrs. Oakes died?" Sarah asked skeptically.

"Well, no. It was one of my oldest friends, but still . . . I'm your mother, Sarah. You must remember where your loyalties lie. Now tell me the whole story."

Sarah couldn't tell her the whole story, so she told the version she'd given Gino, with one small alteration they had decided to make.

"We assume she couldn't live with what she'd done, so she killed herself. They found her dead in her bed this morning."

"How horrible!" her mother exclaimed. "Poor Gerald. She couldn't have been in her right mind."

"I'm sure you're right," Sarah lied. The fact that she'd given the druggist a false name when she bought the arsenic proved she knew exactly what she was doing. But she wouldn't mention that to her mother.

"I'm sure Gerald and Jenny are grateful to Mr. Malloy for figuring out what happened."

Sarah wasn't too sure about that, but she said, "He was glad to help, although I wish we'd found out Charles died from a tragic accident."

"Gerald never would have needed Mr. Malloy if he thought that," her mother pointed out.

Maeve came into the kitchen and sat down next to Sarah at the table. "Catherine is asleep," she reported.

"Are you going to go over to the house again tomorrow to help Malloy with the workmen?" Sarah teased.

But instead of making a face, as Sarah expected, Maeve said, "Didn't he tell you?"

"Tell me what?"

"Oh, I guess he hasn't had a chance yet because he got home so late. Did you know he went to see an attorney after he brought you home?"

"An attorney?" her mother echoed. "Whatever for?"

"He went to see the attorney who used to be Ella Adderly's guardian. He wanted to make sure someone knew that her cousin was trying to take advantage of her and steal her fortune."

"That was very nice of him," her mother said.

"Yes, it was, but I still want to know what Malloy hasn't told me yet," she reminded Maeve.

"Maybe I should let him break the news."

"What news?" Sarah's mother said, her lovely eyes lighting with curiosity.

"Yes, what news?" Sarah pressed.

Maeve gave them a smug smile, and for a minute Sarah was afraid she might have to beat it out of the girl, but finally she said, "The house is finished."

"What do you mean, the house is finished?" Sarah asked.

"Just that. I think the workmen were just dragging things out so they could charge Mr. Malloy more money. He told me he suspected that's what they were doing, and so I asked the foreman to walk me through the house and show me what they still needed to do. He's really a terrible liar."

"He lied to you?" Sarah's mother said. "Right to your face?"

Maeve shrugged. "He thought I was some idiot girl who didn't know anything."

"What do you know about construction?" Sarah asked.

"Nothing, but I know what houses are supposed to look like, and I know a lie when I hear one. I had a nice little talk with the man about how angry Mr. Malloy might be if he knew he was being swindled, and he decided they'd done all they could. Then they packed up and left."

"Maeve, that's wonderful!" Sarah said.

"And if the house is finished, that means you and Mr. Malloy can be married," her mother said.

For a moment, Sarah couldn't get her breath.

Married.

Everything seemed to be happening so fast, which was ridiculous because for weeks they'd been complaining about how slowly things were going. And, of course, they'd waited for years, never even suspecting they might ever get to this place in their lives. But now, suddenly, there were no more barriers.

"Sarah?" her mother said. "Are you all right?"

"Yes, of course. I just . . . We need to make some plans."

"Indeed we do. I'm thinking we only need a week to arrange the wedding breakfast. You'll have it at our house, of course. You'll want to be married from your parents' house."

"Mother, there's something we need to discuss."

"What's that, dear?"

"We . . . Malloy is Catholic."

"Mr. Malloy might argue with you on that," Maeve said with a knowing smile.

"He might," Sarah said. "He hasn't been to church in years, so he doesn't really care, but his mother is definitely Catholic. Unless we're married in that church, she won't consider us legally married."

Her mother considered this for a long moment. "I don't suppose it matters what church you get married in." Sarah could hear the disappointment in her voice, though. She was most certainly planning to have her own minister marry them at her house.

"But you're not a Catholic, Mrs. Brandt," Maeve said. "Will they even let you get married in their church?"

"Actually, no. We'll have to get married in the rectory. That's the house where the priests live, I'm told."

Her mother frowned. "That doesn't sound very big."

"I don't know how big it is, but we were planning just to have our witnesses with us, and maybe Mrs. Malloy."

"But what about your other guests?"

"We aren't having many, and they'll all be invited to the breakfast. We would be very happy if you planned that for us."

"We can certainly do that," her mother said with as much enthusiasm as she could muster.

"I know," Maeve said with another smug smile. "Why don't you get married twice?"

"Twice?" her mother echoed, obviously intrigued.

"Yes. Get married by the priest with your witnesses, then have another wedding at your mother's house with all your guests."

"Aren't there laws about getting married twice?" her mother asked.

"Only if you marry different people," Maeve said, grinning. "What do you think, Mrs. Brandt?"

Sarah could see one possible obstacle. "I think we'll have to ask Malloy if he's willing to go through that twice."

"He'll do anything you want him to," Maeve said with more confidence than Sarah felt.

"What a wonderful plan, Maeve! Who are you going to ask to stand up with you?" her mother asked.

Sarah had been waiting, not quite ready to believe it was really going to happen, but now she thought it was finally safe to say the words. "Maeve, I was hoping you would be my maid of honor."

Maeve gaped at her so long, Sarah was afraid she was going to say no. Then she burst into tears. The next thing she knew, Sarah was crying and so was her mother, and that was how Malloy found them when he came over for his nightly visit.

They tried to explain that they were crying happy tears, but he didn't look like he really believed it.

"Gino didn't cry at all when I asked him to stand up with us," he reported.

THE MORNING OF THE WEDDINGS DAWNED BRIGHT AND cool. Felix Decker sent his carriage to carry his daughter, Maeve, and Mrs. Malloy to the rectory for the Catholic ceremony. Frank and Gino took a cab so the groom wouldn't see the bride before the wedding, because Mrs. Ellsworth had warned them sternly more than once how much bad luck that would bring.

"Are you nervous, Mr. Malloy?" Gino asked as the cab wound its painfully slow way through the city streets.

"No, I'm terrified," he replied, wishing he was exaggerating. What in God's name had ever made him think he deserved a woman like Sarah Brandt?

"What do you have to be scared of? Mrs. Brandt is beautiful and smart and a real lady."

"That's what I'm scared of."

Gino only needed a minute to figure it out. "Oh, because you're"——he gestured vaguely——"not like her."

"No, I'm not."

"But you're rich now. Maybe richer than her father, even." Gino smoothed the lapel of the tailor-made suit Frank had bought him for the wedding.

"Money doesn't make you a gentleman."

"You're right. I've met a lot of rich men who were bums."

Frank looked at Gino in amazement at his insight. "So have I."

"And I don't think Mrs. Brandt would marry a bum."

Frank felt the knot of fear in his chest loosen just a bit. "You're right, Gino. She wouldn't."

"Now tell me again what I'm supposed to do, because I really am terrified. I've never been a best man before."

THE CEREMONY AT THE RECTORY HAD BEEN MERCIFULLY brief. The priest had explained during their earlier meeting that because Sarah wasn't Catholic and they couldn't hold the service in the sanctuary, he could dispense with a lot of the rituals. Even without them, Sarah thought the ceremony was beautiful. She remembered making those same vows when she married Tom Brandt, but she hadn't really understood what they meant then. Now she did. When she looked into Malloy's dark eyes as he slipped the ring on her finger, she knew he did as well.

Afterward they all rode together to the Deckers' house in the carriage. Malloy held her hand, and he couldn't seem to take his eyes off her. Sarah knew she looked beautiful. Maeve had told her often enough this morning when they were getting dressed. Her mother's dressmaker had followed Sarah's instructions perfectly, designing her an elegant gown of robin's egg blue silk taffeta trimmed in lace. She'd wanted something much simpler, of course, but Maeve had reminded her that both Sarah and her sister had eloped and Mrs. Decker had only this one chance left to see one of her daughters married in style. At least she'd been able to forgo a long train, since she wouldn't be walking down any aisles.

"That's a pretty dress, Mrs. Malloy," Gino was saying to

Malloy's mother. It was, too. Sarah's mother's dressmaker had convinced her that dove gray was the perfect color for a woman emerging from mourning after twenty years. She'd trimmed it with black braid stitched into swirls around the bottom of the skirt and the front of the jacket. Her hat sported an ostrich feather dyed to match the dress.

Mrs. Malloy looked up at Gino in surprise. "Why, thank you, young man."

"I don't think I've ever seen you in anything but black, Ma," Malloy said.

"Mrs. Brandt thought it would be all right," she said primly.

Sarah smiled at Malloy's astonished look. He was still getting used to Sarah and his mother being friends.

"You can't call her Mrs. Brandt anymore," Maeve said with a teasing grin. "She's Mrs. Malloy now, too."

"Are you going to call each other Mrs. Malloy?" Gino asked with a teasing grin of his own. "That'll be confusing."

"I've asked her to start calling me Sarah," Sarah reminded her.

"And she can call me Mother Malloy," Mrs. Malloy said, successfully shocking her son all over again.

When they arrived at the Deckers' house, Sarah's parents met them at the door. Sarah's mother embraced her, hugging her fiercely, and when she finally released her, Sarah saw her eyes glistening with just a hint of tears. Then she turned to Malloy, and to his surprise, she kissed him on the cheek.

"Welcome to our family, Frank," she said, then quickly turned to greet his mother so she could pretend not to notice his astonishment.

Sarah's father took both her hands and kissed her cheek. He successfully maintained his dignity, but Sarah knew how deeply his emotions ran by how tightly he squeezed her fingers.

They all knew Frank Malloy was not the husband her

parents would have chosen for her, but they had come to understand he was the right husband for her. Her father shook Malloy's hand with all the warmth she could have hoped for.

Then they moved on upstairs to the drawing room her parents hardly ever had occasion to use where all the rest of the people who were important to them had gathered. Behind her, Sarah heard her mother complimenting Mrs. Malloy on her new clothes.

"I'm so glad you were happy with Susan's work," she said. "She desperately wanted to please you."

Mrs. Malloy murmured something Sarah didn't catch.

"I'll be sure to tell her you said so," her mother replied. "Brian has been wondering where you are. Mrs. Ellsworth and Mrs. Hicks have been doing a marvelous job of entertaining him and Catherine, though."

When they reached the landing, for a moment Sarah and Frank were out of sight of the others. Malloy leaned over and kissed her.

"It's hard to believe that I can do that whenever I like now," he said with a satisfied grin.

"You can do a lot more than that, too," she replied with a satisfied grin of her own and watched in delight as the color crawled up his neck.

"Mama!" Catherine cried. She'd obviously escaped from the drawing room one floor above and came racing down the stairs to them, with Brian close on her heels. She threw herself into Sarah's arms, then pushed away and threw herself into Malloy's arms. "You're my papa now, aren't you?"

"Yes, I am," he told her happily.

Brian went straight for Sarah, but he skidded to a stop and gazed up at her in wonder. He hadn't yet seen her in her wedding finery. Then he ran his thumb down his cheek and held his hands out to the left in the sign for *Mother*.

"Yes, my darling boy," she said, nodding and making the sign back to him. He threw his arms around her.

By then Gino, Maeve, and the parents had caught up, and Gino and Maeve took charge of the children, ushering them back upstairs where Mrs. Ellsworth was fussing at them for getting away from her.

"Everyone's here," Sarah's mother told them.

"Even Roosevelt?" Malloy asked.

"Oh yes, and Edith is with him. He said he was delighted to be invited and wouldn't have missed it for anything."

"He's running for governor now," her father said. "He needs all the friends he can get."

When Frank and Sarah stepped into the room, everyone stopped what they were doing and applauded the newlyweds. Then they came rushing over to greet them.

Mrs. Ellsworth assured them all the omens decreed they would have a long and happy life together. Her son, Nelson, wished them all the best. Roosevelt took the liberty of kissing the bride, since they had been childhood friends. Then he pumped Malloy's hand and slapped him on the back. His wife, Edith, kissed Malloy, making him blush all over again.

Michael and Lynne Hicks were the closest thing Catherine had to family, except for Sarah and Malloy. Lynne was Catherine's much older half sister, but Lynne's own children were much older than Catherine, so Catherine knew her as Aunt Lynne. They declared themselves to be honored to witness the wedding.

Dr. David Newton and his wife, Anne, had been friends of Sarah and her first husband, Tom. David had earned Malloy's undying gratitude when he operated on Brian's clubfoot almost two years earlier. David was thrilled to see Brian running around as a boy his age should do. Finally, Mrs. Keller came forward. She was the matron at the Mission where Sarah had first encountered Catherine and Maeve, and she'd brought several of the girls who had known Sarah the longest. They seemed a bit overwhelmed by the magnificence of the Deckers' home, but thrilled to be there all the same.

When they had greeted all the guests, Sarah glanced around the room. Gino was deep in conversation with Theodore, his former commander, and Mrs. Roosevelt. Mrs. Ellsworth and Lynne Hicks were chatting amiably with Mrs. Malloy and the Newtons while they tried to keep the children under control. Sarah's mother and Maeve were making Mrs. Keller and the girls welcome. Her father had gone to greet Michael Hicks and Nelson Ellsworth.

Her parents' minister was coming toward them with an expression of happy anticipation.

"Are you ready to go through it all again?" Sarah asked Malloy.

He took her hand and gave her a look that curled her toes.

"Yes, I am. I would be glad to marry you twice a day, every single day for the rest of my life."

Author's Note

We've waited a long time for Sarah and Frank to be married. Before you ask, no, this is not the last book in the series! I have many more adventures planned for Frank and Sarah Malloy and their crew. I hope you will share them.

As a reward for your loyalty to the series and your patience in waiting for this wedding, we will be doing a second Gaslight Mystery book this year. *Murder on St. Nicholas Avenue* will be out in November 2015. While Frank and Sarah are on their honeymoon, Gino and Maeve step in to help a young woman falsely accused of murder. When they find they need a little help, every one of Frank and Sarah's family and friends step in to assist.

Please let me know how you liked this book by contacting me through my website victoriathompson.com or "like" me on Facebook at facebook.com/Victoria.Thompson.Author, or follow me on Twitter @gaslightvt. I'll send you a reminder whenever I have a new book out.

Author's Note